I0760370

# Stone Heart

MAEGAN M. SIMPSON

My Lord and Savior Jesus Christ lived the only perfect human life. I have edited this to the best of my ability, but there will undoubtedly be mistakes. Please forgive my lack of perfection. Thank you.

Cover design by MoorBooks Design

Under Jacket Design by Maegan M. Simpson

Chapter Background Artwork by Chicklen Doodle

ISBN: 978-1-966420-01-9

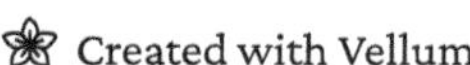

*To my wonderful Mom.*
*This is still your birthday book...just a little shinier.*
*Love you!*

# CONTENTS

# ACKNOWLEDGMENTS

I would first like to thank my Heavenly Father for the talent and love for writing that He has given me, and the time and freedom to pursue that talent. The credit and glory for this story goes to Him.

Thank you to all my friends who encourage and support me in many ways. I especially want to thank Sarah, for sticking with me since the beginning of this whole writing thing, and Lexi, for listening to all my fragmented story ideas and encouraging me that they're worth something. And thank you both for being so willing to read my writing and for not laughing at my crazy ideas and moments of inspiration.

Thank you to my professors at Colorado Christian University for teaching me so much and helping me grow, in soul and faith as well as in knowledge. Throughout my time at CCU, you challenged me to think deeply, to always be learning, and to pursue God with all I am. Thank you for pouring into me, and I pray that the lessons I learned from you are visible in my life and my writing.

And finally, thank you to Mom, Dad, and Levi. Your support allows me to pursue these stories as more than a hobby, and your work behind the scenes is why my books are legible and I am still sane. You help me more than you know, and I continually thank God that He gave me *you* as a family. I love you!

# BARGAINS

Ragged breathing echoed through the shadowy hall, originating from the stocky man collapsed on his knees before the throne. He quivered, fighting not to look up at the monster seated above him. His resistance failed. He couldn't help himself: he'd never seen a living being as strange, or terrifying, as the beast of living stone he knelt before.

The intruder's fear served Dyrerisan's purposes well.

"For the last time," Dyrerisan said. "Why did you steal from me?"

His low, rough tone had more of an effect on the intruder than if he'd shouted. The man flinched, lowering himself a little closer to the floor.

"Forgive me, milord," the man replied, his voice shaking even more than his limbs. *The mighty protector,* Dyrerisan scoffed privately, his lips twisting in a sneer.

"I took it as a gift for my daughter."

"And the ruby rose you chose is my most prized possession," Dyrerisan replied, matching lie for lie.

The trinket was one of many littering his halls, taken from a dusty cabinet he hadn't paid any attention to for years. But it was his, and he didn't take kindly to thievery. Nor to cowardly lies. Dyrerisan leaned forward, making the wooden throne creak.

"I'll have the truth, now."

The man didn't reply, staring at the floor in terrified silence. Dyrerisan waited a breath, then gestured to the masked guard standing on his left. The guard drew his sword, and the intruder flinched.

"I'm in debt," he said, looking up to Dyrerisan. "To the Duke of Sarnere. If I don't repay him in five days...he's threatened to take one of my girls into his service."

"And you resorted to thievery to save yourself."

"Surely...surely, you'll take pity on my family. It's such a *small* piece of your wealth, milord."

"To you it is no small bit of wealth."

The intruder was slow to respond to that. Dyrerisan could see his eyes darting around, could guess at the thoughts churning in his head. He was searching for a way out of his predicament, a way that bore no consequences for himself. *Selfishness.* It was always the most predictable human reaction.

"The Duke of Sarnere," Dyrerisan mused. "I've heard of him...he's known for his cruelty, yes?"

"Yes."

"Entering his service is poor fate for any person, let alone your *beloved* family."

The man rose a little, hope lighting his face. Dyrerisan resisted another sneer.

"Yes, milord. I would do anything to keep my daughters from him."

Dyrerisan knew that already. He also knew the man's dedication didn't protect *all* of his household. Dyrerisan would use that to his advantage.

"And if I offer you a bargain? Enough wealth to repay your debt?"

"I would accept, gladly."

The man spoke eagerly, without any apparent thought to the

cost of such a bargain. Duke Kelan wouldn't have needed to work hard to entrap this rabbit-hearted man. Dyrerisan rose from his throne, accepting the ache that came from forcing his stiff limbs into movement, and stepped toward his victim.

"And in return," Dyrerisan said, "You'll serve me."

The man blanched. Dyrerisan smiled.

"Unless you'd rather serve your punishment for thievery in my dungeons, of course."

"I...I can't," the man gasped, nearly falling over as he leaned away from Dyrerisan, eyes wide in terror. "I can't leave my family, my home..."

"Then send one from your family," Dyrerisan said with a negligent wave of his hand. "You had a victim chosen for the Duke of Sarnere, surely. Send them to me instead."

"I..." the intruder trailed off, the first time in their interaction that he'd taken a moment to *think.* Perhaps if he used that thick head more often, he wouldn't find himself in this situation. But Dyrerisan doubted this sop would ever learn to weigh his decisions...he'd seen this type of man waste away their lives too many times to believe otherwise.

Dyrerisan reached behind him, and his second guard placed a heavy sack in his hand. He tossed it to the ground before the intruder, and the clink of gold coins against the marble floor pierced the silence. The intruder's eyes widened, his fingers brushing against the full purse almost reverently. Dyrerisan's lip curled.

"Your decision?" Dyrerisan prompted.

"I accept your bargain."

Dyrerisan grunted his response, watching the intruder snatch up the gold like his life depended on its cold weight. Perhaps he believed it did.

"I expect my servant in two weeks," Dyrerisan said, gesturing to his guards. They stepped forward to seize the intruder by his elbows. "Don't keep me waiting, Radcliff."

The man finally looked up from his prize, skin ghostly gray as he met Dyrerisan's gaze. "How do you know my name?"

"Does it matter?" Dyrerisan asked with a stiff smirk. "Our bargain is sealed. You dare not disobey me now."

Radcliff allowed the guards to drag him backwards, out of the once-lavish hall. Dyrerisan held his gaze in a silent warning until the doors were shut. Then he returned to his throne with a deep sigh, glancing around the shadow-ridden room as if seeing it for the first time. The statues lining the walls loomed over him from their darkened pedestals, silent witness to his ignoble interview with Radcliff. Dyrerisan sighed and looked away, to his stiff hands.

Radcliff would not return to these halls, but he wouldn't risk breaking the bargain, either. He had a ward he seemed content to leave vulnerable. Dyrerisan had no doubt that she'd be Radcliff's choice for a sacrifice. The only question left was whether or not the young woman would agree to the terms. Dyrerisan doubted she had any idea of the fate that waited for her in Dyrerisan's halls...or the fate left to her if she refused to come.

# CHAPTER ONE

Ember set tea before her uncle, scowling at the way her shaking hand sent waves across the dark liquid. No one else seemed to notice, focused as they were on Uncle Radcliff's delayed and foreboding return. Even Ember had to admit that Uncle Radcliff looked terrible: ragged and stunned. Unlike her aunt and cousins, the sight didn't inspire sympathy. Whatever mess Uncle Radcliff had gotten himself into, Ember was sure he'd foist the consequences onto someone else. It was what he did best.

The tea delivered, Ember retreated to the back of the room and took the chair furthest from the fire. In the dark corner, hopefully she could listen without being observed. The entire house had been in a dizzying rush since Uncle Radcliff had returned, with a sum of gold that exceeded what he'd made in the past three years combined. Gathered in the parlor, waiting for Uncle Radcliff to recover enough to tell his story, brought a comforting silence that *nearly* outweighed Ember's curiosity. She curled her legs beneath her on the plush chair, counting on Uncle Radcliff to distract Aunt Cecile from the grave infraction, and laid her head back to wait for Uncle Radcliff to sip his tea.

"Will you tell us your story, now?" Louisa asked, bouncing in her seat. She'd managed to wait for Radcliff to set his tea back on the table, which was more restraint than Ember would've expected. Uncle Radcliff looked down on his youngest daughter with an indulgent smile. It didn't fully banish the fear in his eyes.

"Yes, my dear," he said, taking her hand. "First, I found no help from our friends. They've all chosen to turn their backs on our good name."

Ember suppressed the desire to snort at that. *What 'good name'? If the Radcliffs had one, it's long gone now.*

"I rode home as swiftly as I dared, but was waylaid by a fierce storm, deep in the forest. It came on suddenly, in a siege of wind and rain that nearly knocked me from my horse. I could smell the lightning in the air, feel the current along my skin."

Ember settled deeper in her chair, willing the knots in her stomach to unwind. Whatever else her uncle was, he was a fine storyteller.

"Just as I gave myself up for lost, I came upon a tall gate, black as night. And through that gate lay a castle, holding against the storm as though it had stood there for a thousand years, and intended to stand for a thousand more."

"Did you find any monsters?" Louisa asked.

Uncle Radcliff hesitated, and Ember's dread rushed back in.

"The castle looked abandoned," he hedged. "Inside, every surface was covered in lavish treasures, buried in dust. If I'd had to guess, I wouldn't have thought any living creature had disturbed those halls for a hundred years. And yet...when I reached the kitchen, I found a lively fire and stew laid out, already served."

Ember assumed he'd helped himself. She hoped that whoever's meal he'd stolen hadn't gone without.

"You didn't see anyone?" Sophia asked, more timidly than her younger sister. She was curled against Aunt Cecile's side, staring out at the room with wide eyes. She was the only one who'd glanced to Ember's place in the corner since the story had begun.

"Not at first," Uncle Radcliff said. "As the storm cleared, I tried leaving the same way I'd come. There were so many treasures filling the halls, all forgotten, I decided to...borrow one. Just enough to save our family."

Ember bit back a groan, lifting her gaze to the shadowed ceiling. Entering a strange castle, eating their food, and stealing their belongings. What did he expect to happen?

"You were caught," Aunt Cecile guessed in a flat tone.

"Yes," Uncle Radcliff said, staring into his tea. "Masked guards appeared from the shadows and took me to their...lord. A monstrous creature."

"What kind of monster?" Louisa asked. Ember couldn't help but wonder the same...what kind of monster had her uncle angered this time?

"Some sort of rock troll from the crags of the north," Uncle Radcliff said. "Too large to be human, but with a man's voice and a man's intelligence. He was...ghastly, with eyes that seemed to pierce my very soul. I doubt even the king could stand against him."

Ember took in her uncle's description with careful thought. *A rock troll?* She'd heard legends about such creatures, had even spoken to an old man who claimed to have seen one in his younger days of wandering. She wasn't sure a rock troll would rule over a castle in the forest, though. At least, not in this kingdom. *Eyes that pierce a soul.* What kind of creature could do such a thing? Or was Uncle Radcliff exaggerating?

"What bargain did he offer?" Aunt Cecile asked. Her suspicion matched Ember's, and Uncle Radcliff still avoided her eyes.

"He threatened to lock me away, as punishment for my attempted theft," he said. "But when I explained our situation, the price against our family, he offered mercy. Enough gold to pay our debt..."

Uncle Radcliff trailed off before naming the price, glancing toward Ember. She leaned forward, hands shaking in earnest now. Surely not...

"In exchange for a member of our family serving in his castle," Uncle Radcliff finished. "They must go to him before two weeks pass, or his wrath will fall on our family."

Ember lowered her feet to the floor, her spine perfectly straight as her mind reeled. Uncle Radcliff had changed debtors, and nothing more. *Why did I expect anything different?* Uncle Radcliff didn't look toward her again, focused on comforting his daughters. They'd reacted to his news as if *they* were the ones expected to ride off and serve some monstrous lord in a castle no one had ever heard of. The glimpse Ember caught of her aunt's gaze showed burning anger. She'd worn that look often, lately. Usually, it came with raving against her husband's foolish ways. Now, only three words accompanied her fury.

"Ember will go."

Ember didn't bother to stand, not wanting to test the strength of her legs at the moment. But she did raise her chin when her aunt and uncle turned toward her, keeping her mouth clenched shut against the torrent of words she longed to let loose, just once. But throwing a tantrum would get her nowhere.

*Leaving is to my advantage,* she reminded herself. *Away from attachment, away from my spoiled, innocent cousins... away from any hearts that could be broken.*

"Do you agree to this, Ember?" Uncle Radcliff asked, when the silence stretched a little too long.

*Do I have a choice?* Ember bit back that bitter question, but didn't bother to curb the sharp edges to her voice.

"It's no different from servitude in Sarnere, is it?"

"Thank you, dear," Uncle Radcliff said, relief plain on his face. "Your loyalty to your family won't be forgotten."

Ember didn't bother responding to that. He showed relief, but no remorse. No sign that he felt guilty for forcing his niece into service to a creature he was clearly terrified of, all to pay a debt that *he* incurred. But then, had she expected that to change?

"I'll go to the duke tomorrow," Uncle Radcliff said, finally looking to his wife.

"Then let us hope he'll accept your payment," Aunt Cecile replied. "Ember cannot serve them both."

# CHAPTER TWO

Ember ghosted past the door to Uncle Radcliff's study, glancing through the open door as she passed. He was speaking to a groom, who held the payment for the Duke of Sarnere. She pressed her lips together and kept walking, not wanting to draw any attention to herself.

Two days had passed since her uncle's return, but he hadn't made any preparations for traveling to Sarnere. His excuse was that he needed more time to recover from his previous journey, but Ember didn't think even Sophia believed that. He was afraid. And now, it seemed, he was sending a servant to Duke Kelan's fortress rather than go himself.

*Listening to Aunt Cecile's reaction could be entertaining.* Not that Ember would tell her...she never volunteered information to her aunt willingly. But she knew the habits of Rookwood manor, and she knew where to be to hear news that would otherwise be kept from her. But what to do in the meantime? Aunt Cecile was busy giving orders to the chief gardener. Louisa and Sophia were hidden away learning history from their crusty and dry tutor. She wasn't in the mood to get in another argument with the narrow-minded man about the veracity of legends and folk stories.

In times past, Ember would've gone for a walk, or asked the housekeeper for a task. They were never important chores, but it was something to keep her hands busy. It had been months since she'd offered herself for those menial chores, though. She hadn't polished some unused chair since she noticed her hands trembling while she worked. She hadn't ventured deeper into the lands surrounding Rookwood manor since she noticed how the paths she once ran for the joy of it now drained her strength even at a meandering stroll.

*Reading it is,* she said, forcing herself from those troubled thoughts. She steered her steps in the direction of the library, hearing behind her the sound of her uncle's voice and a door pulled shut. Just as well she was already turned away. She doubted her uncle would appreciate the thoughts written across her face.

She rushed to the library, lingering in its peaceful presence. It was smaller than Uncle Radcliff's study, but the smallness was comforting, a familiar embrace. Ember meandered past the shelves, reaching out to touch the spines of her favorite books. She'd read, or attempted to read, every one of the tomes gracing those shelves. The last, a book on mathematics Ember fell asleep to more than once, she'd returned during the winter.

She selected one of her favorite novels, fanciful and tragic, and turned back to the door. She took a moment to breathe in the peace of that room before ducking back into the hall, toward the sitting room her aunt gravitated towards whenever she was upset. There was a window seat that was always hidden by drapes. Ember had used that secret space to listen in on her aunt and uncle more than once and had never been caught.

Some might say she shouldn't eavesdrop on her guardians. But Ember had left those qualms behind years ago. Especially now, when any discussion of debts and servitude held *her* life in the balance, she wanted to know what was said. It was Ember's life they bargained away, without even warning her before the deed was done. It was Ember who would serve a monster, whether the refined cruelty of Duke Kelan or the monstrous unknown of her uncle's latest debtor.

But her desire to know what was said waned as the hours passed in silence. The book that had captured her imagination so many other times struck her as too morbid that day, perhaps a bit too close to her real situation. She only made it through the first few chapters before setting it aside and leaning her throbbing head against the glass panes.

It was overcast outside, a dull gray that washed the color from the garden. Ember didn't expect a storm to follow, though: the breeze was too gentle. All the storms this year had been wild, raging things that shook the windows. Ember wished another would come, just so she could watch. Maybe watching the wind rip away at the world around her could rip open something within her, as well. Maybe then she could make sense of the building tension within her, that constant pressure that she couldn't name. Fear, anger, grief... nothing fit.

Voices interrupted her contemplation. Her aunt's shrill voice, and her uncle's pleading response, confirmed her guess: Aunt Cecile wasn't happy with her husband. The door opened in time for Ember to catch her aunt's next words.

"But what if he comes here? What if he wants one of us in Ember's place?"

"Our debt to Duke Kelan is repaid," Uncle Radcliff said. "He has no reason to come here. All we have to worry about is getting Ember to that beast on time."

"Why did you take money from him, Branson?" Aunt Cecile wailed. Ember winced as the shrill tones sent needles through her skull. "You don't even know the monster's *name*. Now we have two villains after our family."

"I didn't have a choice," Radcliff growled. "I took the best option I could."

"And how do you know this monster won't demand more than Ember?"

"The bargain is struck. He has no right to demand more."

"You'll bet our daughters lives on that?"

Aunt Cecile's voice choked on a sob, and Ember peeked around the curtain to see Uncle Radcliff embracing his wife.

"Sophia and Louisa will be safe, I promise."

"And Ember?"

Ember's heart stuttered. *What about me?*

"What *about* Ember?" Uncle Radcliff asked, echoing Ember's silent question.

"She's angry. I can see it in her eyes. She's too defiant to agree to this, and yet she hasn't raised any sort of fuss..."

Ember's pulse steadied, her hands balled into fists on her lap. Of course, that would be what her aunt was concerned about. There was no love lost between Ember and Aunt Cecile, and she'd admit that was as much her doing as her aunt's. Ember wasn't surprised... she refused to think she was disappointed.

"Maybe she really is loyal to us," Uncle Radcliff suggested. "We *did* take her into our home, raised her beside our children. I know she's...taciturn, but I doubt she's heartless."

Heartless. If only. *Or maybe I'd do anything to get away from this place,* she suggested silently. *Maybe I'm tired of being unwanted.* The words rested lightly on her tongue, ready to be spoken. But she didn't...she clamped her jaw shut and huddled behind the curtain, still listening.

"Perhaps you're right," Aunt Cecile said, though she didn't sound convinced. Ember didn't blame her.

"Now come," Radcliff said, steering his wife toward the door. "I'll handle Ember. You have nothing to fear."

Ember doubted Aunt Cecile believed that, either, but her response was lost as they left the room. Ember stayed in her hiding place until she counted to forty, then emerged slowly. Her eyes burned but stayed dry. She had a lot of practice at that, holding back tears. And she refused to break now. She'd sworn to herself, years ago, that she wouldn't let anything her guardians said hurt her, not where it mattered.

Ember had known for years that she was an outsider in their home, that she always would be. She hadn't made any effort to change that fact, either. *I won't be sad. I won't mourn leaving them, or this place.* To Duke Kelan or to this mysterious beast lord, at least she'd be away from this false home. The sooner, the better.

EMBER RAN her fingers over the worn pages, pausing when she found her name, written by her mother when Ember was only a toddler. She'd pulled the journal out of her packed trunk to check a few passages, but she couldn't help but linger over these pages. This journal was all she had left of her mother, and she never could stop herself from rereading the words she'd long ago learned by heart.

As far as her aunt and uncle knew, she was packing for her journey to the mysterious castle in the woods that no one seemed to be able to give directions to. She'd used the excuse of preparing for her journey often in the past few days. It was an easy way to avoid her aunt and uncle, who she'd rather not talk to, and her cousins, who would want comforting despite the fact that *she* was the one who was leaving for an unknown fate.

In truth, Ember had been ready to leave Rookwood manor for weeks. She'd known, thanks to her eavesdropping, the price Duke Kelan demanded to repay her uncle's debt. She knew she would be the one they chose to sacrifice. But Ember would rather spend her last hours alone than wandering the halls, fighting to ignore the fate looming before her.

*Is this better or worse than going to Sarnere?* She couldn't decide, despite the many hours she'd spent searching for an answer. This new villain, rock troll or not, was an unknown. He was the sort to take advantage of Uncle Radcliff's idiocy and greed, but then there were plenty who were. Duke Kelan of Sarnere, on the other hand, had the sort of reputation that made reasonable people shy away from any association with him. Ember had heard too many stories of the atrocities he committed to think she'd be well off in his service. Now, she was walking in the dark. Would this new master be any better than Duke Kelan? Would he be worse?

"Hopefully he isn't as monstrous as Uncle Radcliff described," Ember muttered wryly, safely stowing her journal in the shoulder bag that had once belonged to her father.

"Ember?"

The tremulous voice came from the doorway, and Ember turned to find Sophia standing there with a full tea tray in her hands. Her chin was trembling, and Ember stifled a sigh. She stepped forward to take the tray from her cousin's hands, setting it on a small table in the corner. Sophia followed her deeper into her room.

"You're really going, aren't you?"

Ember turned to face Sophia, gripping the edge of the table behind her.

"I have to," Ember said, willing her voice to stay flat.

"But *why*? You didn't *do* anything."

Ember gave Sophia a bitter half smile. "Unfortunately, dukes and debtors rarely care about what's fair. They care about being repaid."

Sophia's tears spilled over, and she rushed forward to throw her arms around Ember's waist. Ember stiffened, closing her eyes against the lump that suddenly rose in her throat. She should pull away. She should ask Sophia to leave. *One moment. What will one moment hurt?* Ember wrapped her arms around Sophia, pulling her into a tighter embrace and willing her eyes to stay dry.

"I wish I could *do* something," Sophia muttered against the shoulder of Ember's dress.

Ember stroked her hair, smiling. "I know. But I'd rather go than watch you or Louisa be sent off."

That was a truth she'd never admitted out loud, even to herself. She was surprised she was admitting it now. But after all, what could one moment of weakness hurt? One moment of letting her heart show before she left this place forever. *Perhaps there are aspects of life here that I'll miss, after all.*

Sophia drew back, wiping tears away from her eyes. Ember had to do the same. When she looked up, Sophia was digging something out of her pocket, a small square of colorful cloth.

"Louisa and I made this for you," Sophia said, holding out the gift. "To remember us by."

Ember took the cloth, and her throat closed up again as she took in the embroidery stitched carefully across its surface. *"We love you, Ember. Sophia and Louisa."* It was obvious that the letters, precise and delicate, had been done by Sophia. Ember guessed that the haphazard flowers were Louisa's contribution.

"Thank you," Ember whispered. "I'll keep it close."

*This is more than a moment,* she warned herself. *This is more dangerous.* But Ember stowed the cloth between the pages of her journal, anyway, silencing that worried voice whispering to her. What was she supposed to do, toss it aside?

The sound of horses pounding down the drive interrupted whatever Sophia tried to say next. Ember turned toward the window, her breath catching when she caught sight of the mounted knights gathering outside. The standard they bore, a black wolf standing over a bloodied lamb, identified them clearly enough. They were from Sarnere. And the man leading them, dressed in dark burnished armor that looked like it weighed more than Ember, was the duke. She'd heard enough of the black etching on his breastplate, and the two-handed sword that never left his side, to mistake him for anyone else.

"Sophia," Ember said in a calm tone that didn't match the pounding of her heart. "Find Louisa and go to the attic, to the secret room."

"What is it?"

Sophia pushed to the window, letting out a small "oh" when she caught sight of the company below.

"That is Duke Kelan," Ember said, before drawing Sophia away from the window.

"Will he try to take you?"

Ember bit her lip. "I don't know. But you and Louisa need to be safe and hidden until he leaves."

A look of panic passed over Sophia's soft features, before they hardened in determination. She nodded before throwing her arms around Ember's waist again.

"He won't find us," she said. "Just...be safe."

"I'll try," Ember said, squeezing her cousin's narrow shoulders before pulling away. "Now go, before any of them come inside."

Sophia fled the room. Ember took a moment to pray that Louisa was inside, that she'd go with Sophia without a struggle, before turning back to the shoulder bag laid out on her bed. It already had her most precious belongings inside. Now she rolled up a spare change of clothes to stuff inside, along with the biscuits from the tea tray. After gulping down the cup of tea, scalding her throat on the way down, Ember left her room. She didn't bother to take a final look around at the space that had been hers for seven years now. No matter what happened today, it was hers no longer.

As Ember tiptoed to the servant's staircase, her heart continued to pound, making her head feel light. She kept one hand on the wall and kept moving. Only a few minutes before, she'd been unsure whether Duke Kelan or Radcliff's newest debtor would be a worse master to serve. Now that Duke Kelan was on the doorstep, she decided she'd take the rock troll. If she had any choice...

*No.* She had a choice. She wouldn't be a helpless victim, not in this.

Ember darted from the staircase to a closet that was empty except a few broken pieces of furniture. She and a couple of the maids knew that this closet shared a wall with Uncle Radcliff's study, and that a lot could be learned by a quiet individual sitting close to that thin paneling. Duke Kelan's voice was deep and loud, easy to understand even through the wall.

"...received your payment. You failed to include interest."

"I beg your pardon, milord," Radcliff, quieter and muffled, replied. "I was never told about any interest."

"A fault of my servants, I'm sure. Regardless, I'm here to collect."

There was a pause, and Ember held her breath.

"I don't have the resources to pay more. I gave all that I have."

"That is why I've come to offer our previous arrangement: your niece's service until I deem your debt paid in full."

Ember backed away from the wall, nearly tripping on a splintered chair leg. She didn't need to hear her uncle's response. *I have a choice.* She'd *make* herself a choice. But how could she get to the stables without Sarnere's knights seeing her? Ember's mind spun with dozens of ideas, all impossible, as she backed into the hallway.

"There you are."

Ember jumped at the voice, unfamiliar in its hissing whisper. She spun on her heel to find Aunt Cecile glaring down at her, hands on her hips. She looked so out of place, standing in her fine silk dress amid the plain hallway, that Ember choked on a laugh.

"I won't go with Duke Kelan," she whispered back, shutting the closet door behind her.

"Of course not," Aunt Cecile replied, seizing Ember's wrist and dragging her forward. "Your task is to appease that rock troll Radcliff indebted us to. We'll handle Sarnere."

That wasn't the response Ember had expected. She allowed herself to be pulled down the halls while she floundered for a response.

"How do I get past our guests unseen?" she finally asked.

Aunt Cecile stopped and turned back to Ember, still glaring down her long, fine nose.

"I've made the arrangements," she said. "You'll ride now, before they have reason to search for you. Are Sophia and Louisa safe?"

"Hiding in the attic," Ember replied, glancing to the narrow door they'd stopped beside. She knew where it led. Somehow, she'd always assumed her aunt hadn't bothered to learn the secret passages of Rookwood. Apparently, she was wrong.

"Go, now. Before Branson angers him."

Ember nodded, reaching to the small door. But she paused halfway inside the passage, glancing back at Aunt Cecile. Leaving without any sort of goodbye felt...wrong. Yet she had no idea what to say to this woman who'd been her adversary ever since she'd stepped foot in this manor.

She settled with, "good luck." She barely caught sight of Aunt Cecile's wry smile as she stepped into the dark, dusty passage. The door shut behind her only a few steps inside, leaving her in darkness. But Ember knew this narrow tunnel well enough to navigate it by memory even with its strange twists. The entrance made it seem like the passage led to the storage rooms behind the kitchen. In reality, it turned back on itself and led to the outer wall on the far side of the house, closest to the forest. The even narrower exit outside was hidden by massive rose bushes.

Ember didn't bother with caution when she reached the exit, pushing through the branches with a wince at the stinging tears of thorns on her arms. On the other side was a groom with a saddled horse. His name was Rob, and he'd been serving Rookwood for longer than Ember had been alive. He held the horse steady while Ember clumsily climbed into the saddle and handed her the reins with a nod. Ember returned the nod and swallowed the fear clogging her throat. She'd be alone from here on out.

She glanced back, proving to herself that she was out of sight from Duke Kelan and his company, before urging her horse forward. The temptation to send her mount into a run was strong, but she resisted. A horse and rider running away would draw too much attention.

Her shoulders stayed tense long after the manor faded out of sight behind her. The road through the forest was narrow, but well-traveled. If her uncle's story could be trusted, she'd stay on this trail for nearly a day before reaching the overgrown path that led to the castle. Since it was already midmorning, that put her arriving during the night if she held a steady pace. The very thought made her ache.

Ember squared her shoulders. She'd ride as long as she needed to. Duke Kelan's men would likely be searching for her soon, and she wouldn't take the chance of anyone finding her resting and vulnerable. If they wanted to catch her, they'd have to work for it.

That determination held for the first few hours, as Ember glared at the trees she passed as if daring them to reveal her. But by the time the hot afternoon reached her, she was sore and *oh* so tired. She didn't resist when her horse turned aside to a stream that ran alongside the path. Her own throat burned with thirst. Slowly, biting back a groan, Ember threw her leg over the saddle and dropped to the ground. Her legs nearly collapsed beneath her.

Ember took a deep, slow breath, holding tight to the saddle to keep from falling to her knees. The horse drank noisily, oblivious to Ember's struggles. She rested her forehead against the worn leather. *What am I doing?* She couldn't count the number of times she'd dreamed of running away like this, but she'd never imagined she'd be running to a new prison.

She could keep riding, she supposed, and never search for that mysterious castle her uncle described. She could leave them all to their fate and find her own life. Except... *I don't want Sophia and Louisa to fall victim to their father's choices.* Daughters shouldn't face the punishment for their fathers' mistakes.

Ember ached. It was more than her sore legs, unused to sitting so long with a massive animal shifting beneath her. Her chest, her head...all of her ached. Her moment of letting her heart out was having more consequences than she'd guessed. But she couldn't bring herself to regret anything about this day, even running to her own doom. It wasn't like she had anywhere else she could go.

*Serving in a looming castle is as good a way to spend my final years as any, I suppose. Fewer people, fewer chances to fall.* And she couldn't deny that the thought of this mysterious lord of stone, and his strange castle, drew her imagination. What legends would those walls hold? What could she learn serving within them?

The horse let out a huffing sigh, reminding Ember of her current surroundings. She patted the gelding's neck before kneeling a little higher up the stream, scooping up water to satisfy her own thirst. She splashed more on her face in a vain effort to wake herself up.

*Protecting Sophia and Louisa,* she reminded herself, forcing herself back to her feet. *Finding out what this rock troll of a master wants with a young woman in his massive castle.* Her first attempt at remounting ended with Ember struggling not to fall on her rear. She clenched her teeth and tried again, with little success. *Keeping myself away from any entanglements. I have plenty of reasons to go on, and none to keep me here.* As soon as she could get back into the cursed saddle, that was.

After a third, failed attempt, Ember tugged the horse forward to search for something to use as a step. With the added height of an obliging fallen log, Ember finally made it onto the horse's back. She took a deep breath before urging the horse back onto the unchanging path.

"Here's to hoping no storms come along," Ember said to the empty trees, looking up at the small glimpses of sky. *And no curious wolves willing to take on a horse and his rider.*

Ember shivered at the thought, scolding herself for dredging up *that* legend. Tales of large wolves attacking knights, and *killing* them, were too recent for Ember to dismiss easily. The people who'd warned her about the wolf weren't ones to exaggerate.

Ember started humming to fill the silence, forcing her mind to wonder how much of her uncle's fanciful story was true. What would she find at the end of her journey? What legends would she uncover? Wild imaginings took her mind off dangers for a while.

But when the sun set, thoughts of wolves and blood returned. The image of Duke Kelan's standard, the monstrous black wolf standing victorious over its victim, was branded in her mind. Ember was no lamb, but it wasn't hard to imagine her own form below that predator's paws. She jumped at every sound, wishing she could see more in the dim light of dusk that filtered through the trees.

Her horse stopped. Ember looked back to her mount, nudging him with her heels, but though he shifted his weight he didn't step forward. His ears swiveled around wildly, and with a pounding heart Ember searched the darkness around her. *What does he hear?*

A low growl rumbled through the air at her back.

## CHAPTER
# THREE

Ember turned slowly and found a pair of amber eyes glowing in the darkness. They were nearly level with her horse's back. Ember could barely make out the course fur and long teeth that belonged to those eyes, the shape of a wolf just as large as the rumors claimed. *Almighty, save me*, she prayed, choking on a scream.

The wolf growled, taking a single step forward. Her horse bolted. She snapped back, nearly tumbling from the saddle as she scrambled for something to hold onto. She settled for a fistful of mane. Her breath caught in her throat, warring with her thrumming heartbeat. Wind tore tears from her eyes, branches whipped against her skin. But there was no stopping her mount now: Ember's one attempt to tug on the reins did nothing.

And behind her, looming like the shadow of death, the wolf followed. Every moment Ember expected to feel the weight of that predator on her back, feel his fangs tearing out her throat... But the attack never came. Minutes passed as years. Her horse's breathing grew ragged, his sides wet with sweat. Still the wolf didn't pounce.

Ember chanced a look over her shoulder and found the amber

eyes still behind them, still at a distance. Why? Were there others on the road ahead? Ember tried pulling back on the reins, and the horse slowed to an uneasy canter. The wolf slowed as well.

*What game is this?* Ember turned forward again, hands trembling as she gripped the sweat soaked reins and horse mane. None of the stories told anything like this. The wolf attacked, and its victims died. It never *pushed* them anywhere. The idea of going where the wolf wanted made her sick with terror. *But what choice do I have?*

Another snarl sounded from her left, and Ember flinched away. Her horse did the same, shying away onto a narrow trail lined with pines that scratched Ember's bare arms. She tasted blood where she'd bitten her tongue. Another branch loomed close, and Ember barely ducked in time to avoid being knocked off her horse's back. Her heart stuttered. If she fell now...

Her thoughts were interrupted by the horse skidding to a stop before massive gates. They rose from the trees like they'd grown there, a solid barrier between Ember and safety. Ember glanced over her shoulder in search of that amber glow...and found nothing. She shivered. Was the wolf scared of the master of these lands? Or was this where he'd been steering her?

Her horse shifted uneasily, lifting his front legs off the ground in threat. Ember scrambled from his back. Her legs folded when they hit the ground, and Ember barely managed to catch herself on the saddle. She refused to be trampled, not at this late stage of her journey. Thankfully, the gelding settled a little once she was off his back. Ember took a deep breath and stepped toward the gates, casting another glance toward the road in search of the wolf. The night was still empty. She turned her attention to the gates.

They were made of a metal that was black in the darkness, solid and gleaming dimly. Ember reached out a shaking hand to take hold of the latch, but a shock made her pull back. A shivering power traveled from her fingertips through her body, reverberating through the ancient gates. Ember held her hand to her chest and stared wide eyed at that entrance. The power trembling through their air was dark, sorrowful...and too familiar. *What have I done?*

The horse reared suddenly, tugging the reins from Ember's grasp.

"No," she gasped, trying to snatch them back. But the gelding had reached his limit. He spun around and ran back down the overgrown drive, disappearing into the night. Ember was left staring after him, heart pounding. *Please let the wolf have moved on.* After a moment of listening, and hearing nothing but silence, Ember turned back to the gate.

*This is my part...I won't try to run.* No matter what malevolent powers lay on this place...she would face it head on. *Just as I always have.*

Ember squared her shoulders and reached her fingers back toward the latch. No strange power lashed out at her this time, and she managed to pull them open wide enough for her slim body to slip within. The metal was cool and smooth under her touch, making her shiver when it brushed her. They pulled shut on their own.

Ember refused to look over her shoulder, walking forward as steadily as she could manage. She held the idea of Sophia and Louisa, safe from this terror at least, at the front of her mind. No matter what happened with the Duke of Sarnere, she'd spared them this place. And she examined the castle as best she could in the darkness, trying to match it to one of the many legends she'd heard through the years. Without the trees blocking her in, she could see to identify most of the larger shapes in the moonlight.

The castle was a tall, block structure clearly designed for defense, not beauty. She couldn't make out what stone made up its walls, but her mind filled in the rest: stone blocks larger than her horse, all in a weathered gray. Behind, Ember thought she could see craggy bluffs of a mountainside rising far above everything else in the landscape. Four towers rose from the castle, one in each corner. Ember thought she caught a flash of light in the tallest tower, standing in the northern corner. Her steps stuttered.

"I won't be afraid," she whispered, forcing her left foot forward. "Whatever is in this castle, I will face with dignity."

She paused again when she passed beneath the wall and into the courtyard. Ahead, steps rose to the main entrance, framed with stone carvings Ember was careful not to examine too closely. Ember couldn't see much of the courtyard, and she hurried through it to the steps. She continued whispering to herself as she climbed the wide staircase.

"I'm safer here, anyway. I'm serving in an abandoned castle, possibly under the control of a true *rock troll*...hardly the setting for a romance."

It sounded like the setting of a fairy tale, but Ember ignored that. She enjoyed reading about happy endings and hope winning out, but that didn't mean she thought they were real.

Ember stopped for another deep breath before knocking on the wooden doors. They were nearly twice her height, bound with the same smooth metal as the gates and adorned with spikes as long as her forearm. Her knock barely made a sound.

When nothing happened, Ember hesitantly tugged on the door. It swung open with surprising ease, allowing Ember to slip inside. Like the gate, it closed on its own, though this time Ember softened its fall. Then she turned to face the room.

Torches high on the walls cast a dim glow over her surroundings, revealing a grand foyer filled with lavish decoration beyond Ember's imagination. Statues, tapestries, vases holding jeweled flowers that glinted in the light... The careless show of wealth made Ember shrink in on herself, an insignificant stain on the worn carpet running down the room. She understood, now, why her uncle had thought his theft might go unnoticed...how could someone keep track of it all?

But the beauty was marred. Dust covered everything in a thick, muffling layer. Cobwebs, also covered in dust, hung down from drapes and corners. Only the floor was disturbed, a few trails of footprints interrupting the dirt. *How long has this castle stood, untouched? How long since life filled these halls?* The question made her shiver.

Movement on her right made Ember jerk back, her shriek muffled to a gasp just in time. A masked guard had stepped into the torchlight, looming tall and silent as her uncle had described. Ember was beginning to wish her uncle *had* exaggerated his story.

The masked man beckoned her forward, turning away without waiting for her response. Hesitantly, Ember followed. She tried not to gawk as they passed through more rooms full of treasures. By the time they stopped outside a set of ornate doors, where a second guard waited, Ember wasn't sure what overwhelmed her more: the sheer wealth laying around, or the neglect that hung over everything like a thick shroud.

The second guard opened one of the doors, while her silent guide beckoned her through. Ember eyed him warily. She didn't like following orders from shadowy guards who never spoke. But what would the consequences be if she refused? Ember stepped forward.

Though she watched the guards carefully, they did nothing but close the door behind her. She couldn't resist turning to examine her new surroundings. In a way, it was the most intimidating sight yet.

They stood at one end of a great hall, tall enough that the ceiling was lost to the shadows. There were no treasures carelessly spread around this room; the walls and floor were devoid of the decoration she'd seen along the way. But along each wall leading to the front of the room were alcoves where statues of men and women stood eerily on their pedestals. Ember could almost imagine them turning to watch her as she took her first steps into the room.

But the only eyes Ember could see were on the far end of the room, from the figure sitting on the throne. Cast in shadow, Ember couldn't see much of the man seated there. But his eyes...his eyes seemed to burn in the darkness. Once Ember looked up, she could hardly tear her gaze away. Dazedly, she stepped forward. The scuff of her boot on the stone floor woke her a bit, and she raised her chin. She stood tall as she made the way past those still figures toward the dais, and when she stopped she gave a deep, flourishing curtsy.

"You're early."

Ember fought not to flinch at that *voice*, deep and gravelly. She could hear his annoyance. She rose from her curtsey, wobbling slightly, and kept her head lowered in deference. This wasn't a promising start.

"My apologies, milord. It wasn't my choice."

"Explain."

"Duke Kelan of Sarnere came to my uncle's estate to claim the *interest* on my uncle's original debt."

"I don't see how that would require you to come early. You didn't long for more time to spend with your family?"

Ember stiffened at the sarcastic edge in his voice, raising her chin without lifting her eyes.

"*I* am the interest Duke Kelan demanded. If I hadn't come today, I wouldn't have come at all. What difference does a week make in the span of a lifetime?"

The throne creaked as her new master leaned back. She dared to raise her gaze to his boots, but no further. The darkness around his throne was unusually thick, and she didn't want to find out whether or not her eyes could see through that veil.

"You chose coming here over service to Sarnere? I suppose I should be flattered, but I can't help but wonder why."

Ember resisted the urge to sigh audibly. "Because that was the bargain. I *know* what I would've faced in Sarnere, and I preferred coming here. At least now one threat to my family is eliminated."

"*Do* you know?" the figure on the throne muttered. He spoke louder before Ember could make sense of those words. "You're that loyal to a family that sends you as their sacrificial lamb? Your uncle sent you off to serve a villain...obviously a caring guardian."

Ember gritted her teeth, struggling to keep her voice steady. "My relationship with my uncle isn't your concern. You wanted a servant, and here I am."

Tense silence followed. Ember knew she'd left subservience behind her, but she couldn't bring herself to care. At least, not yet.

She kept her chin raised and her eyes lowered as she waited for her new master to respond.

"Here you are," he repeated. "What's your name?"

"Ember Kendrick, your lordship."

"Ember Kendrick. Do you intend to spend our time together staring at my feet?"

"I was under the impression nobility don't appreciate servants making eye contact," Ember snapped. "It isn't as if I could see anything, even if I did look up."

"I'm not nobility. Not anymore."

His voice had lowered to a snarl, and it took every scrap of courage Ember had left not to flinch under its weight. *Not anymore.* What did that mean?

"As for the darkness," he said in a steadier tone. "That's solved easily enough."

With that he stood and stepped down, toward Ember. She stiffened her spine and stayed where she was, refusing to retreat. Her eyes lifted without her permission, taking in the figure as he left the strange shadows. He paused on the last step before fully entering the light. And Ember was left somewhere between captivated and terrified as she took in the creature before her.

Her uncle had been wrong...this man was no rock troll from the crags of the north. He was a statue come to life. He was tall and broad shouldered: built like the knights she'd seen ride through the countryside, but larger than she would've expected. No towering giant, but enough to be thoroughly intimidating. The sword hanging from his side drew her attention as the onyx stones in the hilt winked in the torchlight. A warrior, then. She could well imagine men cowering before him, fearing the sting of that sword in his grasp.

But she couldn't help but look to the rest of him... his skin that was the dull gray of river rocks, chalky and stiff. She wondered what it would feel like to touch the back of his hand, where darker lines gave the illusions of cracks through the stone. Would it feel like stone, as well? Would it give like flesh? The hand she was staring at clenched into a fist, and Ember's gaze darted up, to his face. His features, haughty and severe, were weathered like she imagined the stone of the castle would be. His eyes were the only feature that wasn't dull and worn: blue gray and fierce, full of life. She quickly looked away, afraid of looking into those eyes for more than a heartbeat. She focused instead on his disheveled hair, also gray and hanging around his face, not quite to his shoulders.

"Well?" he asked, harsh with contempt. "Do I live up to the horror stories?"

Ember swallowed and forced herself to sound calm, at ease. "My uncle exaggerated."

His harsh laugh shouldn't have been comforting, but she relaxed anyway.

"That doesn't surprise me," he said. "Let's go over your duties, shall we?"

He turned and walked forward, not looking to see if Ember followed. She wondered what he'd do if she stayed behind, but moved to walk after him anyway.

"I have servants who work in the kitchens and stables," he said. "But no one seeing to the maintenance of my castle. I'm leaving that to you. Start anywhere you like, and see Helen if you have any questions. The only areas off limits to you are my personal rooms, my study, and the dungeons. Understood?"

"Yes," Ember said, though her mind was spinning. Did he expect her to clean this *entire* castle? But that wasn't the question that left her lips. "How should I address you?"

He stopped and whirled around so quickly, Ember nearly ran into him.

"What?" His eyes glared down at her, making Ember draw back a little.

"I don't even know your name," she said, trying to sound harsh. Her voice still trembled.

He narrowed his eyes, and crack-like wrinkles appeared to

surround them. "My name is Dyrerisan. You may address me as 'milord.'"

"Yes, *milord,*" Ember said, bobbing a shallow curtsey.

Dyrerisan narrowed his eyes further, watching Ember for a heart stopping moment, and she wondered if he'd caught the sarcasm in her gesture. But he turned again without punishing her, and Ember followed with a breath of relief.

"Ben will lead you the kitchens," Dyrerisan said, gesturing to the masked guard on the left. The pair had followed them across the room, and now Ben stepped forward. "Helen will show you to your rooms and explain your duties further."

He marched away without so much as a glance back or grunt of farewell. Ember stared after him, blinking slowly. *What have I gotten myself into*? She turned back to Ben, the guard, who bowed and led her on. She followed him closely, trying not to gape at the new hallways he led her through. These were obviously servant passages, bare and serviceable. Unlike the rest of the castle she'd seen, these places had obviously been cared for. It was all a little worn, and little ragged, but no dusty cobwebs hung from the ceiling.

*This is one place I won't have to clean,* she thought with an edge of hysteria. She swallowed back the urge to laugh, knowing she wouldn't be able to stop once she started. She didn't want her new companions to think she was crazy.

*Why are the servant passages the only clean place in this fortress?* That was a better turn to her thoughts, the mystery she'd walked into. Why would the master of a castle allow his halls to fall to disrepair?

That question brought Dyrerisan's face to her mind. A statue come to life. Had she heard legends of such a thing? What would the servants of such a man be like? She knew of the two masked men, but who else lingered in this place? What sort of people served a lord like Dyrerisan?

*People like me, I suppose.* Air lodged in her throat, choking back what was either laughter or sobbing. Ember wasn't sure which. *I'm here now. I'll face whatever comes.*

Voices fell silent as Ember stepped inside the kitchen after her guide. Three women stood from a table, and Ember stuttered to a halt a few steps inside the door. *They look normal.* Perhaps that should've reassured her, but the wobbly feeling in her stomach didn't feel like reassurance.

Her guide, Ben, continued forward, dropping his mask onto the table as he took the hand of one of the younger women. Meanwhile, the oldest stepped toward Ember, a smile lighting her whole face.

"You must be our new companion," she said, taking one of Ember's hands before Ember could react. "It's a pleasure to meet you. I hope your journey here wasn't too rough."

"It was fine," Ember said, her voice strained against that looming hysteria.

"My name is Helen," the woman said, pulling Ember deeper into the toasty kitchen. "I'm the head cook. At the table are Miri, and Freya."

The other two women nodded as their name was called. Miri dropped her sewing to the table, looking away when Ember tried meeting her eyes. She held tight to Ben's hand. But Freya met Ember's gaze boldly, smile lines gathering around her eyes.

"It's good to meet you," Freya said.

"Good to meet you, too," Ember replied automatically. "My name is Ember."

Helen released Ember's hand only to shove a slice of thick bread into her grasp.

"I'm sure you're hungry," Helen said, when Ember looked to her blankly. "We have more substantial fare, if you want it."

"This is fine," Ember said, drawing the bread closer to herself. She didn't move to take a bite, turning instead to the other faces in the room. The two young women had retaken their seats, and Ben had settled close to Miri. Ember thought she saw something in Ben's face, something that reminded her of Dyrerisan...but she couldn't be sure in the dim light. Freya caught her staring, but only smiled. Ember looked down to her hand.

She should be better at this. She should be saying something. But what could she say? She couldn't pretend that she was excited to live here...this was the better of two options, not something she would've chosen on her own. And Dyrerisan...her meeting with him had left her off balance.

"You're trembling," Helen said, reappearing at Ember's side.

Ember looked down at her hand and saw that she was, indeed, trembling. She stared at her shaking hand for a moment before she found her voice to answer Helen's concern.

"I'm a bit tired."

"Of course. I'll take you to your room so you can rest."

Ember followed Helen back into the hall without comment, following close to the woman's back. Only a short distance from the kitchen, she turned left through a thin door, beckoning Ember to follow her. Ember ducked into a little room, with a narrow cot and trunk tucked against one wall and a wardrobe and washbasin against the other.

"It isn't much," Helen said apologetically. "We weren't sure what you'd like added, so we left it bare. As you get settled you can do what you like to make yourself more at home."

"Thank you," Ember managed, and hoped desperately that Helen wouldn't stay for more conversation. She was reaching her limit. She needed to be alone...desperately. On some level, Helen must have understood, because she left with a wish for good sleep, closing the door behind her. Ember stood silently as she waited for the steps to retreat down the hall.

The bread in her hand crumbled, and Ember looked down to see she'd tightened her hand into a fist. She cupped her hands to catch the crumbs, raising what was left of the bread to her mouth. It was fresh and flavorful, making Ember suddenly realize that she was starving. She ate the rest as she stepped deeper into her new room, laying her shoulder bag on the cot and sitting beside it.

There wasn't much to look at. *What do they expect me to decorate with, I wonder? Treasures from the upper halls?* The thought made her want to laugh again, and Ember pressed her fist to her mouth to stop it from escaping. She couldn't fall apart, not even here. She couldn't forget that she wasn't really alone.

Ember turned to her shoulder bag, digging out her journal and the worn yarn doll she'd kept on her bed as a small child. With those treasures in her arms, she crawled under the covers and closed her eyes, begging her mind to be silent for a few hours. Just a few hours of rest...then she'd face her new world.

# CHAPTER FOUR

The next morning, Ember stayed in her room longer than necessary. She'd already changed into her spare dress and stowed her items away. Most of her meager belongings went in the trunk. Her shoulder bag and journal went in the frame of the cot, where it was a little better hidden. She'd washed her face with the water someone had provided before she'd arrived, she'd redone her hair...now she sat on the edge of her cot trying to catch a bit of the light that made it through her shuttered window. If she had to guess, it was already late into the morning. Some servant she was.

Ember closed her eyes. *Stop stalling, stupid girl. You'll never get anywhere hiding in your room.*

Still, it took a few more quiet moments before Ember could make herself stand and leave the room. Her steps were slow as she neared the kitchen, but she made herself stand tall as she entered the warm room. All three of the women she'd met were present, and neither of the men. Ember inched further inside.

"Good morning," Helen said, smiling when Ember looked to her. "Feel rested?"

"Yes," Ember replied. "Thank you for letting me sleep in."

"No trouble. Come, grab some breakfast and I'll answer any questions you have."

Ember obeyed, unable to resist the smell of pumpkin bread that had overwhelmed her since she'd stepped into the hall. She stood near the counter, across from where Helen worked, and organized her thoughts.

"Lord Dyrerisan said I'll be cleaning the castle?" Ember said.

"That's what he told us," Helen said, glancing up with a wry smile. "I know it's an overwhelming thought, but not much of it is used, these days. You won't need to do anything in here, or any of the servant halls on this floor."

Ember nodded, looking around. That still left most of the fortress for her. Her mind spun.

"Who else lives here?" Ember asked, looking back to Helen. She almost missed the uneasy look Freya and Miri exchanged.

"We're the only servants left," Helen said, staring at her hands as she transferred bread from the counter to the oven. "The only one you haven't officially met yet is John, Freya's husband. He and Ben see to the stables and gardens, while the three of us work here, mostly. There's too much for us to take on cleaning this whole place."

*If three people can't see to it, why did he give the task to one girl?* But Ember didn't ask that question, wary of her place here. They were being friendly, welcoming even, but she shouldn't let it lull her into complacency. There was a lot they weren't telling her. Of course, that was only fair...there was a lot she wouldn't tell *them*.

Ember caught Helen watching her and tried to smile. "Where do I start?"

Helen thought a moment, brow furrowed.

"The towers," Freya offered. "There's not much to clean, but the view is stunning."

"It's a decent climb," Miri said, with a darting glance at Freya that Ember thought was a silent scolding. Freya didn't react.

"Learning the layout might be your best starting point," Helen said. "It's easy to get lost in this place, if you're not familiar with its ways."

Ember tapped her fingers against the counter, glancing between the three women. It didn't escape her notice that none of them volunteered to show her around themselves. *A* lot *they're not telling me. But maybe I can learn some of it for myself.*

"That's probably a good idea," Ember said, taking a step away from the counter. "I won't do much good if I can't find anything."

"Don't forget to come down for lunch," Helen said. "And come to us if you have any more questions. We'll be glad to help you."

Ember nodded as she backed away, out of the kitchen. Once she was out of sight she turned away, examining the hall around her as she tried retracing her steps from the night before. She found the door to the great hall, which was empty, but after glancing at those statues standing in the darkness she returned to the corridor and went on. After trying a few doors, she found the foyer.

Ember stepped quietly as she left the servant halls, wary of coming across Dyrerisan. She had her excuses ready if he questioned her purpose wandering the halls, but she'd prefer not to use them. When it came to it, she'd rather not face *him* at all.

Ember spun slowly, taking in the foyer and wondering which path she should take. Freya's suggestion wouldn't leave her mind. *What view waits for me up there?* Ember climbed the stairs on the left, hoping they'd lead her to the passage toward one of the towers.

But the stairs only led her to the next floor, spitting her into a hall that dead ended in a door to a cobwebbed guest room. A peek inside the other doors of that hall showed the same. Ember checked every one, anyway, taking in their interior and wondering at the vast difference between outside the castle and within. The structure was obviously a fortress built foremost for defensibility, and yet the rooms within were decorated like an emperor's palace. Why?

Ember closed the door to the last guestroom, decorated in shades of green all faded to gray with dust, and stepped toward one of the curtained windows. She pulled aside the heavy curtain, squinting to see through the grime coating the glass panes. All she could see were blurred shapes of green and gray. Just washing the windows would take days. And how long until they'd be covered in dust once more?

Ember dropped the curtain into place, turning to an adjoining hall. If she kept wandering, she'd stumble upon the towers eventually. She'd handle one problem at a time, one mystery at a time.

This hall was lined with more guest rooms, with a few sitting rooms interspersed. It ended on the other side of the fortress, at a wide window with a cushioned seat. Ember set a hand on the cushions and disturbed a cloud of dust. She frowned and withdrew her hand, glancing around.

"What was he thinking?" she whispered.

She couldn't clean this entire fortress. Even if she managed it, how long would it take her? Months, surely. By the time she finished, she'd need to start over. The never-ending cycle stretched before her, looming to swallow her remaining years in monotony and toil. That wasn't how she wanted to spend the rest of her life. But she was trapped, enslaved...no way out.

"I was thinking one maid is better than none."

Ember jumped at the low voice behind her, spinning on her heel and dropping into a curtsy. Her heart pounded. She hoped Dyrerisan hadn't seen the terror on her face as she lowered her head...she had no idea when he'd come up behind her.

"Forgive me," Ember said.

"For? And stand up. I don't want you falling to your knees every time we pass in the hall."

Ember obeyed, raising her eyes until she found Dyrerisan where he stood in the shadows. Their eyes met and held. Dyrerisan looked almost surprised, but Ember wasn't sure why. Did he expect her to keep her head down? Well, she hadn't, and now...now she was remembering Uncle Radcliff's story. *Eyes that can pierce your very soul.* Ember believed it. But she wasn't sure she wanted her soul to be seen.

Ember forced her eyes away, looking back to the cushions. She cleared her throat, pressing her legs to the window seat to steady herself.

"I didn't mean to disturb you," Ember said, glancing to Dyrerisan only briefly. He was still watching her.

"You didn't," he said. "And don't tell me you're the type to apologize if I step on your foot. I have no use for a terrified mouse."

Ember met his eyes again, this time with a glare. "Then tell me what you *do* want, *your lordship,* since you obviously aren't asking for a typical servant."

Dyrerisan's lips twisted in what could *almost* be called a smile, but his eyes hardened to the same granite as his skin. "Fire. Good. What I want, Ember Kendrick, is someone who won't cower when I pass. I despise false subservience."

Ember couldn't help her own smirk rising to the surface. "Who said it would be false?"

Dyrerisan raised a single, imperious eyebrow, though the effort seemed to nearly crack his skin. Ember wondered morbidly if he could bleed. How far down did the stone go?

"You are not your uncle," Dyrerisan said. "And I would have respect, not groveling."

He took a step forward, and Ember leaned back, her heels hitting the edge of the window seat. The action was involuntary, but still Dyrerisan's face twisted. He turned away before Ember could decide what his expression meant, stalking silently down the hallway.

He called over his shoulder, "If you're looking for the north tower, start at the foyer. Second hall to the left."

Ember's thanks went unsaid, as she stared numbly after her strange new employer. She waited until he'd disappeared before turning back the way she'd come, retracing her steps to the foyer. But though she glanced to the hall Dyrerisan had named, longing to explore a little more, she turned back toward the kitchen. She wouldn't risk running into him again...not yet. She needed time to make sense of what had just passed between them.

Slowing her steps as she neared the kitchen, Ember worked to pull her expression into some kind of composure. She'd ask again what she should clean first, and she'd disappear into mindless tasks for a few hours. Maybe scrubbing at stone floors would give her a chance to think through her confusing new life.

Only Freya and Miri were in the kitchen. Both women looked up at Ember's entrance, and she took a moment to remember her planned words.

"I was wondering what rooms Lord Dyrerisan uses most, and which you'd recommend I clean first?" Ember said, striving for an innocent sort of confusion that would cover any lasting unease. She didn't want them asking questions about what she had, or hadn't, found.

"The dining room is closest," Miri said slowly, looking to Freya.

Freya nodded and started pulling dough from her hands. "I'll show her."

Miri accepted that easily enough, and Ember stepped back to let Freya pass. And she followed the woman's brisk pace back down the hall, to the fourth door on the right, which opened to a large and predictably lavish dining hall.

"Do you know where the supplies are?" Freya asked, as Ember glanced around the room.

"No," Ember admitted.

"This way."

Freya led her to a door across the hall that led to a large and well stocked supply closet. Ember leaned in the doorway, taking in the inventory with relief that she'd have supplies, at least. The question of why a castle that hadn't been cleaned in decades still had furniture polish was something Ember would ponder later.

"Thank you," Ember said, glancing back to Freya.

Freya nodded but didn't move from the doorway. She was staring at Ember, and the look she had made Ember straighten and grab the doorframe.

"What is it?" Ember asked warily.

"I just...I wanted to say you don't need to fear Marquis Dyrerisan. He's a protector at heart. And...his callousness is caused by many years of sorrow."

Ember took that in, watching Freya closely. It seemed she expected Ember to respond.

"Who said I fear him?" she asked, aiming for a flippant tone.

"It's expected, given what you know of him so far," Freya replied, nodding like she approved. "But he has his reasons. I've known him... longer than you'd expect, and I know he's an honorable man. As long as you're at Nyxwood castle, you have nothing to fear."

Ember blinked, holding tighter to the doorframe. *Nyxwood...* Freya smiled at Ember's reaction, nodding again as if she somehow knew the thoughts that were flying through her head.

"Happy cleaning," Freya said, turning back toward the kitchen.

Ember stayed at the doorway, not bothering to respond as she took in this new revelation. Could she really be in *Nyxwood* castle? Ember had wondered what legends she'd uncover in this place...but *Nyxwood.* That name rang through dozens of legends, was carved into a hundred monuments. Every dream of protection, every story of valiant heroes had Nyxwood at its center.

*And its broken.* Thoughts of clouded windows and dust filled halls echoed through her mind. The image of *Marquis* Dyrerisan, a living statue amid the forgotten fortress, stood before her like one of those ancient monuments. *What happened here?*

# CHAPTER FIVE

Numbly, Ember donned an oversized apron and tied a clean rag over her hair. She managed to find what she'd need for sweeping and returned to the dim dining hall Freya had shown her. Ember took it in with new eyes. *How many heroes have stood on this floor? How many legends have eaten at this table?*

As Ember stepped inside, the room looked the same as the rest of the castle: lavish with decoration, and dim with neglect. She stepped toward the far wall and pulled back the drapes to let in the murky sunlight, blinking at the clouds of dust disturbed by her action. *They'll need to be washed.* But she left that thought behind for the moment, turning to take in the room.

It was twice as long as it was wide, filled with a massive table surrounded by chairs to seat dozens of people. *How long have they sat empty?* The only part of the table that looked used was the head, where an ornate chair and half-used candlesticks stood out as the only *lived in* part of the space.

The wall where Ember stood had ten narrow windows, all covered with dark curtains, and directly across stood a massive fireplace empty of all but dust. The rest of the walls were covered in tapestries and mounted weapons, leaving only glimpses of the wood paneling beneath. The servant entrance Ember had used was hardly noticeable, tucked in a corner beside wall hangings that could be pulled over to hide the door. The main entrance had double doors with twin battle axes hanging above them.

"At some point," Ember muttered, pulling open more curtains. The windows were all barred from the outside. "I'll have to ask who was in charge of decorating this place."

It only took a few more sneeze-inducing dust clouds for Ember to go back for a step ladder and pull the curtains to the floor to be washed. The resulting pile of faded cloth was almost to her waist, and Ember stared at it with dread. *Nyxwood or not, those won't be enjoyable to wash.* With a slight hesitation, Ember dragged them into the hall. She'd ask where the laundry was later. For now, she had other cleaning to do.

Ember worked more slowly than necessary, her mind still alive with the stories she knew by heart regarding the fortress where she now stood. She stared up at mounted swords and axes she'd need to dust, wondering if they had names, whose hands had wielded them before they'd been turned to trophies high on a wall. She beat dust from the tapestries and watched their scenes come to life, wondering who'd woven them. She was almost sure she recognized a few of the stories they told.

On one tapestry, a company of men and women on golden horses rode toward the sunrise, monsters and sorcerers chasing after them only to shrink back from the light. Was it recounting Marquis Montague leading his people out of the shadow lands? He captured this castle and renamed it Nyxwood, establishing it as a foothold for the kingdom's defense. Ember had fallen to sleep listening to tales of his valiance, his concern for the people who were withering away under tyrants and monsters. His descendants had followed in his footsteps.

Until Nyxwood disappeared. Then men like Duke Kelan had risen back into power. The concept of *valiant* leaders, lords who *protected* their subjects, had faded to little more than a bedtime story. People like the man who taught Sophia and Louisa claimed Nyxwood itself hadn't existed...it had been merely a fairytale, a way for people to bring a little joy to their dreary lives. Ember had argued with the tutor more than once about that.

*Where does Dyrerisan fit in to all of this?* Ember paused her dusting, glancing back at the head of the table. Could the legends surrounding Nyxwood's disappearance really be true? She'd always thought they were myths, explanations for why the land's greatest fortification disappeared so suddenly, without a trace. She'd assumed those who told the stories were desperately trying to find a reason that the regions greatest protectors had abandoned them. Ember had never understood how anyone could *know* what had happened. But standing on these stones, knowing she was now servant to at the very least a *descendent* of the Nyxwood masters... those legends felt more real.

Ember pondered that as she retrieved a broom and attacked the stone floor. There were several legends about Nyxwood's disappearance, all with their own explanations for *why*. But the common factor was a curse, on the Marquis and his domain. Ember didn't doubt that *that* part of the story was true. She could feel the curse at work, hanging over this place along with the cobwebs and neglect. Dyrerisan was cursed. Perhaps his servants were too, though Ember couldn't identify *how*.

That cloying magic had already brushed against Ember more than once, trying to decide what her place was in all this. Even now, as she looked up to the murky windows, the curse searched for a way within her mind, a way under her skin. But it ran into a barrier she thought it hadn't expected, if curses could be said to *expect* anything. Unsuccessful, it withdrew back to the shadows. Ember smiled, ignoring the bitter satisfaction it dredged up, and kept sweeping.

"Ember?"

Ember turned from the window she was scrubbing, grasping at the frame to keep herself steady. Miri was at the door, looking around the room with wide eyes.

"Helen sent me," Miri said, looking up to Ember on her stepladder. "It's past time for you to eat."

Ember stared back a moment before dropping her rag into the bucket of soapy water, climbing to the floor to follow Miri out of the room. A small break wouldn't hurt.

When Ember reached the hall, she found Miri staring at the pile of dusty curtains, prodding at them with an expression of distaste.

"I'll clean those this afternoon," Ember said. "I was only waiting for someone to show me where to take them."

"I'll wash them."

Ember blinked. "You don't have to."

Miri looked up, offering the first smile Ember had seen from her. "I'll wash them. It's the least I can do. You have more than enough to do without worrying about laundry."

"Thank you." Ember hesitantly offered a smile of her own to accompany the words, glad when Miri turned back toward the kitchen.

Freya and Helen were laughing together when Ember entered, going straight for the washbasin to clean the dirt and suds from her hands. Miri joined the conversation, sitting at the table with a new sewing project, mending a man's shirt.

"You missed the boys," Helen said, handing Ember a bowl of stew with a slice of heavy bread. "Lose track of time, did you?"

"Yes," Ember said, taking a seat across the table from Miri. "There's...a lot to do."

Freya snorted. "That's an understatement."

"I'm going to wash the curtains and whatnot," Miri said, without looking up from her sewing. "Care to help me, Freya?"

"Only if threatened."

Miri glanced up with a smirk to where Freya was making a gigantic bowl of batter. "Threatened with what?"

Freya thought about that a moment, stirring slowly. "Death or dismemberment. Anything less, and it isn't worth it."

"I'll let you get out of it if you'll take over harvesting the garden for the next few weeks."

"Done. Give me dirt and sunshine any day over endless yards of drenched fabric."

Ember listened and ate quietly, glad that they seemed content to leave her out of the conversation for now. Keeping her distance in this place would be more difficult than Ember had guessed. Perhaps she should be grateful for whatever odd reasoning kept Helen and the rest away from most of the castle.

"Did you find your way around alright?" Helen asked, distracting Ember from her thoughts.

"I suppose," Ember replied. "I found the guest rooms, at least."

"There's twenty-seven of them, if you can believe it," Freya said.

*Twenty-seven?* Then this castle was even larger than Ember had guessed. No wonder she'd gotten turned around.

"It's hard to imagine so many people here," Ember said, thinking of the disarray and endless silence. She watched the women closely for their reactions, noticing that they all paused in their work a moment.

"It used to be commonplace to have most of them filled," Helen said.

*How long ago was that?* Ember longed to ask, but shoved bread in her mouth to keep herself silent. *Small nudges. One question at a time.* The conversation took a while to pick up again, and this time Ember only listened. She finished her food quickly, taking her bowl and spoon to the half full basin of dishes.

"Thank you," she murmured, as she headed for the exit.

"Bring whatever you need washed to one of the servant halls," Miri called after her. "I'll take care of it from there."

Ember repeated her thank you a little more fervently, ducking out of the kitchen quickly. She was glad to return to the dining room's looming silence, even if it meant going back to work. She returned to washing windows, her mind spinning again. The bucket felt heavier as she hauled it back up the ladder, but Ember ignored the sensation. Seeing the view into the gardens uninterrupted by dust and age was worth sore arms.

The afternoon sun had warmed the room almost beyond comfort when Ember moved on to scrubbing the floors. The endless buckets of water she carried back and forth, alongside the repetitive scrubbing required to lift unknown years of grime from the stones, was enough to make her entire body ache, but Ember kept working. This was what she was here for. And she didn't want Dyrerisan to find a half-cleaned room when he came for dinner, as the half-burned candles indicated was his habit. She liked even less the possibility of him coming while she was still working, but she tried not to think about that.

The aching, more than familiar, wasn't enough to silence her mind. She concentrated on recalling all the legends and ballads she'd learned about Nyxwood castle, leaning on those stories to keep her company through the rest of the day. She kept her thoughts away from Nyxwood's disappearance, though. She wasn't ready to consider the full implications of *that.*

It was late afternoon when Ember pulled out the furniture polish, leaving too little time to give attention to every one of the chairs surrounding the table. She settled for polishing the top of the table, a task that required her to climb on top of the vast wooden surface to reach the middle. She had to scrape wax from the wood at the head of the table.

Surrounded by the warmth of sunlight and the nostalgic smell of the polish, Ember unconsciously relaxed. She hummed quietly to herself, a ballad she could remember her mother singing while she cleaned. Ember had sung it to Sophia and Louisa a few times, usually when a storm was battering the house and they couldn't sleep. Not often, though...she hadn't done anything with her cousins *often*, mostly keeping to her own company. *I wonder if my absence has even made a difference.*

Ember frowned, a new ache arising in her chest as she climbed back to the floor. Her mind went to a square of embroidered cloth still tucked in the front flap of her journal. She didn't *want* anyone to miss her, didn't want them to mourn her. So why did that little square of cloth make her eyes burn every time she thought of it?

Maybe because she'd failed, and her cousins were paying the price. *Ember* was paying the price. *But I won't fail in this.* Ember dropped to her knees, turning her attention to polishing the chair at the head of the table. And she did her best to push aside all thoughts of grief or simple mementos.

Dyrerisan's seat at the grand table provided a suitable distraction. Unlike the rest of the chairs that she'd have to see to tomorrow, *this* seat was full of carved detail all across its surface. Ember used her thumbnail to push the polish-soaked cloth into every crack and crevice, scowling as she concentrated. It was likely a good thing Dyrerisan didn't come inside the dining room as she worked. She might've given him a tongue lashing on excessive decoration. She didn't want to find out how he'd react to that.

Ember finished just as the last sunlight disappeared behind the horizon. She took the matches she'd stowed in her pocket and lit a few of the lamps hanging on the wall, as well as the candles at the head of the table. Then she stood back to admire her work for a moment, pulling in a deep breath and grateful no dust tickled her nose. She wondered if Dyrerisan would notice. She wondered if he even had memory of living in a space that was *cared for*, clean and lived in. But then, perhaps he cleaned his own rooms.

Ember stifled a snort at that thought, gathering the last of her cleaning supplies to return to the closet. Her tired arms protested even that effort, but Ember gritted her teeth and ignored it. She wouldn't let that small pain ruin her sense of satisfaction. When was the last time she had accomplished something *tangible*?

Leaving her dusty apron and kerchief in the closet, Ember ducked into the kitchen and washed her hands. Two men sat at the table beside Freya and Miri. She recognized Ben. The other must be John. Their conversation faltered when Ember entered, but picked up soon after.

"Ember," Freya said as Ember turned to dry her hands. "This is my husband, John. I don't think you've officially met yet."

"Not officially," John said, nodding to Ember. He had kind eyes, and Ember looked down to escape their sympathy.

"Good to meet you," Ember murmured, stepping over to where Helen was already dishing out a serving of stew for her.

A glance around showed more bread and confections cooling on the counters than Ember would've expected for a household of six people. *Seven now, I suppose.* The thought struck her that the amount of food Ember had seen Helen and Freya cooking since she'd arrived was *far* too much for seven people to consume.

But Ember let that mystery drift away, more interested at the moment with examining the two men seated at the table. They looked...different. Almost as if they were caught halfway between stone and flesh, their skin tinged gray and their voices rougher than one would expect. But why would the curse only catch them halfway?

Ember sat on the edge of an empty chair, eating her dinner automatically as she listened to her new companions talk about their day. She learned that Dyrerisan had a stable with over a dozen horses, though not what use he had for them. She learned that the recent storms had been hard on the garden, but that the roses would still bloom. And she had confirmation that, as welcoming as they were, these people weren't telling her everything.

It was by accident, it seemed like. John made a comment, debating when to take certain horses out for exercise, that *they* would be returning soon. At that Ben glanced to Ember and John turned the conversation back to what needed to be pruned along the garden paths. *Just one more mystery.* She wished John had been more specific, at least with the timing. But then, it shouldn't be hard for Ember to notice when *they* came.

"Alright," Helen said, setting a tray on the counter. "It's ready. Whose night is it?"

Ember glanced around and found everyone else doing the same.

"Ember should go," Freya said.

Ember raised her eyebrows. "Go..."

"Serve Marquis Dyrerisan his dinner," Freya said. She looked up to Helen. "It's later than usual, isn't it? He might already be there. And Ember's already familiar with where the dining room is."

Freya smiled at that last bit, but Helen hesitated, glancing to Ember with a concern that had her stiffening.

"I'll go," Ember said.

Her interest was piqued...now she wanted to know what all this was about. And she had a feeling if she asked anyone here, they'd try to brush off her questions. No one argued, at least. Helen handed Ember the tray as soon as she stood.

"Don't rush, now," Helen said, shifting the dishes on the tray just slightly. "Don't want to burn yourself."

Ember tightened her grip on the tray to keep her arms from trembling with the weight of it. She smiled as brightly as she could manage.

"I'll be back in a moment."

She turned into the hall without waiting for any of them to respond, her thoughts turning to more questions. Always more questions. Ember wondered if she'd ever find *answers* to all the mysteries she was uncovering.

Ember made it to the dining room with ease, though shouldering the door open with the tray in her arms proved a little tricky. The clink of dishes announced her presence, and Ember did her best to walk gracefully as she approached the table she'd so recently been perched on top of.

Dyrerisan was already seated at the table, with his back to Ember's entrance. He didn't bother to look up, making Ember narrow her eyes. She set the tray on the table a little harder than necessary, making the dishes clink again.

"Good evening, *milord,*" Ember said, forcing cheer into her voice. Finally, he looked up.

"Ember. I wasn't expecting you."

Ember lifted one shoulder artlessly, sliding the tray in front of him. He said nothing else, even when Ember took a step away from the table and waited. She watched Dyrerisan for a moment, wondering if she should retreat in silence. But a wild part of her, stirred up by all the secrets and troubles filling her mind, kept her where she was.

"Do you forbid your servants to enter your presence?" Ember asked before she could think better of it. A flash of satisfaction burned through her to see him stiffen. It helped her ignore the accompanying fear.

"I don't *forbid* them," Dyrerisan replied, but not in the harsh tone Ember had braced herself for. He sounded almost...wry?

"But you discourage it."

"For their own safety, I assure you. It's dangerous for them to be in my presence."

That wasn't the answer she expected. It took her a moment to think of a response, and by then some of the fire had faded from her voice.

"Is it dangerous for me?"

"No," he said, glancing up briefly. "No harm will come to you here."

His voice quieted. Ember wasn't even sure she'd heard him correctly, but those words...they made her chest ache again. What did he know about her safety?

"Why should I believe you?" Ember asked in a whisper, the words dragged from her lips without her permission.

Dyrerisan turned toward Ember, looking up to meet her gaze. "Are you afraid of me?"

At that moment, Ember wasn't sure. She covered her sudden confusion by tossing her hair over her shoulder, leaning back on her heels.

"Should I be?"

"That doesn't answer my question."

Ember smiled. Annoyance she could deal with. "Who's to say I owe you answers? You bargained for my labor, not my mind."

That wasn't strictly true. The wording of her uncle's bargain only said Ember was to serve him, not *how*. But Dyrerisan didn't call her on that detail. Instead, he chuckled and turned back to the table.

"Then we're at an impasse. Good evening, Ember."

"Good evening, *Marquis* Dyrerisan."

Ember left before he could respond to that, insisting to herself that she wasn't fleeing. But as soon as the door was shut between her and Dyrerisan, she leaned against the wall and closed her eyes. Ember supposed she should be terrified. Any servant who'd talked to Uncle Radcliff or Aunt Cecile like that would've been facing harsh punishment. But it wasn't fear making her heart pound.

When was the last time she'd spoken her mind? When was the last time she'd allowed the words that *burned* in her mind to pass her lips? If she could get away with it in these halls...well, she definitely wouldn't cower. Dyrerisan might come to wish he'd set a few more guidelines for her behavior.

# CHAPTER SIX

Ember took a slow breath, taking in the scent of rain and earth. All around her were green shrubs and budding flowers. Wandering the paths of the garden, she found no sign of the neglect and age that filled the interior of the fortress.

Several days had passed since Ember's arrival at the mysterious Nyxwood castle. Nothing spectacular had occurred: she hadn't discovered any forbidden treasures in her cleaning, the mysterious "they" hadn't arrived, and no one had dropped any more hints about whatever curse was haunting the castle and its occupants.

Her progress cleaning on the ground floor provided a way for her to measure her days, as she declared war on the dust and disuse filling the entire castle. But the closest she came to any excitement or variation were her interactions with the enigmatic Dyrerisan.

She'd asked to take over serving his meals, and Helen had agreed without much convincing. Ember still wasn't sure if she fully believed Dyrerisan's explanation for keeping his servants from his presence, but if there really was a danger Ember would do what she could to minimize it. She didn't want to watch Miri or Freya slowly turn to stone.

Of course, those interactions were predictable. Ember hadn't initiated conversation since that first night, nor did he comment about her progress. But twice now he'd sneaked up on her while she was cleaning. He'd offered a few vague comments, which Ember had responded to with the first words that came to her mind. Ember wasn't sure if those interactions could be called *friendly*, but they were civil. Dyrerisan hadn't punished her for her loose tongue yet. Ember thought he might actually enjoy it.

That was a disturbing thought. Ember slowed on the path, staring at the flowers near her feet. Now that she thought of it, she enjoyed her verbal matches with Dyrerisan as well. But she shouldn't...she shouldn't be engaging with him, for multiple reasons. *I'll have to be more careful.*

Ember turned her feet back toward the kitchen entrance, thinking of the hall she'd started cleaning that morning. She'd already taken all the drapes to Miri for washing. Now she had long hours of dusting ahead of her.

She still didn't understand the amount of decoration littering the inside of the castle. It was as if the rulers of Nyxwood had decided at some point that impressing visitors with their wealth would take the place of effective defense. Of course, the exterior of the structure was still forbidding...

As Ember wiped down vases and statuettes, she thought again of what she'd heard and read of Nyxwood castle. The Marquises had been prosperous...but all the stories said they took their role as protectors seriously, as well. So where did the legends fall short? Or was there merely more to the story?

*Would Dyrerisan tell me if I asked?*

Ember pushed the thought away, forcing her concentration on the small end table she was rubbing down. She wouldn't initiate conversation. She wouldn't invite any more interaction than was necessary.

Ember wiped her forehead with the back of her hand, standing back to appreciate her work. It had taken a few days, but the hall was finished. Newly washed curtains were pulled back to let in the light, the floors were so clean they almost *shined*, and the many trinkets no longer looked like they'd been abandoned in a storeroom for a few decades.

"Well done," Dyrerisan's voice echoed up the hall.

Ember flinched and turned, spotting his large form striding up the hallway. Her heart echoed in her ears, and it took her a moment to realize she ought to respond.

"Thank you," she said.

Dyrerisan glanced at her as he stopped near her side, turning to look out the windows. Ember followed his gaze, though the view was only of a stretch of open field where the horses grazed, and the forest pressing against the wall surrounding the castle lands.

"Are you finding everything to your liking?"

"Of course," Ember replied. "I've always wanted endless hallways and useless riches to clean. It's my favorite pastime."

He didn't rise to the bait. "You haven't moved anything."

"I know the consequences if anything goes missing."

There was that strange chuckle he sometimes gave, that sounded a bit like rocks crashing over each other in the distance. Ember glanced up to see him watching her and quickly looked away again.

"I don't care if you take anything" he said. "It's not as if it'll go beyond my domain."

With that declaration, he left. And Ember stared after him, caught between anger and plain confusion. Had he cared about Uncle Radcliff's thievery, then? Or had his bargaining with Radcliff had another purpose?

Ember turned away from the window, leaving in the opposite

direction as Dyrerisan. *Keep my head down, do my job. What's done is done.*

DYRERISAN PUSHED BACK from his desk, rising to set the book he'd been consulting back on its shelf. A glance at the piles stacked haphazardly in front of the shelf made Dyrerisan sigh and raise a hand to his forehead, wincing at the sensation of stone against stone. He hadn't sorted those books to their proper places in years. His desk was little better.

*And for what?* He wondered. *Nothing's changing. It's all the same as it always has been: different lives making the same choices.*

He stepped toward the window, wondering—not for the first time—how long he would continue like this. How long would this cursed existence stretch on? Hadn't his watch lasted long enough? On the other hand, the only escape he could trust wasn't a path he was anxious to explore. He didn't enjoy thoughts of where death would take him, after the life he'd lived.

He looked down from his tower, examining the land below for a distraction from those unwanted reflections. He found a blonde head wandering the gardens that succeeded in drawing his thoughts elsewhere.

*Ember Kendrick.* She certainly wasn't what he'd expected. *Fierce. Outspoken. Determined.* She seemed to be everything her supposed guardian was not. And yet...she was hiding something. The more Dyrerisan interacted with her, the more he was convinced that she had reasons for coming to his castle that had nothing to do with Radcliff, or Sarnere. And he couldn't fully banish the desire to tease out those secrets as he had so many others, to discover what was behind the guarded look in her eyes.

*Tread carefully*, he reminded himself. He couldn't afford to add

Ember to his list of failures. He owed too much to ever repay as it was.

Below, Ember stooped to examine one of the many roses John insisted on maintaining. As far as he could tell, she never even touched the flower. He tilted his head, leaning against the window frame as he watched her.

Having her within the castle had been...unnerving. She was another life within the halls he wandered, another heartbeat always close by. Ember was the first person to live in Nyxwood that he could *talk* to without guilt in...he didn't want to consider how long.

*There's no harm to a little conversation.* Especially when their interactions usually ended with Ember's eyes flashing in annoyance, fearless as she snapped at him. Yes, he would be cautious...but after two hundred years of solitude, he could allow a few moments of companionship.

Ember pushed open one, massive door, her bucket of soapy water knocking against the edge of it. She ignored the water that sloshed on her skirt, keeping her eyes on the room before her. As far as she could tell, the long hall was empty save the statues. She took a few steps deeper within, holding her breath until she saw the shadowed throne was empty.

She'd been avoiding this room for days. She hadn't stepped foot within it for over a month, since her arrival at Nyxwood. But it was the last area left for Ember to clean on the first floor, and she didn't believe Freya and Miri's assurances that she could leave it be. Even if he only ever used it to intimidate people, Dyrerisan *did* use it. She wouldn't leave any way for him to accuse her of falling short of the bargain. But that didn't mean she enjoyed being in here.

Narrow windows high on the walls let in indirect light from the bright day without: revealing the patterns in the marble floor but leaving the alcoves in shadow. Watching the statues more closely than she really needed to, Ember approached one of the sconces mounted on the walls between recesses. Unlike most of the other spaces Ember had explored so far, the lamps were clean and filled already. All Ember needed was to light them with the matches she still kept in her apron pocket.

Ember lit most of the lamps, ignoring the voice in her head that said it wasn't necessary. She didn't like the shadows of that room. She didn't like how the statues stared out from their darkened coves like ancient judges waiting to condemn her. She only hoped none of them came to life while she was cleaning to scold her for her impudence. If there were anywhere a statue *could* talk, Ember was convinced by now that it was this place.

*One statue already does talk.*

Ember muffled the laughter that thought summoned, knowing it would sound too desperate echoing in this vast space. She returned to the first statue, wringing out her rag and setting to work. She had to climb onto the pedestal to reach the statue's head, leaving her in the awkward position of half embracing the stone as she cleaned his head and crown.

"Pardon my reach," she muttered, more to bring some sound to the vast space than anything. "Your crown certainly has a lot of crevices for dust to hide."

He didn't answer. Ember narrowed her eyes as she dug dust from every fine, maddening detail. There was a reason the statues in this place looked half alive...whatever sculptors had shaped them had carved practically every hair on the patriarch's face. It might've been unnerving, if Ember hadn't been faced with the task of cleaning it all. Her newfound hatred of dust helped her ignore the lifelike quality to the stone, though it didn't silence her imagination.

*Who was he?* Ember assumed the statues were of famous Marquises or other heroes, but she hadn't seen any name plate to identify them. Was this the likeness of Marquis Montague? One of the kings of old? Or someone she hadn't heard of before?

Ember twisted a little further, swiping dust from around his collar. At this rate it would take her weeks to finish this room.

"I see you're getting acquainted with my great-great grandfather."

Ember startled and had to wrap her arm around the statue's neck to keep from losing her balance. She took a breath, clenching her rag tighter, and went back to work.

"I'd be more honored if his beard didn't collect so much dust," Ember muttered, ignoring the way her heart still pounded from Dyrerisan's unexpected entrance.

"Don't blame him," Dyrerisan said wryly. "That's the cleanest I've ever seen him. And once there was a team of servants to keep down the dust of this place."

Ember twisted around to glare down at Dyrerisan. It was an odd angle, looking *down* on the hulking man. He stared at her, one stiff eyebrow raised as he waited for her response. Ember raised her own eyebrow and tossed her rag into the bucket. She tried not to be disappointed that Dyrerisan didn't flinch from the dirty water that sloshed onto the floor.

"I won't bother, then," she said. "A quick once over with a dry rag will be enough, yes?"

"Whatever you think is necessary."

Ember narrowed her eyes. She hadn't figured out yet why he was willing to give her free rein of his castle, or why he seemed so unconcerned with the state of things. Dyrerisan smirked under her glare, then shifted his eyes to the statue. Ember leaned back against the wall of the alcove, crossing her arms over her chest and examining the statue as well. Dyrerisan's ancestor, was he? She thought she could see some resemblance in the nose, maybe in the brow.

But of course, that wasn't the most obvious similarity. If Dyrerisan had his own alcove, Ember would've been hard pressed to tell him apart from the silent stone.

"Say it."

"Say what?" Ember asked innocently.

Dyrerisan switched his eyes back to Ember, piercing her. Ember worked not to squirm beneath his attention.

"Whatever you're thinking. I want to hear it, now."

"No, you don't."

Dyrerisan narrowed his eyes. "Speak. Or else I'll show you to the statues we have in storage that could use your attention."

"That's cruel.

"I never said I wasn't cruel."

Ember blinked. He hadn't, had he? And yet, she hadn't expected him to take her accusation seriously. Nor had she expected the haunted look to his eyes interrupting his commanding glare. Ember tightened her arms around her chest, leaning carelessly against the edge of the alcove.

"Fair enough. I was noting the family resemblance. Your skin tones are *remarkably* similar."

For a heart pounding moment, silence filled the vast hall. Had she gone too far? But then Dyrerisan thawed, smirking.

"You think I'm handsome?"

Ember straightened. "I never said anything about that."

"There's no need to be bashful, Miss Kendrick. My ancestors were known for their...fine looks. It's an honor to know you believe I possess the same."

Dyrerisan bowed and turned away, leaving Ember sputtering beside the statue.

"Rock troll!" she called after his back. He only laughed.

Ember stared after him, looping her arm around the statue to keep her steady. *Where did that* come *from?* Had something changed that she wasn't aware of? Ember was a little disturbed to realize her racing heart was caused not by anger, but by the *thrill* of it. *I don't think...I don't remember anyone teasing me like that.* She watched his retreating form a little closer, wondering...she didn't even know what.

She waited long after his footsteps disappeared before jumping down from the pedestal, nearly falling to her knees when she landed wrong. She blew hair from her eyes and snatched her rag back from the bucket. Her face was still warm from Dyrerisan's words. *Handsome? Not hardly.* She wouldn't let him distract her from what she was here for.

Climbing back onto the pedestal, Ember took up where she'd left off, giving attention to every tiny, maddening detail. Perhaps it wasn't necessary to be so thorough...but these statues were carved to resemble *real people.* People who'd lived and breathed and hoped to be remembered. And Ember wouldn't leave them lingering in the dust, not if she could help it. Even if it meant long, tedious days of cleaning.

Ember shouldered open the door to the dining room, her mind only peripherally on her task. Freya had mentioned something to Miri about sticking closer to the kitchen for the next few days, and it had made her wonder of the "they" she'd heard mention of were arriving soon. Would Helen try to hide Ember away, as well?

Ember set the full tray on the table, noticing only afterward that Dyrerisan wasn't sitting. Instead, he stood beside the windows, staring out toward the gardens.

"I brought your lunch," Ember said, backing away from the table.

"Thank you, Ember."

Ember froze, turning her eyes to Dyrerisan's back. He never thanked her. Normally he hardly acknowledged her when she brought his meals. *First* teasing *me, and now* thanking *me? What's changed?* Ember took another step backward, longing for escape before he said anything else. But she'd hesitated too long.

"Something you want to say?"

"Where's the library?"

It was the first safe question that came to mind. Ember *had* been wondering, having explored the second floor without any sign of a library. But now, as Dyrerisan turned to face her, Ember was regretting not just leaving in silence.

"Why do you ask?" he replied.

"The nights are long," Ember said slowly. "I was wondering if this place would have any new books for me to read."

She was sure it would...this place was ancient. There were bound to be books on its shelves that Ember had never heard of, even if they were dry records. She'd take whatever she could find.

Dyrerisan looked her over. "I wasn't aware you were an accomplished reader."

Ember straightened, fire rising in her chest. "I wasn't aware you knew every detail of my existence."

He smirked, stepping up to the table to lean on its surface, still staring at Ember. She took another small step back.

"Let's see how much I do know, shall we?"

Her mind warned, *danger.* Her heart commanded, *flee.* But Ember stayed where she was, tilting her head. Did he really think he knew her? How could he?

"What are the stakes?" Ember said, her voice barely more than a whisper.

Dyrerisan smiled, his teeth too bright against his gray skin. "If I know less of you than I think, then I'll show you the library. But if I can name eight truths about you...you have to join me for dinner. Every night."

Ember laughed, ignoring how breathy the sound was. She wasn't scared. She *wasn't.*

"Or I could search for the library myself and be done with it."

"You *have* searched."

Ember scowled. How had he known that?

"Come, now," Dyrerisan said, beckoning to a chair near his own. "You want to prove me wrong. I can see it."

"And you want to prove *me* wrong," Ember countered, staying where she was.

"Perhaps."

He beckoned again to the chair, still leaning toward her with intense eyes glinting in the light. Ember stared back at him...and stepped forward. *What am I doing?* She couldn't find a good answer as she took a seat at the table, watching as Dyrerisan sat so near she could reach out and touch him. He poured tea into the china cup, stirring in a bit of sugar and cream. And then he set it before her.

Ember narrowed her eyes. "I don't usually drink my tea with sugar."

Dyrerisan's smirk didn't falter. "We won't count this as the first truth, then."

He leaned back, watching Ember in silence. Ember looked to the table to escape his gaze. After a moment, she pulled the tea closer and took a cautious sip, annoyed when she enjoyed it.

"Only child."

Ember glanced up to Dyrerisan, saying reluctantly, "Yes."

"Impatient."

"By who's standard?

Dyrerisan flashed another smile but kept going.

"Bold, unlike your uncle."

Ember snorted at that.

"Dedicated to whatever responsibility is set before you."

*Am I?* She supposed if one only saw her work in the castle, she was. *But what responsibilities have I been trusted with before now?* Only the ones she inflicted on herself...only the promises she'd spoken to no one.

"You have two cousins..."

"That doesn't count," Ember said, straightening in her chair. "That's too general."

Dyrerisan raised an eyebrow. "You have two cousins, who you try to protect, despite the poor way you've been treated by their parents, your so-called guardians."

Ember shrank back in her chair a bit, but her glare was fierce. "How could you possibly know that?"

"Why else would you come here so easily? Why else would you be willing to go to Sarnere? Not for Radcliff, surely."

No, not for Radcliff. But was Dyrerisan right? *Only partly.* But she had admitted, to herself and Sophia, that sparing her cousins was one reason she'd come. She supposed that could count as a kind of protection.

"Fine," Ember said. "You have three more."

She tried to ignore the unease swirling low in her stomach. She should've made her escape when she had the chance. The shift in Dyrerisan's expression, the edge of almost *sorrow*, only increased her dread.

"You were orphaned at twelve."

Ember nodded, not trusting her voice.

"Your father was killed in a tavern dispute, and your mother died of illness a few months afterward."

"You're wrong," Ember said, voice choked. She traced the grain of wood on the table. "My father was *attacked*. He didn't mean to start a fight. And my mother died...of grief, you could say."

She was glad he didn't debate her on that or ask her to say more. She wasn't sure she wouldn't run if he tried discussing her parents.

"Two more?" Dyrerisan asked. Ember shrugged, and Dyrerisan cleared his throat.

"You only follow the rules when it suits you."

That brought a weak smile to Ember's face. She couldn't deny it. She looked up before that smile could die, leaning forward.

"Alright, one more," she said. "But this one has to be something deeper. Something you couldn't learn from asking my *uncle*."

"I didn't learn any of that from Radcliff."

He spoke the name with a note of disgust that Ember understood well, and her smile grew. "My challenge stands."

"Very well."

That unnerving intensity was back in his eyes, and Ember took another sip of tea to escape it. He took a long time to answer, long enough that Ember considered insisting that he'd failed. But she stayed silent. Perhaps...perhaps she was curious what he'd say.

"You're afraid of something," he said quietly, his voice musing. "You're running from more than your uncle."

Ember's breath caught. Her heart beat steadily on, whispering *it's true. He's right.* But she wouldn't give in that easily.

"And what," she murmured, "am I afraid of?"

"Love? Loss? If you watched your mother die of grief, then maybe you're afraid of sharing her fate."

Ember turned her eyes to her lap, a ghost of a laugh escaping through her lips. *If only that were something I could escape.* She looked up to Dyrerisan.

"You're wrong," she said, half-strangled. "I don't want to *cause* grief, Marquis Dyrerisan."

They stared at each other, the only sound Dyrerisan drumming his fingers on the table. Slowly, he nodded.

"Even so, I've won. You'll find suitable clothes for dinner in the rose room."

Ember was beyond the point of arguing. She stood and stumbled to the door, turning away from the kitchen toward the nearest door leading outside. She needed air. She needed to be alone.

Outside, a fierce wind dragged clouds across the sky, blocking out the sun. It howled in Ember's ear, whipping her skirts around her legs. She accepted its attack gratefully, plunging further down the paths to where she knew she would be hidden. All the way, her heart screamed at her.

"Why did I say that?" she whispered, ducking onto a worn bench. "*Why did I say that?*"

She looked down at her hands, held open to the air. They trembled. But was it leftover nerves from her dangerous games with Dyrerisan, or something more? She tucked them around her waist and rocked forward, staring at the gravel blankly. What had she done? This was more than a moment of weakness, more than pushing her boundaries for some sort of freedom. This was a deadly dance she'd entered into.

How had he known...any of that? Some of what he'd said he could've guessed, but not all of it. Not unless he was far more observant than Ember had given him credit for. *How had he known?* And what would he do with the weaknesses he'd uncovered? She didn't trust him to keep it to a light wager. What was he playing at? What would Ember lose if she kept at this?

She took a deep breath, fighting to steady herself. She wasn't lost yet. He'd won this round, but that was all he'd be getting. *I haven't come this far to fail now, have I?*

# CHAPTER SEVEN

Ember stood before the wardrobe, the door gripped tight in her hand, and wondered how far she'd get if she tried running away. Would she even make it past the stables?

She wouldn't have any help from her companions. Freya and Miri, after laughing at the very concept of the wager, had said she needed to go through with it. Miri had even offered to help Ember dress and adjust anything that might not fit. Helen, though more subdued, had also insisted Ember fulfill her side of the wager. Ember hadn't lingered long enough to decide if the worry in Helen's gaze was for her or for Dyrerisan.

She'd climbed to the extensive guest wing early, to give herself time to prepare for the strange night that lay before her. Now she was beginning to think that Marquis Dyrerisan had a twisted sense of humor: the "suitable clothes" he'd mentioned were all gowns meant for a princess, outdated styles notwithstanding.

Ember took a hesitant step closer, brushing her fingers lightly over the fine fabrics, the rich colors...she'd never dreamed of dressing in anything so beautiful. The thought of doing so now terrified her.

Her hands were trembling again, her nerves already ragged from the conversation that had started this whole mess.

*A twisted joke. That's all this is...it has to be.* She should serve him dinner in her dusty apron just to spite him.

Ember's hand paused on a lavender satin that shimmered in the candlelight. She'd never get a chance to wear such a dress again... what could it really hurt? She could pretend, just for one night, that she belonged in a place like this. She could pretend for one night that she had no reason to fear.

*I'm taking too many risks.* Her resolution from the garden loomed before her, reminding her of the true stakes to this odd game. *But this isn't him winning...if I want to wear a pretty gown, what harm is there in that?* She pulled the lavender gown from the wardrobe, holding it up to examine. And what resistance she had left crumbled to dust.

She flipped her damp hair over her shoulder and set to work dressing. Soon she was arrayed in the borrowed dress, standing before the large mirror and twisting back and forth to admire the shimmer to the fabric.

The neckline was high but wide, dipping just low enough to show her collarbones. The sleeves were fitted and ended just above her elbows, edged with a small trimming of lace. And the skirt draped from the fitted waist in wide waves, turning light and shadow into its own decoration as it shifted with Ember's movement. It was simple, elegant...and it made Ember stand a little taller, knowing that it *fit* her, in more than waist size.

She smiled at herself in the mirror, warm and delighted with the way her pale hair looked loose against the silk, at the way her eyes lightened to match the rich color of the gown. She could get used to wearing such a dress...at least when her work was done. The thought of dusting in such a gown was enough to make her roll her eyes. She wondered what Dyrerisan would say to such a spectacle.

A smile edging her lips, Ember collected her cast-off work dress and retreated from the room, ignoring the quiver to her chest that suggested tonight would cost something. One night of living. Then she'd retreat back to the shadows.

Ember's smile finally faltered as she entered the kitchen only to be met with five pairs of eyes that suddenly looked like they'd seen a ghost. Ember's steps faltered, sudden fear thrumming in her chest. What had she done wrong? Ember's eyes settled on Freya, who was biting her lip and looking like she'd just come face to face with her own doom. She looked away when she caught Ember watching.

"You look lovely," Helen said, breaking the silence to step closer.

Ember was too lost in bewilderment to respond. She stepped further within the room, watching the table's occupants warily.

"Is something wrong?"

"Nothing you need to worry about tonight."

Helen was the only one who'd meet her eyes. Ember stared back, seeing sympathy, sorrow...guilt. Why, all of a sudden, did Ember feel like she was back to being the sacrifice?

"Are you sure about that?" Ember asked quietly.

"Don't let us ruin your night," Freya spoke up. "Enjoy yourself."

*Not likely.* But Ember couldn't find any words to respond with. She made do with nodding, automatically taking the tray Helen handed her. The fact that it was twice as heavy barely registered as she looked once more around the kitchen. The grave atmosphere didn't change. No one said anything else. After a moment, Ember gave up and turned away, toward the dining room. Tomorrow... tomorrow she'd get answers.

Ember paused when she reached the dining room door, taking a deep breath to reorient herself. Whatever was going on, whatever they were hiding from her, she would deal with later. For now, her focus was needed elsewhere: fulfill her end of the lost wager and try to minimize the damage. It was only one night.

She shouldered open the door, her step light in the wide skirts as she crossed the room. For once, it was brightly lit, every sconce holding a flame. Dyrerisan was waiting with his back to her, staring out the windows again. Ember set the tray on the table as quietly as she could manage and straightened, waiting for him to say something.

But instead, he turned without warning, his eyes bright as he examined Ember in her borrowed dress. Ember fought the heat rising to her cheeks, gripping the back of a chair to keep herself steady. Dyrerisan approached the table silently, finally meeting her eyes.

"Your eyes look violet tonight."

Ember smiled weakly. "A gift from my mother's family."

"Hmm."

Dyrerisan kept staring, and Ember found it difficult to look away. What was he waiting for? Was she supposed to say something? She pressed her lips tight together, unwilling to initiate any sort of conversation. She was here, and that was all that was required from her.

"Sit," he said, gesturing to the chair.

Ember mutely obeyed, hands limp in her lap as Dyrerisan set her food before her. When he ate, she ate. When he looked at her, she made attempts to smile. But that was all. Her food might have been ash for all she could tell through the bundle of nerves and dread sunk deep in her stomach. She pinched the satin of her skirt between her fingers, rubbing it back and forth and wishing the night were over already.

"What sort of books do you enjoy?"

Ember looked up, eyes wide. "Pardon?"

"You enjoy reading," Dyrerisan said. "What books do you choose?"

Ember looked down at her plate. She'd read anything she could get her hands on...but what did she enjoy most?

"Adventures, romances...stories with hope, mostly."

"With a happy ending for all, I suppose," Dyrerisan said bitterly.

Ember glanced up, eyes narrowed, and wondered at that response.

"Not always. Sometimes the *right* ending isn't a *happy* one."

"You enjoy tragedies, then."

"Not usually."

Dyrerisan set down his fork, staring at Ember with mingled confusion and annoyance.

"Explain."

Ember smirked, wondering what he'd do if she refused. But instead, she set down her own fork, leaning back to meet his eyes.

"I don't enjoy stories where the characters fail for no reason other than some twisted 'fate.' If a hero's end is tragic, I want them to go down defiant, determined to bring hope to *someone*, even if they have none for themselves."

"And if there's no hope to be found?"

"Then they haven't looked hard enough."

Dyrerisan's lips twisted into a mocking smile, and Ember stiffened.

"That's unrealistic," he said.

"And who said we need all stories to match reality?" Ember fired back. "You'd leave us all withering in despair and call that realism?"

"Do you truly think hope exists in every situation?"

"I don't know."

Ember's voice broke, and she looked down, biting back tears. Dyrerisan stayed silent, and after a hushed moment Ember raised her head again.

"I don't know," she said, glaring at him. "But if we aren't allowed to hope for *something*, even if it's only for an *end* to all this suffering... why bother living at all?"

Ember held her glare at Dyrerisan as he stared at her. She

couldn't tell if he was baffled, or if he was still judging her for wanting to hope. But she wouldn't back down, not in this.

"Perhaps you're right," he said, slowly. "Only I haven't found hope in much of life so far."

"Have you *looked* for it?"

His expressions shifted to a sardonic smile, but this time it seemed to be aimed at himself. "No."

Ember returned her attention to her plate, letting her silence speak for her. Neither of them spoke again until their plates were empty and piled back on the tray. Dyrerisan stood, and Ember followed, keeping her eyes lowered.

"Tomorrow," he said. "Tomorrow, I'll show you the library. Under one condition."

Ember sighed but lifted her eyes. "What condition?"

"You remain there until evening."

"Why?"

Dyrerisan's eyes danced, and she wondered if he was silently laughing at her. Ember went back to glaring.

"I have visitors coming, and I'd prefer that you didn't cross paths."

So, the mysterious "they" were finally arriving. Did he think it would be that simple to keep her from sight?

"You said yourself, I only follow rules when it suits me," Ember replied. "What's to stop me from leaving when I please?"

"The door to the library locks."

"You'd lock me in?" Ember asked, her eyes flashing.

Dyrerisan smirked. "Perhaps. I could also lock you *out*, should you disobey me."

*Oh.* That was well played. The idea of seeing the library only to be kept away from it made her wither inside. *I could give in for books, just this once. I might be able to make my time there useful, anyway.* And it would be separation...she was supposed to be finding some kind of separation.

"Alright," she said. "I'll behave. This time."

"How obliging you are."

Ember ignored that, reaching for the tray. Dyrerisan stopped her with a hand on her wrist, making Ember freeze. Her heart pounded in her ears as she stared at that gray hand on her wrist, as she felt the course sensation of stone against her skin. His grip was light. She could pull away if she wanted.

"Helen will take these back to the kitchen."

"Why shouldn't I?" Her voice wavered, and Ember swallowed.

"Because I'll be showing you to your new room."

Ember looked up, eyes narrowed. Dyrerisan might as well have been wearing a mask for all his expression gave away.

"And my belongings?"

"Already taken there by Freya and Miri."

Panic made her heart beat faster. *Even my journal?* They wouldn't read it, would they?

"Why do I have to move?"

"Helen brought it to my attention that your previous room is in a section of the castle that stays cold. She's concerned for your health and asked that you be moved to a room with a fireplace."

Ember leaned back, pulling her hand from Dyrerisan's grasp. Her chest felt hollow, suddenly emptied of all but a numb sort of dread she really should've been used to by now.

"You don't allow them in your presence," she muttered.

Dyrerisan offered one of his close-lipped smiles, this one tinged with sorrow. "Once again, for their protection."

*Separation. I need separation.* Ember nodded. Dyrerisan stared down at her without moving for a long moment, but Ember didn't speak. He finally turned toward the door, leaving her to follow at her own will. Ember kept her distance as he led her through the halls.

Somehow, she wasn't truly surprised when he led her to the same room where Ember had chosen her dress earlier. He stopped at the door, which bore a gilt rose to identify it, and turned toward her.

"I'll take you to the library after breakfast."

Ember nodded. Her head was throbbing, and she barely resisted the urge to close her eyes against the sight of Dyrerisan standing there, waiting for her answer.

"Good night."

He turned away, and Ember didn't bother responding as she pushed open the door. Inside, the room was transformed: clean linens were already turned down on the bed, the furniture and floor had been wiped clean of dust, there was even a fire in the narrow fireplace. Ember looked around blankly, finding her belongings piled on a table. She stepped forward to pull her shoulder bag from the stack, glimpsing inside to see her journal and other treasures undisturbed. She pulled it to her chest and slowly went to her knees.

*I'm playing with fire.*

The dress, the wager, the dinner...even her verbal battles with Marquis Dyrerisan. Her resolution in the garden that afternoon had gotten her nowhere: she'd *still* pushed too far. And not just with Dyrerisan. Helen and the others...they were concerned for her. But they shouldn't be...they shouldn't notice if she was cold, they shouldn't care enough to put themselves in danger for her sake.

*What am I doing?* She pulled the bag closer to her chest, breathing in its familiar scent and blinking away tears. *Almighty, what am I supposed to do? Are You even listening?* Ember lowered her face to her arms. She felt alone...just as she'd always been.

# CHAPTER EIGHT

Ember descended to the kitchen later than usual the next morning, dark circles beneath her eyes from a nearly sleepless night. She'd paid the price for her evening of freedom in more than dread and tears. She'd considered, briefly, not bothering to rise from her bed that morning. But she needed a distraction...she needed something to draw her out of her own mind.

Helen was alone in the kitchen when Ember entered. She offered Ember her usual warm smile as Ember took a seat at the table.

"Freya and Miri are with the boys," Helen explained, setting a plate of eggs and sausage before Ember. "They deserved some time to themselves."

Ember didn't bother to ask if their absence had something to do with whoever was arriving today. She was sure it did. Instead, she picked at her breakfast and watched Helen bustling around the kitchen. As usual, she was making enough food to feed a small army. Would Dyrerisan's guests stay to supper?

"Why move me to the guest wing?" Ember blurted. "I wasn't unhappy in my other room."

Helen paused her work, looking up to Ember with a motherly disbelief that made Ember shrink back.

"Dear, you've added three blankets to your bed since arriving, and you *still* tossed and turned all night."

Ember couldn't deny that. But she wasn't ready to give in yet, either.

"But why move me upstairs? I'm not...I don't need anything as fancy as that place."

"It's not doing any good rotting away, though, is it? Someone might as well get some use out of it."

"So why don't the rest of you stay there?"

Helen's hands paused again, but this time her eyes stayed on her work. "Stubbornness, mostly. It seems pointless to change things after this long."

"So, it has nothing to do with the curse over this place?"

Helen looked up sharply, while Ember sat easily and met Helen's eyes. Helen stared at her a moment before huffing out a laugh and dusting flour from her hands.

"I don't know why we expected you to stay ignorant. It's not as if you're blind, is it?"

Ember stayed silent as Helen took a seat at the table, moving with an unusual weariness. When she looked up to Ember, she seemed to have aged thirty years.

"How much have you guessed?"

Ember tapped her fingers on the underside of the table, wondering how much she should say.

"There's a curse over Nyxwood, centered around Marquis Dyrerisan. You all are caught up in it somehow...but not fully?"

"We're as trapped in the curse as the Marquis. But the part we play is different...we turn to stone gradually, only as we interact with Dyrerisan."

"Which is why you all stay away from him," Ember murmured, mind bright with sudden understanding.

"As much as possible, yes. John and Ben take their post as

Dyrerisan's guard willingly, but you can see that it's taken a toll on them."

So that was why the dusty halls, the clear separation, the masks and few words...it really was for their own protection.

"And me?" Ember asked.

"You're safe," Helen said, stretching a hand to lay across Ember's wrist. "The curse only has power over those who were in the castle when it was cast."

Ember had guessed as much already, but her heart still lightened at hearing it confirmed. That was one threat she had no need to fear, at least. Ember glanced back to Helen, wondering what else she could learn.

"Why stone?" she asked. "Why was this place cursed?"

Helen's face softened, her smile returning. "That is the Marquis's story to tell. I wouldn't share it any more than I'd share yours."

Ember leaned back, pulling away with sudden wariness. How much had she guessed? How much had she *read*? Helen's gaze was too understanding, too attentive.

"I haven't pried into your secrets, Ember dear. But I'm no more blind than you are."

"It's that obvious?" Ember asked, her lips twisting to a grim smile against her will. She'd successfully hidden her troubles in her Uncle's house...but then, she supposed she hadn't counted on anyone actually *looking* for her story.

"To me. I can't speak for the others."

Helen stood, returning to the counter and to the tray set off to the side. Ember stood as well to receive it, avoiding Helen's eyes as she wrapped her hands around the tray's edges. But Helen didn't release it right away, and Ember finally looked up to meet her gaze again.

"I won't take more than what's offered," Helen said. "But whatever sorrow is on your heart...we'd all share the burden with you, if you'll let us."

*That's what I'm afraid of.* But she couldn't say that...nor could she bring herself to brush off Helen's offer with callousness. Perhaps that was where she failed: she'd never learned how to push people away, only how to keep her distance. A lump rose in Ember's throat, and it took her a moment to be able to answer.

"I know," she whispered.

Helen nodded and released the tray. And Ember fled the kitchen as quickly as she dared while holding a tray of breakfast and tea.

Inside the dining room, Dyrerisan was standing by the windows. He waited until Ember set the tray on the table to turn.

"Ready?" he asked.

Ember glanced from the food to Dyrerisan, not saying a word. Dyrerisan smirked.

"I'll come back for it," he said. "For now, I'll see you settled among your treasured books."

Ember bit back her retort at that, still raw and wary. *Separation. Necessary interaction only.* Those reminders pounded in Ember's head alongside her heartbeat, until Dyrerisan offered his arm to her. Ember stared at it in dread. Could she refuse? The stony look to his eyes that Ember caught only a glimpse of suggested she couldn't.

"My touch won't turn you to stone, you know," he rumbled when Ember still hesitated.

"I know."

"Well?"

Ember reluctantly took his offered arm, glaring up at him.

"Kind gestures don't count when you're *demanding* to be accepted, you know."

"Is that so?"

Dyrerisan led them on in silence, and Ember paid close attention to the path he traced. Wherever the library was hiding, Ember was determined *not* to need directions twice. Still, when Dyrerisan led them up the stairs past the second floor, Ember was surprised. And chagrined. After her conversation with Helen, Ember didn't want to take the chance of Dyrerisan noticing her pace was slowing the higher they climbed. She gritted her teeth and pushed on, glancing to Dyrerisan and glaring when she found him watching her.

"I thought the third floor was storage," she said, to keep the attention off herself.

"Of a sort."

They stopped at a landing, Dyrerisan pulling her toward the first door in a long hall. Dyrerisan paused before the door, and the fanciful part of Ember's mind wondered if he'd ask her to close her eyes. She grimaced at the thought of that kind of theatrics, quickly schooling her expression when Dyrerisan turned toward her. He still quirked an eyebrow as he pushed the door open, gesturing for her to enter first. Ember watched him warily as she passed, only to lose her breath when she turned to the sight in front of her.

The room they'd entered must've taken up at least half of the third floor, divided by hundreds of shelves, all full of books. Two walls bore dozens of narrow windows to provide light, while lamps and sitting areas were dotted around the room. But even with those small allowances for light and comfort, the room held more books than Ember could've ever guessed were gathered in one place. She stepped deeper into the room, drinking in the overwhelming sights, the smell of paper, the reverent hush of the room.

"How?" she whispered.

"At one time, this castle held the chronicles of the kingdom. Traveling scholars donated most of the other tomes as a payment for using this space."

It must've taken hundreds of years to fill that room, no matter how many scholars came seeking knowledge. *I wonder what they did after Nyxwood disappeared?*

"This shelf contains the catalogues listing the contents of the library," Dyrerisan said, and Ember turned to see the shelf he gestured to. The tomes filling that shelf were all thick and, expectedly, covered in dust. Ember nodded, not sure she could speak at the moment.

"Read whatever you'd like," Dyrerisan said, backing toward the open door. "I will return when it's alright for you to leave."

Ember nodded. After a moment, Dyrerisan left, and Ember held her place long enough to listen for the sound of a key being turned in a lock. She heard nothing. Relieved, she turned back toward the endless shelves and smiled. She stepped forward without another glance at the catalogues, intrigued with all there was to explore.

She hummed as she ran her fingers over the spines, taking in the titles with a smile. She breathed in slowly, the smell of books soothing her heart. For a while, she'd forget curses and mysteries. She had reading to do.

EMBER PRIED her eyes open to meet dusky shadow, slowly aware that her neck was propped in a rather *odd* position. She winced, closing her eyes again as she sat up. She rubbed a hand over her sore neck, her other hand busy keeping a thick book from slipping to the floor.

"Have a productive day?"

Ember didn't have the energy to jump. She lifted heavy eyes up to find Dyrerisan leaning against a nearby bookshelf, smirking down at her. She tried to return the smirk, fighting to pierce through the fog that came with heavy sleep. The headache that had made her lay down in the first place still lingered on the edges of her mind, making thought difficult.

"Sure," she finally replied, stretching her arms. "And you?"

"Productive enough."

Dyrerisan stepped forward, moving more quickly than Ember thought possible to catch the book sliding off her lap. Ember blinked at his sudden proximity. Dyrerisan didn't seem to notice, turning the book over to look at the inside cover.

"An interesting choice," he said, sitting on the table in front of the sofa where Ember had taken up residence. "I thought you preferred adventure and romance."

"I never said that was all I read," Ember said, her heart beating faster.

Did he recognize the volume? It was a local history focusing on Nyxwood and the surrounding Rausbane forest, during the time of a Marquis that Ember *thought* might be included the statues downstairs. He certainly had enough exploits to warrant a memorial of some kind.

Dyrerisan set aside the book without another comment, standing and offering his hand to Ember. She took it hesitantly, her head spinning as he pulled her to her feet. She closed her eyes again, standing still and hoping he didn't think anything of it. If he did, he hid it well. He wasn't even watching her when Ember's mind settled enough to open her eyes again. But he did lead her rather slowly through the library.

"You may come here whenever you'd like," he said, adding after a pause, "as long as it doesn't interfere with your work, of course."

"Of course."

They walked down the stairs in silence, though Ember glanced at him in confusion when he turned down the hall to her new room, stopping outside the door.

"It's nearly time for dinner," he said, dropping her arm.

"And?" Ember said slowly, heart sinking.

"I specified every night, didn't I?"

He had...but she'd hoped he'd been joking.

"Are you opposed to spending time with me?"

That was a dangerous question. Ember knew she should say yes...she *was* opposed to it, just not for the reasons he likely believed. But...she'd never heard that tone from him before. It made her shiver. And ache. And before she could fully think it through, she found herself turning toward him.

"That's not it. I just...don't understand."

He smirked, but his eyes were still heavy, dark with something Ember couldn't fully see.

"You don't understand my desire for a conversation partner? After two-hundred years of near isolation?"

Two-hundred years. Then he was admitting it. *I suppose he never denied it...* But even knowing where she stood, even knowing a curse was at work, hearing those words from Dyrerisan's mouth was unnerving. More so than it should've been. It took her a moment to remember where they were in their conversation, and this time she was sure Dyrerisan took notice.

"Is it a matter of availability, then? I'm merely the only person around who isn't endangered by your presence?"

"Mostly. Apologies if that offends your sensibilities."

Ember snorted. She *wished* she could believe that was all.

"Are you going to stand here and wait for me?" she asked, raising her eyebrows. "Lead me to the kitchen as if it's my first day again?"

She was rewarded with a flash of a smile as Dyrerisan bowed shallowly. "I'll see you in the dining room."

Ember slipped into her room as soon as he turned away, wishing she could turn the lock for good measure. She stood with her back to the door a moment, leaning her head against the wood and closing her eyes. Her headache was still lingering. But now that she knew her guess was correct, that every interaction they had with Dyrerisan turned Helen and the rest a little closer to whatever Dyrerisan was, she couldn't use that as an excuse to stay upstairs.

She took a deep breath before pushing away from the door, opening the large wardrobe to decide what lavish creation she'd wear that night. She pulled an emerald green gown from the depths, fingering the gold and black lace decorating the bodice and skirt. It would do.

Ember almost changed her mind when she was trying to put it on, though. The buttons closing up the back weren't designed for a woman to put on alone, and the neckline was...daring. By the time she finished closing the back and digging through drawers until she found a gold toned shawl to wrap around her shoulders, she knew everyone would be waiting.

"Suitable clothing," she muttered, pulling her skirts free of the door before pulling it shut. "If it weren't so pretty, I'd flat refuse."

She supposed that was her own weakness...she wanted to try them all. But that didn't mean she enjoyed the process, or the feeling that she was dressing up for him. Ember rushed down the stairs, holding the wide skirt high enough to keep her feet free, and scowled at the pleased feeling that crept over her at the affect. She walked faster, turning down the first hall that went toward the kitchen. She was nearly running when she reached the large, warm room.

"Ember," Freya said with a smile. "We were just wondering where you went."

Ember smiled, pressing an absent hand to her chest.

"Took a while getting this thing to cooperate," she said breathlessly, flourishing her skirt.

She took a step forward and froze. All of a sudden, she wasn't sure she was quite touching the ground. Miri's words were lost to a rushing in her head, and the next she knew hands were catching her by the elbows and pulling her toward the table. Ember closed her eyes against the rush of movement, putting all her concentration on breathing.

Voices. Voices she couldn't comprehend slowly entered her awareness, along with a hand on her forehead, and another on her back tugging on the edge of her dress bodice.

"It isn't too tight," Miri said. She sounded worried.

"Ember?" Helen said, gentle as usual but oddly insistent. "Ember, can you hear me?"

"I'm alright," Ember whispered, forcing her eyes open again. She met five worried faces all staring down at her. She resisted the urge to close her eyes again to hide from that concern.

"You fainted," Freya said. "*Something* caused it."

*Oh yes, something caused it.* Ember gripped the table edge with one hand but didn't move to stand quite yet. She looked around the room.

"I...rushed down here. It must be that."

Helen's eyebrows furrowed, her eyes tight with worry. No one looked convinced.

"You didn't take any lunch with you to the library, did you?" Helen asked.

Ember shook her head. Helen squeezed her hand, backing away.

"That might do it. Sit there a minute, alright?"

Ember didn't argue. The others weren't so quick to move away, and Ember shifted uncomfortably. She checked her shawl to ensure it was still pinned across her chest, watching Helen adding the last touches to the dinner tray.

"I'll carry it in," Freya said.

"No." Ember forced herself to her feet, holding onto the table until she was sure her legs would hold her. Everyone watched her closely as she stepped toward Helen and the tray.

"I'm fine now," Ember said. "I'll take it."

They all stared at her like they were expecting her to collapse again. Ember stood tall, gritting her teeth. After a moment of Ember standing without swaying, Helen reluctantly placed the tray in her arms.

"I'm at least walking down the hall with you," Freya said.

She stepped ahead of Ember before she could argue, and Ember followed in silence. *Of all the bad timing,* she bemoaned, clutching the full tray tighter. Freya paused at the door and pushed it open, murmuring "don't push yourself" as Ember passed her. Ember didn't respond, stepping carefully into the dining room. The door closed behind her, and Dyrerisan turned away from the windows. Ember set the tray on the table with a breath of relief, busying herself arranging their plates so she didn't have to look up at Dyrerisan.

"You're late."

He sounded more musing than annoyed. Ember took a moment before answering, hardening her voice as she stared resolutely down at the table.

"Always so hard to please. Would you rather I'd come down in a dressing gown?"

Ember bit her lip, regretting those words as soon as they left her mouth. What if he chose to tease her again? She was struggling to hold her balance as it was...she didn't want to face more kindness, not right now. But he didn't respond. Ember glanced up as she took her seat to find him staring at her from his own overly ornate chair.

"Why the shawl?" he asked.

Ember resettled it around her shoulders, making sure the pin held.

"You're uncommonly observant this evening," she bit out.

"I don't think so."

He stared at her for a long moment, until Ember turned to glare at him.

"I'm waiting," he said.

Ember sighed, but she didn't have the energy to sound angry as she spoke. "Whoever designed this dress had a different definition of modesty than I do, and I didn't have time to change back."

"Was that so hard?"

Ember glanced up to find laughter in his eyes. She resisted the urge to pull the shawl tighter around her shoulders. Instead, she fingered her silverware and glared.

"You can't stab me with your butterknife," he said, a smirk pulling across his lips. "Though you're welcome to try."

Ember didn't laugh, though a part of her wondered what he'd do if she *did* try. But she didn't ask, looking down and pulling her hands onto her lap.

"Did something happen that I'm not aware of?"

He must be confused. Here he was, actually speaking to her, *teasing* her no less, and she was being a taciturn shrew. She should keep it up. Maybe he'd give up on the idea of sharing meals if she wasn't a pleasant companion. But she made the mistake of looking up and found him watching her again, but his countenance had softened to concern. *Concern.* And she found she couldn't continue being shrewish under such a look.

"I got a little breathless coming down the stairs," she said, picking at the lace under the table. "Everyone in the kitchen was... overly concerned about it."

"And you don't like when people are concerned about you."

She looked up, straightening her spine as she met his eyes. "No. I don't."

Dyrerisan nodded slowly, his eyes piercing through her to where Ember could swear he saw her beating heart. She couldn't tear her eyes away. Then he broke the trance by leaning back, smirking as his eyes closed off again, like shutters across a window.

"Should I have a talk with them?" he asked lightly. "Order them to limit their kind gestures, ration their friendly exchanges?"

Ember allowed the change of tone, rolling her eyes. "Obviously not."

"If you're sure."

And with that, the conversation died away. Each of them ate quickly, allowing the silence to swallow the room. Ember had almost convinced her dread to unwind by the time they were finished. Until Dyrerisan offered his arm to her again, and it all came rushing back.

"Can't have you fainting on the stairs," he said with a half-smile that Ember didn't return.

She took his arm, though, and didn't bother to protest. Their walk to her room was as silent as supper, and Ember pretended not to see when he bowed before leaving. She was already slipping within her room.

With the door closed firmly behind her, Ember crossed to where she'd stashed her journal in the drawer of an end table, sinking to the floor in a pouf of fabric. She kicked her shoes off, leaning against the side of her bed as she flipped open the pages.

Ember wasn't sure why she bothered. There was no new information she could glean from these pages, no secret escape. This book was nothing more than a record, written by desperate mothers hoping their daughters could somehow be saved. And a dozen different handwritings stared back at her, testifying to the failure of that hope again and again. Each one told the same story, the same tragedy, the same futile, broken hope for an end. Ember read them again, anyway.

If nothing else, it reassured her that she wasn't alone. She wasn't the only young woman to feel the curse sinking around her bones, slowly stealing her life. She wasn't the only one fearing the day it would silence her heart. And she wasn't the only one hoping that one day the curse would break.

"It will end," she whispered, running her fingers over those faded words. She wished the women who'd written their stories could somehow hear her, especially her mother. "The curse will end."

Ember was the last of her family line, and the last girl born under that cruel curse. She couldn't escape it any more than her mother could—her increasing weakness proved that much. But like the women before her, she still had hope. She was the last...and when she died, the curse died with her. She closed her eyes, holding the journal to her chest. And silently, she vowed, *no more broken hearts.*

# CHAPTER NINE

Breathing in deeply, Ember left the taste of dust behind her. Her steps were slow and measured, a steady beat below her as she wandered the garden paths. After several days airing out and cleaning lavish guestrooms, even the stale breeze was refreshing.

There were flowers blooming now. Their bright faces swaying slowly, their perfume filling the warm afternoon, made Ember feel like she walked through a dream. The ache in her arms and back told her otherwise.

That morning she'd tried washing the bedding from her current project, the Jade room, rather than make Miri take care of it all. It proved more than she could handle. Miri was finishing it now, while Ember escaped to the gardens where she could air her frustration in private. Even flexing her hands made her muscles ache.

"I should be able to wash a quilt," she muttered, crossing her arms over her stomach.

A few months ago, she could've washed it on her own. A few months ago, it wouldn't have even been a *question. A few months ago, I was hiding in my room at Rookwood and not flirting with cursed nobility.*

Ember flinched at her own thoughts, retreating. She'd expected this. She'd sworn she'd stay strong to the end. *But it turns out feeling the curse eat up my life is far different from watching it happen.* Beneath all the frustration and anger at her own weakness, she couldn't ignore the flickering terror at what she was becoming...at what she knew came next.

*Separation. Distance. I won't fail now...I knew this would happen.* But somehow, she never expected it to happen so quickly. Was it the result of that second curse darkening the air around her? Was Dyrerisan's curse strengthening her own, feeding it? Had she walked into her own tomb when she entered those gates?

She paused on the path, closing her eyes and taking a deep breath of the flower-scented air. Pessimistic thoughts wouldn't help her. It wasn't as bad as all that...she hadn't fainted again in the week since her first visit to the library. *But I haven't tried running since then, either.*

Ember shook her head and continued down the path, taking the next turn leading back toward the castle. She needed to get out of her own head, before she drove herself to hysterics. If more work wouldn't help, she'd visit the library. Surely, she could find a book to fall into so that she could escape her dreary existence, at least for a few hours.

DYRERISAN SAT LIMPLY in the ancient throne, elbows planted on his knees as he hunched forward to stare at the floor, to stare at his empty hands. Once, he'd taken up his place in this hall with pride, surrounded by hundreds of people praising his name. Once, he'd looked out over those empty stones to see dozens of courtiers all vying for his favor. Once, all of that pomp and glory had meant something. Now it was just an empty room.

Clenching his hands into fists, Dyrerisan looked up. Afternoon sunlight filtered in from high above his head, lighting the hall enough to see that the dust and ruin was gone. Ember had cleaned the room until it shone, including each of the statues she claimed gave her so much frustration. It should've brought him satisfaction, to see the grand hall of Nyxwood restored to its former glory, to look over it and remember how it was long ago in the days of his renown. Instead, looking out upon that hall made him feel heavy, tired...like he was no more than stone.

*"You aspire to be one of them, do you? Then one of them you shall be... nothing but stone and memory."*

Dyrerisan ground his teeth together, pushing back against *that* remembrance. But still her voice echoed, her laughter cutting through the air as he'd hardened into living stone, as his existence had been reduced to shadow and misery. He closed his eyes against the pain that shivered across his flesh at the memory. But all he saw was a pair of vibrant eyes, their violet depths fierce in her cruel victory.

He pushed to his feet, opening his eyes as he dropped down the stairs to the main floor of the room. Dyrerisan's steps echoed on the marble, as he glanced to the statues lining the hall. Free of dust and cobwebs, bright and formidable...in that dim light they seemed more alive than him. If they could speak, what would they say? Dyrerisan could imagine all too well the condemnation they would give him...a sentence perhaps worse than any curse his enemies could inflict. But no worse than he deserved. *Almighty, have mercy.* He turned his gaze away as he passed those silent witnesses, leaving behind that grand hall that was a testament to his past...and his failure.

Ember looked up from her book, blinking in surprise as Marquis Dyrerisan sat in a chair across from her. He didn't acknowledge her even with a glance, merely opened a book and began reading. She watched him for a breath, wondering what had brought him here. The library was one place they seldom met.

When Dyrerisan continued to read silently, without even glancing up at her, Ember returned her own eyes to her book. And when she was sure he wasn't looking, she slipped a piece of paper inside her apron pocket. The contents weren't particularly condemning, merely a quote about Nyxwood Castle's function in the region, but she didn't want to answer the questions it would bring.

She'd begun researching Nyxwood and its leaders weeks ago, as something to think about other than her own troubles. So far, she'd found a lot of history, as well as legends almost beyond imagining for anyone but Ember. But she hadn't found anything about the curse that had hidden Nyxwood away and sealed its marquis within. She was beginning to think that if she wanted answers to *that* mystery, she'd need to find them at the source.

*He's sitting right there. I could ask him...the worst he could do is refuse.*

But Ember stayed silent, watching Dyrerisan more than the words of her current book. *Does he want something?* If he did, he didn't seem to be in a hurry to ask.

"Enjoying your reading?" Dyrerisan asked, turning a page.

Ember glanced back to her book. "Yes."

It was a book of local legends, full of stories the editor claimed were embellishments of the true history, fanciful additions to make the past seem less bleak. So far, she hadn't found anything more unlikely than her own situation. She wished she could sit down with the editor and explain her own past, her own future...perhaps then he wouldn't think these "legends" were so impossible. *Perhaps if he met Dyrerisan his take on these histories would be different.*

Ember looked up, realizing that Dyrerisan was staring at her, his book held limply in his lap. How long had she been lost in thought?

"Are you enjoying your reading?" she asked, wanting to draw his attention elsewhere.

"No."

He snapped the book shut and held it up for her inspection. It was a romantic novel, one Ember had finished reading only a few days before. Ember fought a smile and failed.

"I wouldn't have guessed you're the romantic type."

Dyrerisan grimaced. "I thought I'd try your sort of reading. I've found it shallow and dull."

"Of course you have," Ember shot back. "You chose the worst book I've found in this place."

Dyrerisan narrowed his eyes, and Ember closed her own book and set it on the cushion beside her. Folding her hands in her lap, she met his gaze and waited for whatever response was building behind those eyes.

"You read this book through," he said slowly.

"Yes."

"But you didn't enjoy it?"

"Not particularly," Ember said breezily. "That author somehow manages to combine a dry style with hysterical characters that can't be taken seriously. I wished I could reach in and strangle the heroine the entire time I was reading."

Dyrerisan's eyebrows drew together, but Ember could've sworn a touch of a smile pulled at the corners of his mouth. "Then why finish it?"

"There's value in following a story to its end, even if the journey is less than satisfying."

"Even when surrounded by more books than you ever dreamed existed?"

Ember narrowed her eyes, but she couldn't contradict his assumption...this library *was* more than she'd ever imagined. But as for his confusion...perhaps she could help him understand that.

"Turn to page two-hundred and forty-three."

Dyrerisan looked suspicious, but he flipped to the named page and glanced over it.

"The bottom of the page," Ember said. "Read what Alyssa says to Lamont."

Ember waited. Her heart beat faster as she watched him, waiting to see what he made of the passage.

"You think me naïve and vain," Dyrerisan said, his low voice sending a sudden shiver down Ember's spine. "In some ways, you may be right. But do not equate my innocence with foolishness. I know this world as well as you, what it offers and what it takes. If I choose to live with my head high, dauntless in the face of its attacks, shouldn't that make me courageous? And yet you judge me as shallow and thoughtless. Do not presume that your past makes you superior to me, or that our futures cannot look the same. I have as much life burning in my veins as you."

Dyrerisan didn't look up from the page, though Ember could see his expression had turned thoughtful. Ember gave him a moment to think before speaking, her own voice soft in the hush of that room.

"That one passage makes the book worth reading. Because there's *something there.* It gives the story a depth of possibility far beyond what the author actually wrote."

"But it *is* beyond what the author wrote," Dyrerisan argued, looking up to Ember. "How can a single paragraph redeem an entire book?"

"Because it makes the story *mean* something, even if I have to develop it in my own imagination."

Dyrerisan didn't look convinced. Ember's lips twisted in a smile as she leaned forward. She didn't stop to wonder why it suddenly mattered so much that Dyrerisan understood, that he saw what she saw. Her mind was alight with all the possibilities that had been dancing in her head since she'd finished that disappointing novel.

"Imagine if everything you knew about Alyssa began with that quote, if her conduct in the story was how she describes herself here: a woman who uses her innocence as a shield, who *burns* with life and is determined to find a way to make her existence mean something. Now think how such a woman would interact with the rest of the story, the choices she'd make and the changes it would cause. Wouldn't that be a story worth knowing?"

Dyrerisan stared at her for a long moment, his fingers tapping lightly against the book's spine. Ember held his gaze, *willing* him to understand. He slowly nodded.

"It would."

Ember leaned back, giving in to the urge to smile. Dyrerisan's own mouth flickered with a matching smile, even as he closed the book and tossed it to the table.

"But I won't mine the depths for that meaning, now that you've done it for me."

Ember shrugged. "Fair enough, *milord*."

She wasn't sure why she added the title. Perhaps as a reminder to herself to keep her distance. But the result was Dyrerisan leaning back in his chair with an unsettling grin, his eyes almost *dancing*.

"Call me Dyrerisan."

Ember raised her eyebrows. "Servants don't call their masters by their given name."

"But you're not truly a servant, are you?"

Ember sat in silence, unsure how to respond to that. Part of her wanted to agree that she was no servant, that she wouldn't bow to him as master. She never had, really. But another part of her was wary, unsure what implications hid in those words. Perhaps the separation required between a servant and a member of nobility was a protection she wanted to keep.

Dyrerisan snorted, still lounging in his chair as he stared at her. "You're here as your uncle's bargaining chip. I demanded the presence of someone from his family, but your place within these walls is still up for me to decide."

"And you've decided I'm no longer a servant?" Ember asked quietly, breathlessly.

"Yes."

"Then what am I?"

"I'm not sure." He tilted his head, and a distant sorrow passed through his eyes. "Perhaps that's yours to decide."

Ember looked away, thrown off balance. *Mine to decide?* Was it really? She snorted, a smirk threatening across her lips. One thing she could decide...perhaps it would make Dyrerisan think twice before offering her more freedoms.

"I'll call you Dyre," she said, looking up in time to see the grimace that crossed his face.

"No," he growled.

Ember's smile grew. "Yes. The name Dyrerisan is archaic."

"*I* am archaic."

Ember resisted the laugh bubbling up at that, amused by his growing displeasure. She forced her tone to be even, matter of fact.

"Dyre is *much* easier to say."

"But my name is *Dyrerisan.*"

"Have you never had a nickname?"

Ember's amusement grew as a new grimace overtook his expression. Was he remembering pet names from childhood? The imperious tone he took when he spoke next wasn't convincing.

"I haven't allowed that kind of liberty in over two centuries."

"Who would you have offered it to, the lamp shades?"

He ground his teeth together. Ember tried to temper her own amusement, not wanting to arouse his true anger, but it was difficult. She wondered if his objection to the nickname "Dyre" was because of its meaning, "dear heart."

*That was another dangerous move.* Some of her amusement froze over. What would she have done if he'd read into her choice more deeply? What if he'd assumed calling him "dear heart" was an endearment, rather than a way to get under his stony skin?

"Fine, *Dyrerisan,*" she said, deciding to retreat. "We'll discuss nicknames more later."

"Have a more pressing engagement, do you?"

Ember glanced pointedly at the nearest window, where the sun was tipping toward the far horizon.

"If you want dinner before midnight, I should start preparing," she said, standing.

"Still bitter over my dress code?"

Ember smiled but didn't reply. In truth, she was still enjoying dressing up in ball gowns like a princess. But she didn't intend to let him know that.

"Fine," Dyrerisan said, crossing his legs and looking up at her. "I'll see you at dinner, then."

Ember nodded and made her escape, glad when walls separated her from Dyrerisan's piercing gaze. She never could help herself, could she? She always had to push farther, take another risk, go where she didn't belong. Ember was lucky she hadn't stepped off a precipice, at this point. She shook her head as she descended a floor, suddenly wondering why he put up with her.

*"I am archaic."*

Dyrerisan's words echoed through her mind, and along with it that brief glimpse of sorrow interrupting his annoyance. It had come and gone so quickly she wasn't sure she'd actually seen it...except this wasn't the first time his eyes had flashed with something broken. Ember couldn't help but wonder if he really believed that he was archaic: that he didn't belong to the present, only to the past.

*Over two centuries.* Would Ember *want* that many years of life, if she knew they'd be spent in lonely exile? Her heart whispered, *yes.* Of course, she'd want those extra years...a long life, a *full* life, was more than Ember had ever dreamed for herself. But was his life full? *No. I don't suppose it is.*

Thoughts of Dyre's half-life still occupied her mind when she entered the dining room, draped in sage green velvet that whispered as she walked. She watched Dyrerisan more closely as they took their seats. How much of his worn look was the curse, and how much was the result of two hundred years of loneliness? For by now she was convinced that he *was* lonely. Why else would he invite her into his life: *her,* the castoff of a cowardly debtor?

She'd always assumed, with her family history, that the richness of a life was measured in years. Now she wasn't so sure. But what would the measure be, then? Satisfaction? Joy? Pleasure? Her mind shied away from the answer she knew her mother would've given, one her father would've agreed with. But she did conclude that, when it came to the *fullness* of life, perhaps she and Dyrerisan were on equal ground.

"Still comparing me to my ancestors?"

Ember startled at the sound of his voice. "Pardon?"

Dyrerisan looked up, laugher in his piercing eyes. She almost thought she could see a smirk pulling at his lips.

"You've been staring at me for some time. Admiring my appearance?"

Ember snorted and turned her eyes to her untouched plate, picking at her salad with her fork.

"Hardly."

"I could take offence at your tone."

"I wouldn't expect *you* to have such thin skin."

Dyrerisan chuckled, and a smile flickered across Ember's mouth unconsciously. She glanced up at Dyre again, her eyes darting over his features. Handsome? Definitely not. But he had the sort of face people remembered. And she had to admit that, when his eyes were dancing, he didn't look so bad. It made her wonder what he'd looked like before he'd been changed to a living statue.

He caught her staring and raised an eyebrow. Ember looked down again, her face warming, and scolded herself.

"Well?" he asked.

"Well, *what*, Dyre?" Ember asked breezily, glancing up to meet his glare at the unwanted nickname.

"Annoying me won't allow you to escape the subject. What are you thinking of so intently?"

"You expect me to share?"

"Eventually."

How long would he press the issue? She didn't intend to offer her thoughts, any of them. Her mind was her own. But did she want to test her stubbornness against his?

"My patience far exceeds yours, Ember," Dyrerisan warned. "I have plenty of practice at waiting."

Ember gave up avoiding his gaze and planted her chin in her hand.

"Is that what you do all day? Wait?"

"Is *that* where your curiosity took you?"

Ember shrugged. "It's related."

And it was, in Ember's mind. Two hundred years of lonely life... how did he spend his hours? How had he not gone insane? She had already seen the toll it had taken on Helen and the rest, in their weariness and long silences. But Dyre was, for the most part, alone. And he apparently hadn't spent his years devouring the library's contents as Ember would have.

"I see to my own matters," he replied, in a tone that said the topic was closed. Ember wasn't satisfied.

"Picking roses," she said, "weaving tapestries, staring at yourself in mirrors..."

"Ember."

"'Seeing to your own matters' could mean anything," Ember said with a shrug. "If you won't explain, I'll just guess."

"My private matters are not for your prying mind."

"You've pried into *my* life."

"Careful," Dyre growled. "There are many questions about you that I've chosen to overlook, Ember. Don't make me take back that decision."

Ember snapped her mouth shut against her next retort, heat flashing through her face. Would he follow through on that threat? Ember couldn't take the chance.

"Fine," she bit out, her voice not as steady as she would've liked.

She pushed her chair out from the table, ignoring her shaking hands as she stood. "I think I'll retire early."

Her goal was to escape Dyre's presence, but as she stepped away from the table he followed her. Ember ignored him and followed the path to her bedroom, keeping her eyes on the floor even when she felt his gaze on her. He walked by her side all the way to the door, but he didn't speak, not until she reached for the doorknob, and he reached out to stop her.

"You don't want to know all that my life has held," Dyrerisan said roughly.

Ember kept her eyes on Dyre's hand, barely brushing against her skin. She took a deep breath.

"And you don't want to know everything in *mine*."

After a moment of silence, Dyre took a step away. Ember pushed through the door without a backward glance, sighing deeply when she was sealed in the empty room. She waited to hear his footsteps as he left, feeling oddly hollow when they faded down the hall. And once again she wondered...*what makes a life worth living?*

# CHAPTER TEN

Ember stepped lightly down the hall, looking around at the dusty contents as if she were planning how to clean it. There were fewer riches scattered heedlessly here. This place wasn't meant for the public eye. However, a track in the carpet hinted that this route wasn't as untouched as most of the hallways within the castle. Ember hoped that would keep her own presence from notice.

She didn't have to worry about Dyre sneaking up on her at the moment. She'd seen him walking outside the castle walls with a fierce looking man a while ago. His "visitors" had come again, and as far as Dyrerisan knew Ember was safely ensconced in the library. And she *had* been in the library, intending to stay there for most of the day at least...but she couldn't settle. No book held her attention, and no position on the sofas allowed her to relax. She'd been pacing in front of the windows when she'd spotted Dyre outside and decided to take advantage of the rare opportunity to explore one of the forbidden places within Nyxwood: Dyrerisan's study. At the very least, it would distract her from the endless loops of her thoughts.

Ember paused beside a statue of a young woman with a dove in her hands, listening for any sign of company. The stairs ahead of her were silent, but she hesitated. Should she be doing this? What would Dyrerisan do to her if he caught her? She wasn't naïve enough to think he wouldn't care; he guarded his privacy closely. But this was one of the few parts of Nyxwood where she hadn't already explored, other than the higher towers and their endless stairs. And she needed something new today.

With a deep breath, Ember stepped forward. She resisted the desire to glance around her as she approached the stairs, knowing that would make her look suspicious. No one was here, but even if she *was* caught, she hoped to pass off her presence here as innocent curiosity. *That excuse will only work if I'm not inside his study.* But she didn't need to worry about that...she wouldn't be caught.

There were fewer stairs than Ember had guessed, and she emerged on a landing with a dark wooden door looming over her before she was quite ready. She stared at that door a moment, taking one more moment to reconsider, before reaching out to the knob. The door was unlocked, swinging inward on well-oiled hinges. Ember held her breath until she could see that the room was empty.

The three large windows in the room were all covered in thick drapes, blocking most of the light from the room. Ember stepped inside and put her back to a wall until her eyes could adjust to the dimness. The door she closed behind her.

Ember edged around the walls of the room first, taking in the dozens of thick books without titles embossed on the spines. She dared to grab one off the top of a stack, where the dust was already disturbed. Inside were financial records going back to before Ember was born. She glanced over it, wondering how much contact Dyre had with the outside world if could buy new bridles from a town Ember *knew* was at least a week of travel away from Rookwood.

Ember returned the book to the stack. Was that the right angle? She adjusted it, staring at the stack for a moment before forcing herself to move on. Surely, he wouldn't notice a single book slightly out of place. She examined the bookshelves for a moment more before turning to what had truly caught her attention: his desk.

It was massive, carved from dark wood with a forest motif surrounding three sides. The surface was covered with half used candles and loose papers. If the arrangement had any order to it, Ember couldn't figure it out. But she was still wary of disturbing them too much. She planted her hands on the edge of the desk and leaned over, reading what she could see of the papers on top.

Reports from figures with names like "Wolf" and "Badger" dominated her view. They recounted events that seemed to come from the pages of an adventure novel: infiltrating fortresses, interrogating suspects, observing targets. It was the sort of thing only spies and assassins would engage in. The bottom of one page reported that a threat was "eliminated." Ember leaned back, stomach churning.

*I should get back to the library.* But as she turned away, something caught her eye: a stack of papers, with what Ember had thought was a normal stone resting on top. Looking closer, Ember realized that it was more than that...it was rose quartz, carved into a heart. And on its surface were words, carved and filled with silver: "a gift for the living monument." The last word had been scratched out. Ember didn't try to decipher what it had once read. She'd seen enough.

Ember stepped backward, toward the door. But as she spun to face the door, she moved too fast...her vision turned hazy as vertigo struck. She stopped, blindly reaching for the wall to lean against. She ended up leaning her whole body against the door, squeezing her eyes shut and waiting for it to pass. Her whole body trembled. She took slow breaths, counting her heartbeats as they passed, and the world slowed its wild tossing.

She reached for the doorknob, hoping the staircase was really as short as she was remembering, and heard voices. Again, she froze.

*Not Dyre,* she thought, hearing them approach. She didn't know if she should be relieved or terrified. Had those voices coming toward her been the ones to "eliminate" Dyre's enemies? She didn't have any more time to wonder before they reached the door.

Ember stepped to the side, hiding behind the door as it swung open. The voices entered the room, and Ember held her breath.

"I don't need an escort," a man growled, stepping within Ember's view as he approached the desk. His back stayed toward her.

"That's for the Marquis to decide," the second voice purred, also stepping further into the room.

Ember pressed closer to the wall, wondering if she should dart into the hall now, while they were distracted. She took a hesitant step...and froze. She couldn't do it. The first man was sorting through papers on Dyrerisan's desk, with the second looking on, only steps away from where she stood.

"What happened before was a complete misunderstanding," the first man said in a smoother tone that sent shivers along the back of Ember's neck. But it was the other man's response, eerily calm, that sent true fear spiking through her.

"The Marquis doesn't allow anyone to interfere with his staff."

"I was hardly interfering."

"Miri was in *tears.*"

"Are you going to help me find this report or not?"

"He sent *you* for the report. My task is making sure you don't stray elsewhere."

The first man scoffed again, glancing at papers only to discard them. His companion stepped back, closer to Ember's hiding place, and she stiffened. Glancing between his broad shoulder blades had her wishing she'd stayed in the library. There was no way she could fight off either of these men, if it came to that. She reached for the edge of the door, pulling it closer to the wall. A flimsy protection... and a mistake. The second man turned, locking bright amber eyes on Ember.

Her heart thundered in her ears, fingers tightening on the edge of the door. She silently implored him not to say anything. He blinked slowly, looking her over. Then he turned away, taking two large steps toward the desk, subtly blocking the other man from turning around.

"Now you decide to help," the other man muttered.

"It seems you need it," the amber eyed man said. Behind his back, he motioned for Ember to move.

She didn't need to be told twice. She rounded the door, darting into the hall and down the stairs as fast as she dared. She didn't stop until she was within the library, huddled on a stuffed chair with her knees tucked to her chest. She closed her eyes and rested her head against the back of the chair. *That was more adventure than I bargained for.* She snorted. And she'd been so sure she wouldn't be caught.

She shook off thoughts of what the amber eyed man would tell Dyrerisan. Ember was sure she'd have plenty of time to ponder her doom...again, she wondered how far she'd get if she tried running away. But with Dyrerisan's visitors around, she knew she wasn't desperate enough to try. At least, not yet.

"SARNERE HAS RETREATED from the villages he controlled in the south."

Dyrerisan grunted, staring at the forest's edge. "The duke of those lands finally returned to check his holdings. Kelan likely doesn't want his activities brought back to the king."

"You believe the king is ignorant?"

Dyrerisan slowed, glancing to Badger. "The king hasn't set foot in his own kingdom for near a decade. There's no doubt he's ignorant."

"Forgive me milord, but that would imply *your* ignorance as well."

Dyrerisan scowled, continuing his path along the walls of Nyxwood. "Indeed, it would, if I didn't have the Aerie to be my eyes and ears."

A moment of silence passed before Badger continued. "If the King is ignorant, and someone *does* inform him of Sarnere's actions... what would he do? Rumor is, he isn't expected to return for another year."

Dyrerisan thought for a moment.

"I don't know," he admitted. "But neither does Kelan, I imagine."

That was the issue: this king was an unknown. Raised outside the kingdom he was destined to reign over, crowned when he was little more than a boy...he'd spent only half a dozen years inside his kingdom. And yet, those half a dozen years were enough to convince everyone in his domain that he wasn't someone to trifle with. If Duke Kelan possessed any sense of fear, he wouldn't cross the king lightly. And he'd already committed enough crimes to rouse the king's ire, should the monarch ever hear of it. Dyrerisan had considered sending a message to inform the king himself. But what self-respecting leader would accept a missive from a figment of folklore?

Dyrerisan clenched his teeth at that bitter thought. The silence carried them around the bend, to where many of his warriors were gathered, sparring. Laughter and conversation belied the sound of clashing swords. He arrived in time to see Fox disarm Tigress and send her sprawling. Tigress rolled and came up on her knees but stayed there, while Fox grinned and lowered her sword. Then she looked up, bowing when she spotted Dyrerisan. The rest copied her and murmured greetings to him as he passed.

"Care for a round, my lord?" Bear asked.

Dyrerisan's hand drifted to the hilt of his sword, fingering the onyx stones on the cross guard.

"Why not?" he decided, pulling his sword from its sheath. It was good to train with a real opponent, once in a while.

But before he could begin, Wolf and Viper came into view. Viper waved the paper he'd gone to retrieve, while Wolf followed. The look in his eyes made Dyrerisan put away his sword. *Something happened.* If Viper had even *spoken* to any of the castle's occupants, Dyrerisan would hang him from the tower by his ankles.

But when Dyrerisan tipped his head toward Viper, showing the report to Badger, Wolf shook his head. *What did Ember do?*

"What happened?" Dyrerisan asked when he'd reached Wolf's side.

"She was in your study when Viper and I got there."

Dyrerisan sighed, pressing a fist against the wall as he shook his head. *Nosy, stubborn...* She'd agreed to stay in the library. *I trusted her too much, it seems.* He knew which papers he had laying out; he knew what she would've read...*perhaps it's good she knows.* But that didn't change that she'd broken her word.

"I don't have to ask what she was doing. Did Viper speak to her?"

"He didn't even see her. And he still insists that entire incident was a misunderstanding."

Dyre snorted. A misunderstanding that would cost him more than trust if anything like it happened again. A knot tightened in his chest, as he imagined what might've happened if he hadn't sent Wolf to ensure Viper didn't...stray.

"Thank you, Collin," he said, staring at the stone in the wall.

"Glad to be of service," Wolf said with a wry half-bow.

Dyrerisan turned back to the Aerie. He still had business to conduct. Afterward he'd consider Ember's actions...and what he should do so it wouldn't happen again.

DYRE DIDN'T COME COLLECT her for dinner. When twilight darkened the library, she assumed it was safe to leave and retreated to her bedroom, choosing a somber gray gown to wear to match her impending doom. But she did her best not to let her dread show in the kitchen, ignoring the way her hands shook and rattled the contents on the tray. Tonight, it had little to do with weakness.

Dyrerisan was standing by windows when she entered. He didn't turn around, and Ember creeped to the table to set down the tray before she dropped it. Her eyes wandered across the table to avoid glancing at his dark silhouette.

"Enjoy your day?"

Ember winced at the frost in Dyrerisan's voice. She stepped back from the table, linking her hands behind her back. It took her a moment to formulate a response.

"I apologize," she said, her voice dry and quiet.

"For disobeying orders or invading my privacy?"

"Invading your privacy."

Ember couldn't say she was sorry she'd disobeyed orders...if she was being honest, she was only sorry she'd been caught.

"Did you enjoy what you found?"

Ember leaned back on her heels, unnerved by the question. It felt like a trap, but she couldn't think of an answer that wouldn't make it all worse. She opted for honesty.

"No."

"Good."

"Do they kill for you?" The words slipped past Ember's lips against her better judgement. She clenched her hands tighter together, heart pounding as Dyrerisan twisted to face her, fire in his gaze.

"What?"

Ember took a deep breath and tried to stand tall, to look like she wasn't afraid.

"Your 'visitors.' Do they kill for you?"

"And if they do?" Dyrerisan prodded, voice low.

"I'd ask who they kill," Ember replied. "Because I can't think of any *good* reason for a marquis to have a private army of *assassins* at his beck and call..."

"And I don't see how it's your concern."

"I want to know whose castle I'm living in," Ember shot back. "If you're some sort of renegade pulling strings from the shadows, I want to know!"

Dyrerisan huffed. “So that’s your fear? That I’m working against the visible order of things?”

“What I *fear* is having dinner with a monster who’d have me killed if I step out of line.”

Dyre drew back. And Ember wondered...if she’d slapped him, would he look so stunned? Even in her roiling anger, she regretted her words, but she couldn’t take them back now. She kept her spine straight as she watched Dyrerisan recover, standing tall so that he seemed to loom over her even from across the table.

“So, you want a monster, do you?” he asked in a quiet voice that made Ember’s heart pound. “Yes, they kill for me. They go where I send them, they say what I tell them, and they do *whatever* I command.”

Ember shivered, her flesh feeling like someone had dumped ice water over her head. She stood in place, silent as she stared at Dyrerisan. His glare didn’t abate. When she finally found her voice, it stayed far too quiet.

“You wanted my uncle to come here.”

“Yes.”

That short confirmation sent another shiver through her. She swallowed. “Did you plan to have me come, then? Did you want *me* as your servant, to play your twisted games?”

There was that broken flash again, there and gone so quickly Ember wondered if she’d imagined it. But his fury seemed different afterward, sharper.

“Why would I choose *you*?” Dyre spat. “A weak castoff, too rebellious and stubborn to be of any use.”

Now it was Ember’s turn to recoil. She took in a shuddering breath, looking down to hide the tears burning in her eyes

“Then why am I here?” she whispered.

He didn’t respond. Footsteps broke the silence, and the sound of the grand door opening and closing. Ember squeezed her eyes shut, reaching out to the table for support. Of all the consequences her imagination had conjured during the afternoon, *this* wasn't one of them.

*Why does it hurt so much?* If Dyre was speaking the truth, then she was the means to some hidden end, an interchangeable piece of a larger plan. And she should be grateful...perhaps she wouldn't need to force that separation on her own, after all. So why did she *ache* at the thought of being nothing to him?

*Side effect of the curse,* she told herself. *It means nothing.* But she knew.... oh, she knew that wasn't it. Admitting it, though, would have consequences. And she'd experienced enough conflict for one night. With a sigh, she forced her eyes open and reached for the untouched tray, not willing to eat in the large room by herself. Dyrerisan's food she left on the table, as she wondered how she could get through the kitchen and back to her room without Freya insisting she explain what had caused her tears. Explaining her argument with Dyrerisan was the last thing she wanted to do.

Dyrerisan paced in front of the dining room door, silently fuming. Heat filled him, white hot fury that failed to cover the other emotions, *other* thoughts that he longed to forget. At this point, he couldn't tell who he was more angry with: Ember, for her pig-headed curiosity, or himself, for letting his emotions overtake him.

*Weak castoff. Useless.* He'd trained for years to find weaknesses and exploit them...he'd never meant for that skill to spill into his personal interactions. He'd left the room to get himself under control, to gather his wits so he could know what to say to clean up this mess he'd made. He'd planned this all so much better in his head...

He *was* angry that Ember had disobeyed him, that she'd snooped through his study on today of all days. But more than that, he knew what might've happened if she'd run into Viper alone. Viper knew what Dyrerisan thought of his methods, and he knew what the consequences would be if he disobeyed a second time. But Ember was...fragile. And hot headed enough to get herself into a fight she had no chance of winning.

Still, his goal for this evening was to *scold* her, to convince her not to try something like this again, not enter into a heated argument. He should apologize. But if he tried speaking to Ember right now, would she listen? Would it turn into another argument? Everything was roiling too close to the surface...he didn't trust himself to react well if Ember was still throwing insults.

A muffled crash came from the dining room, followed by Ember's sharp voice. Already on edge, Dyrerisan reacted without thinking, throwing open the door so it cracked against the wall. Ember jerked to look at him, and candlelight caught the tears gathered in her eyes. She was on her knees beside a pile of scattered food and broken dishes. Dyrerisan took a breath to steady himself and started walking cautiously toward her.

"What happened?" he asked, doing his best to keep his voice neutral.

"I dropped the tray," she muttered bitterly.

Dyrerisan bit back his reply of '*obviously*'. He reached her side and knelt beside the mess. She was already piling shards of porcelain onto the tray. He scooped up the pieces near himself and dropped them on to the pile, grimacing at the remnants of food deposited on his fingers.

"Stop it," Ember snapped. "I can clean it myself."

Dyrerisan didn't reply, but continued cleaning his side of the mess. A few moments of awkward silence passed until Ember gasped, jerking her hand to her chest. Dyrerisan scooped the remains of the mess onto the tray and turned his attention to Ember, who was cautiously examining her bleeding finger.

"How bad is it?" he asked.

She curled her hand to her chest again. "It's fine."

"Let Miri clean it."

"Fine."

Ember reached for the tray, but Dyrerisan pulled it out of her reach.

"Someone else can retrieve this," he said when Ember glared at him. "Go see about your cut."

For a moment, Dyrerisan thought Ember would argue. But she only sighed and pushed herself to her feet. Dyrerisan stood with her, steadying her when she swayed on her feet. She didn't acknowledge the gesture, leaving the dining room without another glance in his direction. And after staring toward the narrow door where she disappeared, Dyrerisan turned back toward the hallway. He needed to get a message to Fox and Wolf before they left Nyxwood lands. He had a new task for them, regarding just *what* Ember was hiding from him.

Ember collapsed on her bed with a deep sigh, letting her eyes slip closed. Her finger was bandaged and still throbbing, but that wasn't the ache that made her wish she could fade into the carpet.

*Dyre, you confusing, infuriating man.* How could he change moods so quickly? From furious to gentle, from imperiously telling Ember she meant nothing to him to kneeling beside her to clean up broken dishes. Which was the truth? Which was Ember supposed to take seriously? *Which do I want to be true?*

That was a frightening question. She should want the distance, the separation. She should want Dyrerisan to see her as nothing more than payment for a debt, his newly acquired servant who causes more trouble than he bargained for. Ember pressed her uninjured hand to her eyelids, willing the tears to stay within her. She was in a dangerous place.

Her moment of weakness, the tray slipping from her numb hands...was that because of the fight? Because, as much as Ember was determined to stay away, she *ached* at the thought of Dyrerisan not wanting her as...as anything. Couldn't they at least be friends? But even friendship had its consequences.

Ember's next breath rattled. She had no idea what she should do. But of one thing she was certain...life here wasn't as simple and safe as she'd thought it would be.

# CHAPTER ELEVEN

Ember delayed entering the dining room as long as she could the next morning. She had no idea what to expect. Would Dyre be cold and haughty? Would he be warm and gentle? Both options made Ember's stomach churn.

Helen and the rest hadn't asked about what had happened the night before, but Ember wondered if they already knew. They were uncommonly quiet that morning as Ember ate and gathered the tray for Dyrerisan. Not unfriendly...but a little more distant. She wondered what they thought of her actions the day before but wasn't brave enough to ask.

Ember took a slow breath outside the door to the dining room, one last moment to gather her courage. She had to face the day eventually...with whatever consequences Dyre decided to rain down on her. She squared her shoulders and pushed the door aside, keeping her head high as she approached the table. Dyrerisan was sitting in his usual place. He hardly moved when Ember entered, glancing quickly in her direction before returning his eyes to the windows. Outside the sun lit the vibrant gardens into a thousand jewel tones.

Ember let her eyes glide over the sight for a moment, wishing she was out there.

"Good morning, Ember," Dyrerisan said, calmly. There was no anger in his words. Would they pretend last night never happened, then? Ember steeled herself to follow his lead.

"Good morning, Dyrerisan."

"Take a seat."

Ember obeyed, arranging her skirts more carefully than usual to avoid meeting his eyes. He didn't speak until she looked up, though. He pulled a key from his pocket and held it up between them.

"This is the key to my study."

He stayed silent, and Ember realized he expected a response.

"Very shiny, isn't it?" she replied, finding that she didn't want to easily play along after all. Dyre's lips twitched, but he didn't smile.

"From now on, my study will be locked and this key on my person. And don't think I won't notice if you try and pickpocket me."

Ember rolled her eyes. "And I suppose I shouldn't pick the lock, either."

"No."

"Great. Am I excused?"

"I'd like you to stay here. There's something I intend to show you after breakfast."

"And if I refuse?" Ember asked sweetly.

Dyrerisan glanced up at her, one imperious eyebrow raised. "I'll come and find you."

The thought of playing hide and seek with the great Marquis Dyrerisan made a smile break through, and she looked down.

"I suppose I won't, then."

"I won't be long."

Ember didn't respond, stepping up to the windows to watch the gardens more closely. From this angle, the gardens looked endless. Trees hid the wall that separated them from the rest of the estate, bright flowers dominated the scene. The most prominent were the roses in half a dozen hues that Ember knew took up *hours* of John's time.

"You're free to take flowers up to your room," Dyrerisan said, making Ember jump a little. She didn't look away from the window.

"I'd prefer to leave them growing," she whispered.

Neither of them spoke again until Dyre rose from his seat, coming to offer his arm to Ember. She stared at his sleeve for a moment, debating whether or not to refuse, but in the end accepted the gesture. No need to start another argument.

"Where are we going?" she asked as they left the dining room.

"The dungeons."

Ember balked, tugging her arm from Dyre's grasp. He turned on her in confusion, while Ember worked to find words around her suddenly pounding heart.

"Why?" she asked, choked. "You want me to see where I'll be going if I disobey you again?"

Understanding dawned in his eyes, and a flash of what Ember could've named regret. But maybe she was seeing things.

"No," he said. "Since you seem so fascinated with forbidden things, I decided to give you a tour before you decide to explore on your own."

"Oh."

Ember looked away to hide her embarrassment from her overreaction. When Dyre offered his arm again, she took it without hesitation. And she kept her mouth resolutely shut as he led her on.

The entrance to the dungeons was surprisingly nondescript, paneled like any other door. To either side hung tapestries of Death claiming souls from a battlefield. *Appropriate.* Dyrerisan had to unlock the door, and when it opened a breeze of damp air followed. Ember shivered, noting that the door was obviously reinforced, nearly twice the thickness as the rest Ember had seen. She studied it more closely than it warranted as Dyre lit a lamp to carry with them into the darkness.

"Ready?" Dyre asked when Ember was slow to move.

"Of course."

But she held her breath as they stepped down into the gloom. That dank feeling to the air grew stronger as they descended, and Ember couldn't help but watch the strange shadows the lamp cast on the walls. Their surroundings seemed to absorb the light, leaving only a small globe around Ember and Dyre. She held onto his arm a little tighter.

The reached a landing and turned down a new set of stairs. Ember thought she saw an empty doorway to their left but didn't ask where it led. She was glad when they reached the bottom of the stairs, despite the dread of what she'd see.

But as Dyre lifted the lamp, drawing Ember further into the space to see, it was merely a hall lined with barred cells, all of which looked as if they hadn't been used since the curse descended. None of the horrors she'd imagined.

"Why is this forbidden territory, again?" Ember asked, glancing around the sparse room. She could see a decaying table and chairs where guards assumedly would've sat to play dice or find other ways to pass the long hours.

Dyre turned around, tugging Ember to follow, and then she noticed the five empty doorways lined up, dark and identical. Ember had no idea which was the one they'd come through.

"Only one of these doorways leads back to the castle proper," Dyrerisan explained. "Another, to a disguised entrance near the edge of my lands, and the other three...are designed to discourage intruders from poking around."

"I take it I don't want to know *how* they discourage people."

"No."

"Right," Ember said, stiff and cold from her sudden imaginings of what she'd find down those passages. "I've seen enough, I think."

"Your curiosity is satisfied?"

"More than satisfied. I won't be coming down here any time soon."

A smile flickered across Dyre's face. "Good."

He guided her back out of the dungeons, and Ember noted that he took the second door from the right. She hoped she wouldn't have reason to come down here...but just in case, she wanted to know the way out.

Ember was glad when they were back in the normal hall, the door locked behind them. She took a deep breath, looking around at their dim surroundings with more appreciation.

"What are your plans for the day?" Dyrerisan asked, slipping the key back into one of his pockets.

Ember glanced at him without turning her head. "Endless dusting and sweeping."

"Care to leave cleaning behind for a day? I have...business I need to conduct in the library. I'd be honored if you'd join me."

Ember's heart stuttered, and this time she turned to face him, swallowing back her sudden dread. "Why?"

Dyre was slow to answer. It looked to Ember like he was thinking of replies, only to discard them. Finally, he met her eyes frankly, and his broad shoulders seemed to sag a little.

"It's my way of apologizing," he said. "For...losing my temper last night."

If that was all...she supposed that was acceptable.

"Then I will come with you," she replied. "As my own apology."

Dyrerisan's only response was to offer his arm yet again. He walked slower than usual to the library, but Ember refused to wonder why. Whatever his reason, she was grateful for the chance to keep her breathing a little steadier up those stairs she was beginning to dread.

She wasn't sure what she expected would happen when they entered the library, but it turned out to be a quiet and relaxing way to spend time. She picked up her most recent book, a tome on local history that had a dry style but enough enchanting stories to keep her turning pages. Dyrerisan sat at a table unrolling fragile maps and taking notes in a small book he pulled from a hidden pocket.

The hours passed steadily, until Ember found her eyes growing heavy. Climbing down to her room was an unwelcome prospect. She set her book on the table and glanced at Dyre: he was absorbed in his maps. It wouldn't hurt to rest her eyes here, then. She doubted he'd even notice.

DYRERISAN LOOKED up from his work, wondering at the stillness from the couch where Ember had taken up residence. Typically, she shifted often, in unconscious reactions to whatever she was reading. He found her asleep, her light hair spilled across the cushions, looking more at peace than she ever did awake. Something about the sight of her laying there, so still and quiet, caused a sharp ache just beneath his breastbone. He rubbed absently at the spot and frowned, forcing his attention back to his work.

A few minutes passed. Dyre tapped his pen on the paper, staring at his notations without seeing them. He glanced at Ember once more, who hadn't moved. He dropped his pen and pushed away from the table.

Dyrerisan approached her chosen seat cautiously, wary of waking her. He knelt slowly, ignoring the ache at the movement and telling himself he was only ensuring that she still breathed. Ember was too still, too pale... He held his breath: watching as her chest rose and fell, listening to the air passing through her lungs. He let out a silent sigh but didn't immediately move away. His gaze fell on the book beside her, and he flipped the cover open to confirm which book she was devouring now.

A history of the region of Rausbane, focusing particularly on Nyxwood and its vassals. A narrow ribbon marked a page describing a feud between two nobles in the neighboring duchy of Artolia, which nearly escalated into war. The matter was finally resolved with assistance from Marquis Patton of Nyxwood, with a combination of diplomacy and reminders of Nyxwood's vow to protect the citizens of the *entire* kingdom.

Dyrerisan allowed himself a smile as he looked from the worn pages to Ember. He didn't doubt that she'd known what castle she was in for weeks. But why research such history? Was it simple curiosity, or something more? *Could she be investigating the curse?* She wouldn't find anything from those days in this room...after Nyxwood was sealed off, there were no more scholars to add their knowledge to this vast space. Dyrerisan certainly hadn't been in a state to record what had happened.

*If she asks...what will I say?* Would he tell her the truth, or keep her in the dark? It was dangerous for her to know too much...but it was also dangerous for her to stay ignorant. Finding the balance wasn't easy. At some point, if he wanted any say in how she discovered Nyxwood's secrets, he'd have to tell her.

But when he *did* tell her his own history...he'd also need to explain why she couldn't stay here forever. Why someday, sooner than Dyrerisan liked, she'd need to leave. When he'd brought her here, Dyrerisan had thought he was offering her safety. Instead, he'd nearly doomed her. He wasn't nearly as strong as he'd thought, at least not when it came to her.

*Not yet,* he thought, tilting his head as he watched her sleep. *I will see this through to the end. And when it's safe, I'll give her everything she needs to build a new life, wherever she chooses. Just not here.* And in the meantime, he'd take his time enjoying her presence and drinking in the unique friendship they'd somehow forged. *Because that's all this can ever be...friendship.*

He closed his eyes, taken off guard by the sudden pain of that thought. He was used to pain; it was a constant companion in this petrified state, frozen in time. But this...this was a different ache; one he hadn't tasted in far longer than he liked to think about.

Ember shifted in her sleep, and Dyrerisan's eyes snapped open. She still slept. And with that strange agony still pulsing through his soul, he acted on impulse: brushing her hair from her face, running the back of his fingers over her face from her temple to her jaw. Featherlight, hesitant.

Her violet eyes flickered open. Dyrerisan froze with his hand still outstretched, caught for a moment as they stared at one another. Then he pulled away with a sharp breath, making his retreat as quickly as his stiff legs would consent to. And he raged against his own selfish weakness as he pulled the library door firmly shut between them.

Ember blinked, pushing herself up on her elbows as she stared at the door Dyre had disappeared through. *What just happened?* She sat up the rest of the way, her fingers going to her cheek where she could still feel Dyrerisan's light touch. A gesture so gentle, so unexpectedly pleasant...

But the longer she spent awake, the more dread rose to drown out that sleepy bliss. The look in his eyes, the *agony* mingled with... no, she couldn't name it. Ember slipped to the floor, digging her fingers into the rug. No. She must be wrong. But every uneven heartbeat whispered that she knew what she saw...she'd seen that look before.

It was an agonizing goodbye. It was a man looking down on one he *loved*...one he knew he'd lose. It was the look her father had worn when he left her mother for the last time.

"No," she whispered, pressing her hand to her ears as if that would drown out the wailing in her mind. *Too late. Too late.* She'd fallen into the same trap as every other girl who wrote her broken life in that old journal. She *was* the trap. Everything she'd fought for her entire life, everything she'd avoided since she'd wept in front of her parents' graves...it had all come to pass.

Dyre *loved* her. Somehow, in some way maybe he didn't even

understand, he loved her. And Ember, who'd spent so many years in isolation, giving everything to *avoid* the fate of her ancestors, had failed. Because even in all her terror, a flame of hope had lit deep within her. A twisted, broken wonder that anyone could see *her* as someone worth loving.

Ember dropped her head onto her knees, letting tears fall unhindered. What had she done? What had *Dyre* done? And why, despite her entire life's effort crumbling around her, did a part of her *rejoice* as her heart crumbled within her?

# CHAPTER TWELVE

Ember stared at the closet a long time, hollow and numb. Did it matter what she wore? Should she even leave her room?

*If I don't go, Freya or Miri will go in my stead.*

That thought finally forced her into motion, grabbing the darkest gown she saw. She didn't care what it looked like, or if it made her look like a ghost. It was simpler to put on, at least.

Her mind still spun, following fragmented trails without relief, without escape. The hope that she'd mistaken what she'd seen was a hollow one. Even if she had, she knew her own heart had betrayed her...because she *wanted* it to be true. That was perhaps the most painful part of all.

Ember glanced in the mirror when she was done, only to do a double take. The dress she'd chosen was no funeral shroud...it was the night sky. The deep blue of twilight, with clusters of silver stars on the bodice, spilling down onto the skirt that flowed around her like autumn mist off the mountains. This...this wasn't the dress she wanted for tonight. It turned her hair silver and seemed to light her skin from within. It made her tearstained eyes turn bright, *alive.*

Ember turned away from her reflection, glancing at the darkened window. She was late already. She wouldn't bother to find something else...what would be the point, anyway? She'd already failed.

If she was truly selfless, this would be the point where she'd push back. If she were as strong as she'd always told herself to be, she'd end this now. There would be less pain for Dyre if she broke off the connection herself, made him despise her and then left this place far behind so he didn't have to watch her fade away. The damage to Ember was already done, but at least she could salvage Dyrerisan's heart.

But her feeble strength failed in that as well, because the thought of leaving was unbearable. Imagining herself dying far away, forgotten and alone, was a worse agony than she already bore. And it turned out she wasn't noble enough to leave anyway, at least not on her own. If he commanded her to leave, she would...but she didn't think she'd ever be able to force the words past her lips to leave by her own decision. *The curse wins again.*

But Ember curled her lips into a bitter smile, thinking that it hadn't won *everything.* Ember would still be the last.

Ember paused outside the kitchen to compose herself. She didn't want to explain why she'd been crying. She didn't want to invite their tender concern. And so, she took a deep breath and entered with a bland mask painted across her face, ready to deflect whatever inquiries they might have about how she'd spent her afternoon. But again, she was taken off guard.

"He took his dinner in his study tonight," Helen said with an apologetic glance Ember's way. "Said he had urgent matters to see to."

Ember nodded, numb again. *Relief. I should feel relief.* But she couldn't find the will to dredge it up. She refused Freya's efforts to draw her over to the table, claiming a headache. It was only a half lie: there *was* a pounding in her head, it merely didn't have the cause it normally did. They let her leave without too much fuss, though she knew they watched her worriedly as she left the kitchen.

She climbed the steps slowly, taking the time to think. What could she do? What course did she take from here onward? She'd already decided she couldn't make herself leave. Perhaps...perhaps she should take her cue from *him*. Tomorrow, whenever he stopped avoiding her, she'd wait for him to make the first move. If he chose to ignore it, good. If he chose to acknowledge what had passed between them...well, Ember would pray for strength to do what she must.

Ember concentrated on keeping her breathing even as she entered the dining room. She kept her eyes on the tray as she approached, glancing once to see Dyrerisan at the table. He wasn't looking at her.

"Good morning," she murmured, setting the tray on the table.

"Good morning," Dyre replied stiffly, still not glancing toward her. "I trust you slept well?"

Ember drew back, clamping down on whatever it was that made her suddenly ache at the tone of his voice. She said she'd follow his lead...and now she would.

"Yes," she said, matching his overly formal tone. "If you don't mind, I'll get to work now."

"By all means."

Ember turned away and left the room, before her biting retort escaped her lips, closing the door a little louder than usual on her way out. Avoiding the kitchen, Ember retreated up to the sitting room she'd been dreading for days. All of the furniture and paneling had detailed wood carvings that would double the time required to clean it all. Now, though, she took that extra time as a gift and set to work with a vengeance.

But scrubbing dust and cobwebs from the wood was only enough to distract her shaking hands. Her mind was free to rage and twist without restraint. It wasn't long before Ember gave up trying to rein in her thoughts.

*Have I given up entirely?* Dyre had, in a sense, done what Ember wasn't strong enough to do: he'd ignored whatever had passed between them, set a new boundary. She should be glad. So why was she so *angry*? She took a huff of breath and leaned back, examining the knot of wood she'd polished to gleaming. Why, in the midst of all of this, had her heart decided to betray her *now*? Why did she *want* to give in to the curse's twisted game, if only to know what it felt like?

She wouldn't. If her own heart was always meant to be broken, so be it. But she wouldn't leave a legacy of misery behind her. She'd find *some* way to make her life mean something.

*What if I could break his curse?*

Ember paused once again, letting her hands fall to her lap. Her own curse was hopeless, that she knew better than anyone. But Dyre's...he might have a way out. Which meant Helen, Freya, Miri, John, Ben...they might have an *escape*, a way to build a new life. And maybe... maybe if she freed them, the joy of it would distract them from Ember's fate. Maybe she could save them some grief, as well.

Ember took a deep breath, going back to her cleaning. Her movements now were slower, more methodical, as she teased out how to go about her new task. She'd searched through the library enough to know she wouldn't find answers about the curse written in any book. What course did she have left? Asking Dyrerisan would be a last resort. She didn't want him to guess what she was planning, just in case...

The rest of the day passed slowly. Ember took her time bathing before dinner, wishing she could soak away her troubles as easily as dust and grime. And she chose a wine-red dress with drooping sleeves, despite the fact it looked like blood. There was a twisted appropriateness to that, after all.

Dyre was standing at the windows when she entered. She ignored him and set to work arranging everything. Slowly, he came over to the table.

"Good evening," he said.

"Good evening," Ember replied, matching his imperious tone.

"How was your day?"

Ember spoke through clenched teeth. "Productive."

She held her silence after that, keeping to monosyllabic answers. Dyrerisan was hardly better, and Ember tried to comfort herself with the fact that she was only matching him move for move. The frigid interactions were still enough to set her on edge. She didn't like stilted politeness. Ember couldn't help but wonder if it might be better to scream and rage rather than continue in this false formality. Or was it only in her head that Dyre felt the tension too? Was she imagining that this was a mask for him as it was for her? She couldn't know for sure, and that kept her quiet.

He offered her his arm at the end of the night. Ember nearly refused. Why bother with appearances when they were the only two wandering the halls? But in the end, she accepted the gesture, insisting it was only to avoid the conversation that would follow her refusal. As they walked, she kept her eyes ahead and her mouth firmly closed. But that only lasted to the stairs.

Despite her determination to act normally, Ember had to pause at the landing. She closed her eyes and leaned against the railing, waiting for her heart to stop pounding. Each step up might as well have been a mountain.

"You overworked yourself," Dyre said.

"I didn't," Ember replied, turning her breathlessness into a weak growl. "I'm tired, that's all."

"Enough cleaning. There's no use in maintaining rooms no one will ever use."

Ember forced her eyes open, turning to glare at Dyre.

"No use? Why tell me that now?"

He met her heated glare steadily, without wavering. "It was a way for you to fill your days."

"A way to keep me out of trouble, you mean."

He accepted that with a nod. "But now it's interfering with your health. You've done enough."

"Have I?" Ember muttered, looking away.

"Are you ready to continue?"

Her heart had steadied. Ember nodded and reached to take his arm, still refusing to look his way. She was more confused than ever. So, she wasn't prepared when Dyre scooped her into his arms, taking the steps two at a time like she weighed nothing. She squeaked in surprise, locking her arms around his neck on instinct. When she glanced to his face, his expression was as stony as his skin. She looked away, closing her eyes again.

"You can put me down now," she muttered.

He ignored her, not stopping until they were at the door to her room. Then he set her on her feet, holding onto her until she was steady. Ember grabbed the doorknob, holding tight as she lifted her eyes to Dyre's. The suppressed worry she thought she glimpsed there was almost more than she could handle.

"Enough cleaning," he said again, turning away to march down the hall. Ember was left staring at his back, torn between the desire to thank him or shake him. She retreated inside her room, once again off balance and unsure.

Ember entered the kitchen the next morning only to be forced into a chair and fussed over. Freya and Miri asked her a dozen questions on how she was feeling and what she'd done to make herself so exhausted the day before, while Helen gathered everything together *far* more slowly than usual. Ember took deep breaths and avoided as many of their questions as she could, insisting she was feeling normal now that she'd rested. It wasn't a lie...this aching exhaustion clinging to her bones *was* her normal. But she didn't manage to ease their concern.

She slammed the door behind her when she entered the dining room.

"Ember," Dyrerisan greeted wryly.

"Dyre," Ember returned in frozen anger. "What did you tell them?"

"That you managed to exhaust yourself to the point you were unable to climb a set of stairs, and that I didn't want you engaging in any strenuous activity for the next few days, at least."

Ember set the tray on the table with a clank. She pretended not to notice the smirk that flashed across Dyre's face.

"You worried them for no reason."

"I informed them of my wishes. If they're worried, that's their choice."

Ember glared, strongly tempted to set her hands on her hips. Dyre only stared back with one, imperious eyebrow raised.

"If you don't want them to worry," Dyre said slowly. "Perhaps you should ensure there's nothing for them to worry *about*."

A broken laugh escaped before Ember could swallow it back. She turned away from Dyre, retreating before she saw his reaction.

"If only I could."

Dyre said nothing, and Ember went straight to the library to escape any more needless orders or smothering worry. And she took a feather duster with her in a small fit of spite.

Entering the cavernous room, Ember went past all the shelves she'd already explored, avoiding the light spilling in from the windows. Instead, she found the darkest corner and set to work dusting, examining each book's title as she went. It seemed she'd found a section recording different organizations and families that had held power over the centuries. Most were biographies of rulers and their descendants. Though she took a few off the shelf to examine more closely, she found nothing related to her search. She dusted the shelf a bit and took to the ladder.

Near the top of the shelf, Ember spotted a scrap of paper sticking out from the pages of a book. She wrapped her arm around the side of the ladder to secure herself and reached for that tome. She'd found makeshift bookmarks in several books around the library, usually with Dyre's handwriting scribbled all over it. Most of those notes had been complaints or corrections to the book he'd marked. He had such a piercing, clear way of writing that she'd come to enjoy reading his thoughts.

*Maybe that's part of my problem.* Ember frowned, book half open in her hands. When had she begun seeking out glimpses into Dyre's mind? When had she begun to value his thoughts, whether spoken or forgotten in musty pages?

She shook her head, turning her eyes to the book. Her curiosity was aroused now...she wasn't petty enough to put the book back without seeing what was written inside. She read Dyre's note first, finding a list with most of the words crossed out. Ember pulled the book closer to make out what he'd written.

~~Gate~~. ~~Tunnel~~. ~~Forest~~. ~~Send one of remaining servants~~. Send carrier pigeon.

The last line was circled, and underneath he'd scribbled more notes.

Made contact. Visitors were only able to approach castle in darkness, with no moon. Their departure had no issue.

Ember flipped the page over, but it was blank. No explanation on who the visitors were. Surely, they weren't the same people she'd seen...unless this note was far more recent than it looked. Ember turned her attention from Dyre's notes to the book itself. At the top of the page, in decorative script, was a title: *The Aerie*.

Below, the author described a mercenary group that specialized in fighting dark magic. The book claimed the group first emerged during the reign of King Aleksander, who ruled when Dyrerisan's grandfather guided Nyxwood. It went on to note a few exploits of the Aerie: mainly hunting sorcerers and breaking curses. And though the author disavowed the group as brigands more concerned with money than with justice, he included the rumors he'd heard on how to contact them.

Ember closed the book as new thoughts spun through her mind. The Aerie. Were those the visitors Dyrerisan had entertained? Mercenaries...who fought curses. But what were they doing for Dyre if they weren't focused on his curse?

She replaced the book on the shelf, the words within still imprinted on her mind. One of the exploits the author had described...the Aerie had fought a man named Heromin Jairvas, claiming he came from a family in the far north known for their work in the "darker arts." Dyrerisan had underlined his name, and Ember was afraid she'd heard it before.

Ember glanced up the ladder, wondering now if any other books had Dyre's notes within them. She climbed higher, holding tight to the slick wood of the ladder. No more bookmarks were visible, but Ember was slow to climb back down. A title caught her eye, and she leaned away from the ladder to get a better view.

But as she leaned, her ears started ringing. *Not now.* Ember closed her eyes, pulling herself back to a more stable position. But already she'd lost connection with the rest of her body, feeling like she was floating through the air. She hardly noticed when her hand slipped from the ladder, coming back to herself as she plummeted toward the floor...

And landed in a stony embrace.

It took a moment for Ember to remember to breathe. She could already feel bruises forming where Dyre's arms had caught her...but better than cracking her head on the cold floor. She looked up without thinking and found him staring down at her with a deep frown carving new lines through his skin. She opened her mouth, but no sound came out.

Dyre walked to the nearest couch, gently laying Ember on the cushions and kneeling in front of her.

"What was it this time?" he asked, but the calm of his voice was frayed around the edges.

"I lost my grip," Ember whispered.

"Why?"

Ember drew her shoulders up, prepared to bluster her way around that question. But the look Dyre fixed on her, a silent warning not to try it, made her deflate again. *Stupid, weak...*

"I got dizzy," she said, keeping her voice stiff at least.

"This isn't the first time this has happened."

Ember didn't speak, but Dyre nodded like that was answer enough.

"Do you know what's causing this vertigo?"

Now Ember looked away, tightening her jaw against any words that might come: reassurances, explanations...even a demand for Dyre to mind his own business. She didn't trust herself to say any of it.

"Ember."

Was that a command, or a plea? Ember only shook her head, her eyes still trained on the floor rather than anywhere near Dyre. He stood suddenly, backing away from her.

"Don't expect this to go away," he said. "I'll ban you from ladders, if I have to."

Ember nearly snorted, tempted to ask how he expected to enforce that. But she held her silence, teeth aching with how hard she had them clenched together. She didn't look up until she heard the door close behind him. Then she leaned back and stared at the ceiling.

How was it she never managed to disguise herself here? Her every weakness, her every struggle...somehow it was all laid bare here, no matter what she did. *Will I ever manage to* stop *causing worry?*

Again, the question arose: how could she make Dyre, and the

rest, *not* care? But just like every other time, her mind closed against every option she thought of. She couldn't hurt them like that, any of them. Even if it would save them pain in the end.

She let out a gusty sigh and pushed off the couch. Her head was firmly settled on her shoulders again, and she didn't falter as she strode toward the door. She needed to *do* something, distract herself somehow...

Ember turned toward the kitchens, where she knew Helen, Freya, and Miri would be gathered. As long as she managed to keep the conversation off herself, they'd keep her mind occupied. Maybe she could pry a few more answers from them regarding the curse still coating everything like a layer of cobwebs.

# CHAPTER THIRTEEN

Ember looked up, breath coming in great huffs as she leaned against the wall. The end of the staircase still wasn't visible.

"Climb the highest tower," Ember muttered, taking another step. "What a great idea."

She'd managed to pry a few more details from the ladies in the kitchen yesterday, including the very *specific* circumstances that were required for someone to find Nyxwood for the first time. Dyre had already admitted that he'd *wanted* Uncle Radcliff to find this place... had he arranged for someone to *lead* him here as well? And Ember couldn't forget that Dyrerisan had never explained *why* he wanted Radcliff to come. It didn't line up...or maybe it did. But Ember didn't like the way it was all fitting together. While she wasn't willing to share her suspicions, she needed some way of learning *something*... and Freya had already suggested, weeks ago, that Ember should go to the towers. But somehow, she hadn't counted on the towers involving *this many* steps.

Ember rounded another corner, finally seeing the edge of a door on the next landing. That sight gave her new strength, and she made it to the doorway before taking another break to catch her breath.

She pushed the door open without waiting, noting that the hinges worked silently. How often did Dyre come up here?

Morning sunlight filled the room with uncommon brilliance, forcing Ember to pause and wait for her eyes to adjust. Her hand still gripped the doorknob, her thumb rubbing across the worn metal. When her eyes could make out the edges of the windows, she took a few steps deeper into the room.

There was no dust here. No unnecessary trinkets taking up space, no displays of wealth. Just an empty room, with windows on all sides and a spyglass set up near the door. Ember stepped up to the nearest window and touched a finger to one corner of the glass. It was spotless. *Does Dyre clean this himself, then?*

Ember looked up from her clean finger, remembering her purpose. Through the window, she could see the fields and gardens of Nyxwood's estate, all the way to the edge of the forest where a tall wall marked the edge of Dyre's domain. Everything within the wall was green and cultivated, a testament to John and Ben's dedication. But beyond...tangled forest, in every direction Ember could see. She backed away, turning to a window across the room. The same sight. The only interruption to those dark, twisted trees was the mountain looming above: a fortress far stronger and more impenetrable than Nyxwood would ever be.

Ember went back to the first window, searching for any end to the trees. She knew where the plains ought to start, where Rausbane forest ought to *end* in a distinct line. But all she could see beyond the trees was a thin line of indistinct green, a lighter shade that stood in a haze in the distance. But she hadn't ridden *that* far. A glance at the front gate showed a glimpse of the trail that had brought her here, but it soon disappeared beneath the towering trees.

Ember planted her hands on the bottom of the window, leaning forward to stare down at the gardens, where spots of color marked the flowers that bloomed there, bright and fleeting. Freya hadn't exaggerated. Neither had the legends.

*The legends...* Stories of Nyxwood, and rumors of a curse, had floated through Ember's memories ever since she'd learned *where* she stood. But what was it those legends had claimed? She hadn't fully remembered, had she? She'd been so enchanted unearthing history from all this dust, so taken with wearing beautiful dresses and letting her heart slip away...had she taken the time to remember those misty memories, when she listened to stories of the tragedy that befell Nyxwood's last Marquis?

Ember closed her eyes, tapping her fingers on the windowsill as she recalled every scrap of legend she could regarding Nyxwood and its curse. She'd assumed that, with Dyre sealed away from the world, legends about Nyxwood wouldn't have the whole story. But if Dyre had managed to contact people from *outside*, maybe the truth made it to the wider world as well.

"Nyxwood's renown was forged by a noble family, relentless in their pursuit of peace and safety for their lands. Known as protectors, guardians of justice, few dared challenge them."

The words slipped past her numb lips in a whisper, and Ember opened her eyes to stare down at the forest, as her memories drifted on...

"There came a young marquis who was cruel and careless. Observing his callousness, an enchantress cursed the marquis to dwell in ruin and grief until he learned what it was to love...until he found a woman willing to love *him* in his cursed state. Still, he dwells there: alone, waiting..."

"Wrong."

Ember spun on her heel to face Dyrerisan, her breath catching. He stood just inside the door, his eyes twin flames as he glared at her with a fury that sent terror down her spine. She pressed her back against the wall. But Dyre looked away from her, stepping toward one of the other windows.

"There once was a marquis who was young and arrogant," Dyre said, in a clipped tone. "The protection he offered his people was for the sake of *family tradition*, a self-righteous belief that it was his destiny to be *admired.* And when the greatest threat in the land rode through his gates, he was too blind to see it."

Dyre turned back toward Ember, who listened with frozen fascination. She met his eyes without thinking, unable to break away from the depths she found there. He continued, taking a step toward her.

"It was only when this danger, a sorceress named Mitzianna, expressed her...passionate 'love,' that I realized who she was. I rebuffed her...and she took her revenge."

Dyre gestured to himself, face twisting in disgust. "She turned me to *this*, living stone that remains unchanging, unending. And the few servants loyal enough to remain with me in my exile she cursed to slowly petrify alongside me. But even that wasn't enough to satisfy her rage. She offered an escape...but one that would turn me into a true monster."

Dyre took another step toward Ember, and without thinking she leaned toward him, her eyes still locked on his. The agony she found there drew her in, making her own chest ache.

"What did she do?" Ember whispered.

"The curse can only be broken when the woman I love is on the edge of death. The love we share must shatter a heart of stone...only then will I, and the rest of Nyxwood, be free."

Ember blinked, stumbling backwards. Dyre had already turned away from her, planting his hands on either side of a window as he avoided her gaze. For a moment, pity overtook everything else. She could see, now...he thought he was the villain of this story. But beyond that pity, pressure built within her, a raging storm of fear and fury. The pieces fell into place. He couldn't know of her own curse...she was the only living being who knew of it. But oh, it fit in with his plan nicely just the same.

"Is that why I'm here?" Ember asked in an icy whisper. "You knew my uncle would send me. The dresses, the dinners, the trips to the library...was this all about your curse? Were you trying to *make me love you?*"

Her voice cut off in a choke, her heart pounding within her. With every beat it sang of betrayal, an agony so sharp she must've been bleeding out inside herself. Because if that was always his goal, he'd succeeded beyond his imagination.

Dyre had turned toward her again during her speech, and the pure bewilderment in his expression made her doubt...but the words were spoken now. He hardened.

"You think I brought you here to die?" he asked, his voice a low growl of thunder.

"Why else?"

She framed the words as a challenge, but within it felt like a plea. *Why else? Name another reason...I don't want to be just a victim in another twisted game.*

"I forced Radcliff's hand to *save* you from death, not kill you myself."

*Save me?* Ember bit back her next words, staring at Dyre with her heart still thundering in her ears. Was she wrong? Oh, she wanted to be wrong.

"If I hadn't bought Radcliff's debt, you'd be withered under Sarnere's sorcery by now. You're *alive* because I brought you here."

For an impossibly long moment, Ember's broken breathing was the only sound in the room. Dyre's words took a moment too long to sink in.

"Sorcery?" she asked. "What sorcery? Duke Kelan..."

Ember trailed off. Duke Kelan was regarded as one of the cruelest rulers ever to grace Sarnere's lands. Would it really be surprising if he'd reached for more power in the darkest places? A surprise that he'd accept the price of blood such an arrangement would require?

"Every time my men strike down his *allies*, more take their place," Dyrerisan hissed. "Bringing you here was a last resort to prevent him from gaining one more life to drain away on his dark bids for power."

Ember's breath left her in a rush, as her anger cooled. Had he really orchestrated all of this for her sake? For the life of a young woman he had no reason to care about, no reason to fight for? And she'd just accused him of... Ember stumbled back, horrified with herself.

"Difficult for you to believe?" Dyre asked bitterly. When Ember couldn't find the words to reply, he snorted and turned away to face the window. When he spoke again, his voice was harsh...stone cold.

"You can trust this, Ember: my curse will be no danger to you."

*Oh.* Ember backed toward the door, finding the frame to lean against. She closed her eyes against the new agony, new betrayal cutting even deeper into her soul. *Then I was wrong.* How could her spirits rise so quickly only to be flung back to the depths? She didn't know...she didn't know anything except that this...this was the sort of pain the curse reveled in. This was heartbreak. *But apparently, I won't need to save Dyre from grief after all.*

Ember pressed her fist to her mouth to hold in a sob, turning around so Dyrerisan wouldn't see. And she fled down the stairs, not caring what he thought of her retreat. Not caring that her head was spinning as her breath came in broken huffs, as her heart pounded in an uneven beat within her chest. The curse tightened around her, strengthened by her new anguish. But even that couldn't rip her mind away from that room, from Dyre's cold voice and broken gaze. Nothing could distract her soul from the sinking understanding that all she'd agonized over for the past days was obsolete. He didn't care. But she did...oh, she did.

A sob escaped her throat, and she misjudged her next step. She slipped, careening down the stairs... But arms caught her, pulling her down to level ground before Ember even processed that she'd been saved. She glanced up, finding familiar amber eyes.

"Steady, there," the man said, leaning her against the wall before he released her. "What's wrong?"

Ember glanced from his face, familiar from her misguided adventure in Dyre's study, to the woman standing a half step behind him. Her green eyes were piercing, too sharp even with the concern dominating her expression.

"Nothing," Ember said, her voice breaking. She looked away, to the hall behind them, so she didn't have to watch their reactions to her obvious lie. But they didn't call her on it.

"I'm Collin," the man said, stepping away from her. "We never officially met. And this is my wife, Izzy."

"Good to finally meet you," Izzy said. Her voice was deeper than Ember expected, warm and rich.

Ember glanced up to find Izzy watching her with a cautious smile. All Ember managed in return was a nod. She planted her hands on the wall behind her, feeling them tremble against the cold stone.

"We should go," Izzy said quietly, after an awkward moment of silence. "We're already late."

"You say that like it's my fault," Collin said. Ember couldn't help but notice how different his voice was here, compared to when he talked to that *Viper* man. Here he was playful, open.

"It *is* your fault."

Ember kept her eyes lowered, willing them to move on. Her whole body was trembling now, everything threatening to come undone. She'd prefer to be alone before she fell apart completely.

"Do you need anything?"

It was the woman who spoke, and Ember glanced up in surprise. Izzy was watching her closely, that worry still there. Ember shook her head. Izzy didn't look convinced, but when Collin pulled her onward, up the stairs, she went. Ember only waited for Izzy and Collin to be turned away before she fled, stumbling down the hall toward the nearest door.

She needed air. She needed sunlight. She needed a quiet corner where no one would find her crying her eyes out. The door wasn't used often, creaking as Ember forced it open. She left it slightly ajar as she dropped down the steps, already pointed toward the open gate. The gardens weren't hidden enough, weren't *far* enough.

A sudden wind from the east twisted Ember's skirts, blowing her hair into her eyes. Ember pushed it away and forged on, shivering under the wind's assault. It dried the tears staining her face, but more joined them.

*I should be relieved.* She didn't want Dyre hurt. She didn't want him to mourn when her life slipped away into the void. She *didn't.* So why did his cold assurance feel like a knife between her ribs? She wasn't in danger from his curse...meaning he didn't love her. That moment in the library was a misunderstanding. A moment of weakness that meant nothing.

But being safe from one curse didn't mean she was saved. Her own curse didn't require love to be reciprocated: the shuddering ache deep in her bones proved that. Her own love, her *weakness,* was more than enough to doom her. A dark thought flickered through her mind...that maybe she should be glad for the curse sinking its teeth in her flesh. She wouldn't have much longer now...the pain would end.

Ember shook her head viciously, stomping farther into the fields. Ahead was a grouping of conifer trees near the wall. She'd be safe there...safe from prying eyes. There she'd let herself fall apart. There she'd find some way to put herself back together. She wouldn't let Dyre, or anyone else, see her like this...see her frayed and broken pieces. Ember wouldn't make them deal with her pain, whether they cared or not.

Dyrerisan paced in his tower, glancing periodically at the storm growing unnaturally quickly from the east and purposefully *not* thinking of Ember. Not remembering that wrenching sob as she fled the tower. He'd hurt her. *It's for her safety.* But that didn't lessen the weight settled in his gut, nor the guilt tightening his chest. None of this had gone as he'd meant it to.

*...my curse will be no danger to you.* She'd misunderstood him.

Dyrerisan had seen her pain: Ember had thought he was saying he didn't care, that he would never care. *That's the last thing I meant.*

He caught a glimpse of Fox and Wolf entering but didn't stop his pacing.

"Good of you to finally arrive," he said, harsher than he meant to. Dyrerisan turned toward the window, fighting for a better hold on his emotions. "Were you successful?"

Dyrerisan waited for their report, narrowing his eyes at the dark clouds rolling in far too quickly to be natural. *Yet another of Sarnere's attacks.* He should send word for John and Ben to stable the horses and take shelter. But not until he heard what Wolf and Fox had to say.

"Not as much as we'd hoped," Collin said. "We had to travel a full day north to where Ember grew up to find anything, and even that was...scarce."

Dyrerisan turned to face his most trusted emissaries, keeping his tone more even. "Scarce?"

"Most of what we found we already knew," Izzy said. "Radcliff is her only living family, her father's half-brother. She was orphaned when she was twelve and sent to Rookwood, where they practically ignored her."

Dyrerisan nodded, raising his eyebrow at the pair when they were slow to continue. *What have they found?*

"Did you learn anything new?" Dyrerisan prompted.

"Yes," Collin said slowly, glancing at his wife. "We questioned some of Ember's old neighbors...her mother had been sick for two years before she died. Ember's father was searching for a cure when he was killed."

Dyrerisan paused, leaning against the wall. He couldn't help but wonder what sort of sickness plagued Ember's mother. Spells of vertigo? Unexplained weakness?

"Anything about her mother's family?" Dyrerisan asked. He was deep enough in his own thoughts, it took him a moment to realize that Collin and Izzy were once again slow to answer.

"Ember's mother came from a somewhat infamous family in the north," Izzy murmured. "Infamous for the illness that takes each girl born of their blood."

Dyrerisan froze, a sudden cold washing through him. Takes each girl...*kills* each girl.

"You have proof?" Dyrerisan asked, looking up.

Collin met his eyes, and his gaze was pitying. "There's nothing left. Ember is the last of the bloodline."

Dyrerisan stared back at Collin, his heart a distant echo. Then he turned to face the window. *The last of the bloodline.* Then whatever answers he needed he'd have to find from her. She wouldn't want to talk about it. She wouldn't want to talk to *him* after what he'd said. But he'd find a way.

Dyrerisan had brought Ember here to save the life of a stranger who didn't deserve the torture Sarnere would put her through. That sense of duty was nothing compared to the desperate *need* he experienced now. He needed Ember to be safe. He needed her to be bright and strong, rather than a thin husk of a woman who grew weaker every day. He needed her to *live.*

He cleared his throat, slow to speak. He didn't trust his voice at the moment, choked by this sudden terror that he might not be enough to save her. Collin and Izzy waited in silence behind him. Dyrerisan searched the ground below, tightening his hands on the window frame as he fought to keep himself together. What was the course he should take next? Where should he send them? He couldn't think.

And then his eyes caught sight of a blonde head halfway across Nyxwood lands. She was pointed toward a stretch of forest that had crept within the walls...toward the storm already descending on the land. Panic, white hot, pierced him to the soul. Ember would never survive a storm like this.

"Follow me," Dyrerisan ordered, lunging for the door.

Collin and Izzy didn't question him, easily keeping pace as Dyrerisan took the stairs two at a time. Adrenaline raced through his veins, urging him to move *faster*. If Ember made it to the trees, if the curse decided that she'd left Nyxwood lands...

"Ember is headed for the eastern wall," Dyre said, and his voice somehow held steady.

"Where the border goes all fuzzy?" Collin asked.

Dyrerisan was glad to hear worry in his voice. It gave him hope that he wasn't going mad.

"Yes." Dyrerisan skipped the last few stairs, wincing as the landing jarred his stiff joints. "When we're outside, shift and cut her off. I don't want to send a search party into the forest with this storm descending."

"On it."

Collin surged ahead, to a door that already stood open, letting in wind and ice. Izzy followed her husband but paused to hold the door open for Dyrerisan. He gritted his teeth, raging against his weakness, and pushed harder. Collin was already in the open field when Dyrerisan reached the outside. He prayed Collin was fast enough. Ember couldn't be lost. He needed her...he needed her safe.

Ember shivered, rubbing her hands along her arms and wishing she'd brought a shawl. But she pressed doggedly on toward the trees. Her head was already pounding...she didn't know how much farther she'd be able to force her cursed body to take her. But she couldn't stop yet, not when that tower was still in sight behind her. She didn't want any reminders.

A howl pierced the air, and Ember turned with her heart in her throat. A giant wolf was bounding toward her. And Ember ran. She knew it was useless: she couldn't outrun a beast like that. But she couldn't help it. She sprinted toward the trees, cursing her weakness.

"Ember, stop!"

Dyre's voice cut through the wind. And, despite the ragged ache still turning her bones to sand, she turned to look.

The wolf passed her, so close she felt its fur against her hand, and spun to face her again. Meanwhile, Dyre and a smaller form Ember thought might be Izzy sprinted toward her, at a much faster pace than Ember had managed. She turned from them to the large predator still stalking her, its amber eyes trained on her.

Amber eyes... Ember stumbled back, and the wolf followed. But as much as the sight sent her heart pounding, she knew from the glance that the wolf wasn't hunting her. She'd be dead if he was. And his expression was...concerned. Cautious. *Aware.* Ember backed further away, her mind rebelling against that unwilling connection. *What if Wolf is more than a nickname?*

"Ember."

Ember resisted the warmth the sound of that voice conjured, still staring at the wolf. Dyre's hands wrapped around her arms, tugging her backward. She gave in but didn't look at him. Izzy had run past them, toward the wolf who sat and waited for her like a loyal dog. She muttered something to the wolf as she tied a red cloak around his neck, and Ember's eyes widened as the wolf let out a low bark that sounded like *laughter*.

"Collin?" she whispered.

The wolf looked up and nodded. Ember fought to keep her mouth from dropping open, as Dyre continued pulling her backward across the field. A new wind cut across the open space, making her shiver. Was that *ice* carried on the air?

"Ember, come," Dyre said. "You need to get inside."

"Why?" Ember asked, through the shivering. Those were definitely shards of ice falling from the clouds. Her skin stung wherever they touched.

"We'll talk inside," Dyre said, forcing her to turn around. He pushed her forward, wrapping an arm around her shoulders to shield her from the ice. Ember closed her eyes as they walked, wishing that small bit of contact didn't send her weary heart racing. The storm grew as they went, until Ember could hardly see the castle through the ice and wind. A chill forced its way within Ember, making her shake so badly she could hardly walk. When she stumbled near the inner wall, Dyre scooped her into his arms and ran the rest of the way to the door, depositing her on her feet only to pull the door shut against the storm.

Ember leaned against the wall, longing to curl up next to a fire somewhere. But Dyre wasn't ready to leave her in peace. He whirled to face her, shaking. Ember didn't think it was from the cold.

"What were you thinking?" he asked.

"That I wanted some privacy," Ember snapped. The effect was ruined by her teeth wanting to clatter together.

"Outside? In the middle of a storm?"

"How was *I* supposed to expect an ice storm in the middle of summer?"

There had been a few fluke storms in the past few years, sure. But it wasn't something *common.*

"You could've died."

Ember rolled her eyes. "I'm not *that* fragile."

Or was she? Dyre didn't give her time to think it over.

"The storm is from Sarnere, Ember. It's designed to weaken and destroy."

Ember took a step toward him, closing her hands into fists as she glared up at him. "And how was I supposed to know that? It's not like you'd ever *warn* me about these things."

"Don't ever do something so reckless again!" he ordered gruffly, his eyes wild. He took a step toward her, reaching out to rest a hand on her arm.

Ember pulled away from him, before her heart could soften. "What does it matter?"

That made him pause. Ember continued, pouring all her torment into the words. He couldn't do this, not again. He couldn't pretend their fight in the tower hadn't happened.

"You made your position clear," Ember growled through the sting of more tears. "So why would you care if I live or die?"

Ember looked up, intending to go on, but the words died on her tongue. And this time it was more than a flash, more than a glimpse...for a heartbeat, Ember could swear she saw straight to his soul.

"I care," Dyre said, and his voice broke. He stretched his hand toward her face, and Ember stayed still as he gently brushed her hair away from her face. "I care."

Those two words, the featherlight touch of his hand on her skin, undid her. She stepped into his arms, burying her face in his chest. He wrapped his arms around her, gently pulling her even closer.

"I'm sorry," he murmured, his jaw brushing against her hair. "I'm sorry I hurt you."

That made the tears more difficult to resist. Ember pressed her face harder against his chest, breathing in scent of books and pine. And slowly, her heart calmed. Still ragged, still in agony...but, for the moment, savoring Dyre's arms surrounding her.

The door slammed open, and Ember pulled away from the embrace. Her cheeks were suddenly warm, despite the chill still making her shiver, as Collin and Izzy slipped inside.

"Sorry for the interruption," Collin said, shaking ice from his hair. "But it's a bit cold out there."

Izzy leaned against the door with a look of disapproval at her husband, but Collin drew her to his side and that look melted to a contented smile. Ember looked away when she realized that under the vivid red cloak Collin wore trousers, but no shirt. *Cold, indeed.*

"Collin, Izzy," Dyre said stiffly. "Get Ember warm. Answer whatever questions she has."

*Whatever questions?* Ember looked into Dyre's eyes, finding more of that warmth under his gaze. But there was something else there... something haunted.

"I'll find you once I take care of something," he said, turning away.

Ember watched him walk down the hall, head spinning from more than the curse. What had just happened? *What does he suspect?*

# CHAPTER FOURTEEN

Ember led Collin and Izzy to the nearest sitting room, where Izzy set to work building a fire that was roaring in the fireplace within minutes. Ember drew near gratefully, accepting the blanket Collin draped around her shoulders without asking where he found it. For a few minutes, no one spoke.

Sitting in the ordered room, with no sound but the wood cracking as it was devoured by flame, Ember's mind slowly cleared. She carefully remembered the scene in the tower, comparing it to Dyre's panic when he'd brought her in from the storm. Which was real? Was he trying to push her away? Or...or was Dyre as confused as she was? *He believes he's the monster of this story...has he decided to play the part well?* One thing she was sure of: at some point, this had to end. The secrets, the confusion, their agonizing dance around each other. They both needed to decide where they would go from here... even if her ultimate end had already been decided for her.

Collin cleared his throat, and Ember raised her head, blinking rapidly as she realized her eyes were filled with tears. She wiped them away with a corner of the blanket, while Collin and Izzy pretended not to notice.

"I'm sorry for scaring you," Collin said, when Ember raised her gaze again. His eyes were earnest, and he offered her a lopsided smile. "See, that section of forest gets a little dicey. Sometimes it's in Nyxwood, sometimes it's not."

Izzy took over when Collin fell silent. "With the storm coming, Dyrerisan didn't want to risk that you'd be caught in Rausbane."

Ember nodded slowly, turning her eyes back to the fire to think that over.

"Were you the one who chased me on my ride to Nyxwood?" she asked, glancing to Collin.

He rubbed the back of his neck, still sheepish. "That was me. We'd been watching to guide you here, but with Duke Kelan following I had to...hurry you along."

Ember looked to Izzy. "And can you...change form?"

Was this some power of the Aerie that book's author hadn't mentioned? Was this the origin of their animal pseudonyms?

Izzy shook her head, eyes sparkling. "No. I have my own special gifts, but nothing as remarkable as Collin."

"Remarkable," Collin scoffed, bumping his shoulder against hers. "That's not how you usually describe it."

"Would you rather I call you an aberration?" Izzy murmured. "A mutant? A rabid pup?"

"Easy," Collin said. "I'll stick with remarkable, thanks."

Ember watched their teasing interaction, relaxing in spite of herself. She scooted back in her chair, kicking off her shoes to curl her frozen feet beneath her.

"What's your story?" she blurted.

"It's...long," Collin said, glancing at Izzy. "I'm not sure now's the time for it."

"Please?" Ember said. "I...I'd like a distraction."

*Let me forget it all for a little while,* she added silently. *Let me dwell somewhere else, in a tale I know ends with happiness.*

"Of course," Izzy said quietly, after a moment of silence. "First, you need to understand where Collin and I came from. Southeast of here, nearly to the Pitch Mountains, there's an isolated town called Kedar. Collin and I grew up there, as orphan wards of the city. For ten years our home was plagued by a curse."

Izzy fell silent, a far-off look of pain overtaking her expression. Collin grabbed her hand and continued.

"Every sixth moon a young man would turn to a werewolf, slaughtering everything in his path until the sun rose. It took two years for us to figure out that in the day before the shift, a mark appeared on the cursed one here." He gestured to a spot where collarbone met shoulder. "And for every cursed boy, there was a girl with the same mark who had...heightened abilities, you could say."

"They'd lock both of them in a tower at the edge of the city," Izzy said, voice low and haunted. "When the boy changed, the girl would fight him until dawn. She kept the wolf occupied while the Red Cloaks protected the rest of the city from other threats that came with the moon. Few survived. Those who did, especially the wolves, didn't live long."

Ember shivered, aching for the grief she could see so plainly in their expressions. *This was their home...I can't imagine what that would be like.* She'd been ignored, she'd been an unwanted burden...but she'd never feared for her life like that, wondering if her own family would kill her.

"I take it you're both cursed?" Ember whispered, when Izzy and Collin seemed lost in their memories.

"Yes," Izzy said, coming back to herself. "On the same moon."

"How did you survive?"

Ember whispered the words, not sure if she should even ask. *How did you survive each other? How did you survive your home?*

Izzy smiled for the first time in the conversation, and Ember was taken back by the fierce pride in her eyes. "Collin overcame it."

"Only because Izzy trusted me," Collin added. "Far more than I trusted myself."

Ember looked away as the couple stared at each other, struggling to bear the love and *hope* that shone between them.

"Do you still have the curse?" she asked, staring at her lap.

"In a sense," Izzy said. "But Collin doesn't lose himself in the shift, and it's *his* decision what form he takes."

"And we made sure the sorcerer responsible wouldn't be hurting anyone else," Collin growled.

"But you couldn't go back home," Ember guessed.

Collin shook his head. "No. But we'd always planned to leave, anyway."

"The Aerie is a better place for us," Izzy added.

Ember leaned back, readjusting her position as she watched Izzy and Collin. They were...unlike anyone she'd met before. *What is it like, to live as Dyre's warriors and spies?* She tried not to think about what their work involved, the lives they might have taken.

"If you have questions, now's the time to ask," Collin said. "I'm not sure Dyrerisan will give us another chance to explain everything."

Ember nodded, taking a deep breath. She did have other questions. If now was the only chance she got, she'd make the best of it.

"I read that, centuries ago, the Aerie were mercenaries. Is that still true? Do you work for people other than Dyre?"

"Not these days," Collin said. "Dyrerisan first hired the Aerie about five years after his curse, to take down the sorceress who cursed him. But Dyrerisan's skill in strategy, and his vast resources, weren't something the Aerie wanted to give up. They've followed his orders exclusively for about a hundred and fifty years now."

"And you're his only contact with the outside world?"

Collin shrugged. "Pretty much. None of the castle occupants can *leave*, so we make sure they have what they need."

"And you primarily target magic practitioners?" Ember asked more hesitantly. She didn't really want to ask...but she needed to know.

"And up and coming tyrants," Collin said. "Basically, we try to fulfill Nyxwood's original purpose from the shadows. Dyrerisan didn't want to leave the region without its protector, even if *he* is stuck here."

Ember turned her eyes to her lap, taking a moment to think. It sounded as if Dyrerisan's work, that the *Aerie's* work, was honorable. Ember knew enough history to understand that protecting sometimes required blood. And if that *was* their purpose, to protect...could she really hold that against them? She looked up again, finding Collin and Izzy watching her. *I think the time for serious questions is over...I've learned enough.*

"I have one more question," she said slowly.

"Ask away," Izzy said.

Ember looked to Collin. "So, you're called Wolf, for obvious reasons."

"That's right," Collin said, grinning.

Ember turned toward Izzy. "And you're Fox?

"Yes."

"I was wondering how you chose that name? Is there a story behind it?"

Izzy smiled, slow and wide, while Collin chuckled at her side.

"Is there ever," Collin said.

"Can I hear it?"

"Of course," Izzy said, settling back against Collin. "But I'll let Collin tell it. He's a better storyteller than I am."

"Excellent," Collin said, eyes bright as he focused on Ember. "It was our first mission, far west almost to the ocean. There was this little cottage that people *swore* was haunted by the ghost of this herb woman who'd dabbled in some *darker* methods..."

DYRERISAN WALKED PURPOSEFULLY through the bare halls, glancing each way carefully before choosing a direction. He refused to get lost in his own castle, no matter how many years it had been since he'd walked these particular halls. Thankfully, the kitchen was easy to find. He stopped at the doorway, hesitating to interrupt the easy conversation within. The sound ripped open something within him. It had been a long, long time since he'd had such easy companionship.

But reminiscing wouldn't get him anywhere. Dyre stepped into the doorway, taking in the warm room as its occupants fell silent with shock.

"I apologize for disturbing you," Dyre said, staring at the wall as he spoke. Hopefully it would lessen the effects of his coming. "Helen, may I speak with you for a moment?"

"Of course, my lord," Helen said, wiping her hands clean as she rounded the counter.

Dyrerisan backed out into the hall, to the shadows where the others wouldn't hear their conversation. They'd learn about it from Helen, of course, but for now he'd prefer privacy.

"What's wrong, my lord?" Helen asked, stopping a few steps before him.

*Where to begin?* He closed his hand in a fist, willing his voice to be steady and calm.

"I have some concerns regarding Ember, especially her health. I'd like your insight."

Helen nodded, slow to speak as she twisted her hands in her apron.

"She's weaker," Helen said. "Though she tries to hide it. She...she tries to keep her distance, as if she's scared to get too familiar."

Dyrerisan had noticed the same. Few things set off her anger faster than someone worrying over her.

"Anything else?" Dyrerisan asked, failing to keep all of the pleading from his voice. Helen noticed, though Dyrerisan saw her trying to hide it. She was reluctant to answer, pursing her lips for a moment as she stared at Dyrerisan.

"She has a feeling about her, similar to you, my lord."

Dyrerisan straightened. "Similar how?"

"It's the feeling of a curse around her. It's been clinging to her like an illness since she first came."

*A curse.* For a moment, Dyrerisan wondered if he'd petrified completely. He couldn't seem to move. But he found his voice enough to thank Helen as he turned away. He left the servant halls, turning toward the sitting room he guessed Ember would gravitate toward. And every step he took, his mind raged.

Ember, cursed? Why hadn't he considered it before? It fit too well...but he still needed to convince her to *speak*. If there was magic draining her life, he needed to know *why*. He needed to know how to *stop* it, before it was too late. *Ember can't die.* Not from his curse, not from her own. Dyrerisan needed her to live. He didn't stop to think why her life suddenly meant so much to him, why even the *thought* of her death left a hole in his chest. That would come later...for now, his focus would be on finding a way to save her.

Dyrerisan slowed as he neared a door, hearing laughter within. Trust Collin and Izzy to get her laughing, even after their argument in the tower. He paused at the door, drinking in the sound, before opening the door. They all fell silent at his entrance. Dyrerisan fought not to look at Ember, focusing instead on Collin and Izzy.

"We need to talk," he said.

Collin and Izzy jumped to their feet. And Dyrerisan's eyes slipped to Ember. She watched him closely, but there was still a shuttered pain in her gaze. Dyrerisan smiled weakly.

"I'll see you at supper," he said, turning away before she could respond.

He didn't trust himself to talk to her right now. He'd wait, he'd plan...and he'd do his best not to make a mess of things again. She wouldn't hide from him anymore. She wouldn't need to.

Ember stabbed a carrot on her plate, glancing once again to Dyre sitting near her. He hadn't said much since she'd entered, only a few pleasantries. So far, Ember had gone along with it. She hadn't decided yet...hadn't decided anything, really. Something needed to change, but she didn't know what.

*Do I tell him what's happening?* She didn't know how he'd react... she didn't know if she *wanted* him to bear that weight. She'd shouldered her fate alone for seven years; perhaps she should keep it to herself even now. Because she was worried how things would change if Dyre knew. She remembered her father's wild agony when her mother grew sick. She remembered the lengths he went to in order to save her, that it cost him his life. Ember didn't want that grief to repeat, no matter what. She refused to be the death of anyone.

But what options did that leave her? If she asked to leave, would Dyre let her? Ember flinched away from the thought of Nyxwood behind. She'd decided she wouldn't...but was that selfishness? *If I really love Dyre, if I love* all *of them, shouldn't I do it for their sakes?*

But where would she go, if she left? What if Duke Kelan took her to Sarnere? *He'd get less use from me than he bargained for,* she thought viciously. But no matter how little life was left to her, she didn't want to help his evil schemes.

Of course, all of this depended on Dyrerisan, as well. What would he do with her after their fight in the tower? He claimed he cared... but what would that care lead him to do? Ember was almost afraid to find out.

"Are you alright?"

Ember startled at Dyre's voice, and realized that she'd been staring at the candles for several minutes. She looked to her plate, still full of food.

"Tired."

"Would you like rest, then?"

After a moment of thought, Ember nodded, pushing back from the table. She wasn't hungry tonight. Time alone didn't sound appealing, but perhaps it was for the best.

Dyre took her arm as soon as she was standing, and Ember accepted the gesture without looking at him. By now, it felt normal to stand this close, walking with his stony arm as support. And she was grateful for the contact as they took the stairs: the higher they climbed, the more she leaned on him, until he was half carrying her. He made no comment on her weakness, but he watched her closely. Ember ignored him as much as she could. Tonight wasn't the time for the questions she could see in his eyes.

But when they paused before her door, when he slipped his arm free of hers, she found she couldn't leave it at that.

"Dyre," she whispered, not looking above his chest.

"Yes?"

"What passed in the tower..." Ember bit her lip, glancing up. "I'm sorry for my assumptions. I don't...I don't really think you'd do something like that."

"And I'm sorry for my fool-headed words. I spoke amiss."

He stretched his hand toward her face, nearly brushing her skin with his fingertips. But he stopped just a breath away, and Ember was left waiting, wondering if she should close the distance. But she didn't. She just watched. And, slowly, he withdrew his hand.

"I'll protect you," he whispered.

He turned away, leaving her in the dark. And Ember slipped silently into her room, trying to pretend that interaction hadn't left her in turmoil.

Breakfast was similar to dinner, with a few pleasantries but no true interaction. Ember retreated to the library as soon as she could slip free from Freya and Miri's well-meaning chatter. The silence that greeted her wrapped around her like an embrace. *Or a shroud.* Ember shook away the thought as she searched for a book to hold her attention, wishing she could truly disappear within the pages for once.

But she'd hardly settled into her seat when the door opened, and she looked up to see Dyre walking toward her. She went still as he approached, heart thrumming in her chest. She knew that look of determination. Neither of them spoke as Dyrerisan stopped, kneeling before her.

"Dyre," she greeted, her throat too dry to give any volume to the word.

"Ember," he said, looking up to meet her eyes. Her breath caught at the sight of torment, buried deep. "We need to talk."

"About?"

"What's happening to you."

Ember looked away. *No.* Her heart pounded in her ears until she thought it would burst from her chest. *Not now. Don't make me.* But Dyre turned her head back to face him, his fingers gentle.

"I'm not blind," he said. "Something's wrong. Please...tell me what it is."

"I..." Ember's voice failed her. Tears stung her eyes, and she blinked them away so she could see Dyre properly. He hadn't looked away. She couldn't make herself go on.

"Ember," he breathed her name. "Are you cursed?"

Ember closed her eyes, shivering at that dreaded word. It was time for her decision.

"Yes."

Dyre's sharp intake of breath pierced through the room, and a knife seemed to go through Ember's chest. She opened her eyes, grabbing onto Dyre's hand where it rested beside her. He was trying to hide his pain. It didn't work.

"What is the curse?" he asked. His eyes said he already knew in part...but he didn't want to accept it. He wanted her to say there was a way out. And that...that awoke a new agony within her, more than she ever guessed she could endure. She held tight to his hand and forced her voice to work. He had to know.

"It started twelve generations ago. A man from a wealthy family fell in love with a girl from nowhere. They married against his family's wishes...and his father cursed his son's wife, and all the women she bore, to weaken and die in their youth."

"And what sets it off?"

Ember looked away. *Not that.*

"It comes at different ages," she whispered, instead. "But the effect is the same...we grow steadily weaker until one day our heart stops."

"How long?" Dyre asked, his voice little more than a croak. She still held his hand, and he tightened his grip.

"It's...it's different for everyone..."

"How long for *you*, Ember?"

He knew how to ask the most painful questions, didn't he? What would be worse: if he didn't know, or if he *did*? But she couldn't lie to him, not in this.

"A few months?" she guessed weakly.

She glanced at Dyre and regretted it...he looked like she'd pulled the world from beneath his feet. He leaned back, passing his free hand over his face. But he didn't let go of her hand.

"What can we do to fight it?" he asked, his hand still over his eyes.

"Nothing."

He dropped his hand, turning to glare at her with fire in his eyes. "Nothing?"

"My father tried," Ember said. "They've *all* tried. Nothing can stop it."

"There has to be something."

"There *isn't*, Dyre," Ember said, pleading now. "I've seen what happens when you try. It's not worth it!"

His grip on her hand tightened to a stranglehold, his eyes flashing. "Your *life* is worth it. Won't you fight for it?"

"I *did* fight it," Ember snapped, ignoring how her voice broke. "I isolated myself from every person who might ever love me. I tried to save everyone from heartbreak. It didn't *work*, Dyre."

Her words were a mistake. She watched him sharpen, his focus shifting. He narrowed his eyes.

"What do you mean, you hid from those who could love you? What would that do?"

Ember bit her lip, leaning back as she tugged on her hand. He didn't release it, didn't look away.

"That's not the point," she whispered.

"What sets off your curse?"

Ember clenched her jaw, staring down at him. *Not this. Don't make me say it.* He didn't give in.

"I'll find the answer, Ember."

She almost laughed. Find the answer where? She was the only one who knew. Unless...thoughts of her journal, still hidden in her room, made her doubt. If he found it, he'd learn everything.

"Ember."

It seemed she had no choice.

"The curse seeks grief, heartbreak. It kills regardless, but..." Ember looked back to Dyre, afraid but needing to see his face. "It truly sets in when we fall in love."

It took a few moments for Ember's confession to sink in. She watched the rising wonder...and then the sinking grief. He jerked away, standing and stumbling backward.

"I'm killing you, then?" he muttered, pulling at his hair as he turned away.

"No," Ember said. "The curse is doing that. This isn't your fault."

"Isn't it?"

Ember pushed to her feet. "This is two sided, Dyre. If you didn't care it wouldn't change anything, because *I love you*."

Dyre turned back to face her, and the agonizing hope in his gaze broke her heart a little more. He stepped closer, then stopped. And that hope faded into determination.

"And I won't let you die," he growled.

"What are you going to do?" Ember asked.

"Save you."

"And if you can't? Will you let *me* save *you*?"

His eyes lit with fury. "*That* is not an option."

"Why not?" Ember challenged, stepping toward him. "I can do it. I can free you. Helen, Freya, Miri, John, Ben...aren't they worth it?"

"We won't be the death of you, Ember. It's too high a price."

He turned away, marching toward the door.

"Where are you going?" Ember asked, panic rising.

"To call Collin and Izzy. No curse is unbreakable. They'll find something."

Ember moved to follow him. "Dyre, wait."

But he was already at the door. And the sight of him with his back turned toward her, wrenching open the door to leave her alone in that yawning cavern of a room...it was too much. It was too similar to that horrid day, watching her father walk out. He'd never come back. She couldn't go through that again.

"If I give you what I have, will you stay with me?"

Dyre paused, turning to face her. "What do you have?"

"Promise," Ember demanded, heart pounding. "Promise you won't leave me alone."

*Don't make me fade in the darkness. Don't make me walk this path on my own.* She thought she was strong enough, but now...now she knew better. *Almighty, I can't do this alone.* Dyrerisan took several long steps, stopping again at her side. He took her hand in his, meeting her eyes.

"I promise."

Ember nodded, swallowing the lump in her throat as she fought to smile. It didn't work.

"I have a record kept by the women who fell to the curse," Ember said. "They wrote down all that they could, hoping it could somehow save their daughters."

"You have it with you?"

"In my room."

His voice gentled, though the torment didn't leave his eyes. "Let's get it, shall we?"

Ember wordlessly wrapped her arm around his, laying her head against his shoulder. Neither of them spoke as they left the library, but Ember still shook with adrenaline. She didn't believe her journal would be any use, except to convince Dyre that there was no escape from this. She wouldn't bother to believe there was any hope for her. But she wouldn't be alone. And, when her time came, she *would* break his curse. Some good would come from her life, even if it killed her.

# CHAPTER FIFTEEN

Dyrerisan turned a page in the worn journal, careful not to rip the paper. It was obvious the pages had been read often, over many years. Some words were blurred, and Dyrerisan couldn't help but wonder whose tears stained the parchment. The women writing, or their daughters? Had Ember cried as she read her own mother's words?

Ember had guided him through the pages of the journal earlier, showing him certain passages that she was convinced were important. Most showed the failed efforts of those before to slow or break the curse. She seemed determined to convince him that his efforts to save her would be hopeless. But he wouldn't give up.

What had Ember seen, that led her to give in so easily? What had she experienced that led such a vibrant woman to accept her death without a fight? He couldn't understand it...in all other things, Ember didn't give in easily. He glanced up, to where Ember slept on one of the couches. She looked so fragile...

Dyrerisan forced his eyes back to the journal, scanning the page with the ease of years of practice. Without Ember hovering over his shoulder, he intended to read every word. There must be something, some hope to break this. He was still on the original entry, written by the woman who'd received the curse. She was remarkably brave about the situation, determined that the curse weakening her wouldn't take her children. Her words reminded him of Ember.

Turning the page again, Dyrerisan's eyes read quickly. But a single, faded word made him pause and look closer. *Surely not.* But his eyes weren't deceiving him: this woman's husband was a Jairvas. She spoke of her husband's family, and how they continued to plague them even in their exile: *The Jairvas's eyes linger everywhere in the north. And it seems Edmund isn't satisfied with the curse he forced on us...he still believes he can lure my husband back into their arms.*

Dyrerisan tore his eyes away, looking to Ember's sleeping form. Violet eyes. "A gift from my mother's family," she'd said. A gift from *Mitzianna's* family. Mitzianna Jairvas, darling of the north and gifted sorceress...the one who'd cursed him to this endless existence.

Ember shifted in her sleep, murmuring inaudibly before going still. His pulse thudded in his ears as he watched her, now comparing her to his old tormentor. In looks, they weren't similar, except their eyes. In personality...he didn't want to consider that. Dyrerisan flipped the pages of the journal, turning to a random page near the back. His focus was needed elsewhere.

His eyes moved over the page, not truly taking anything in until he found another familiar name. *Ember.* Dyrerisan flipped back to the beginning, noting the woman's name. *Ember's mother.* He glanced once more to her on the couch, still fast asleep, oblivious to the world. And he returned to his reading, letting thoughts of the name *Jairvas* fade before this glimpse into Ember's childhood.

Ember's mother, Agnes, began her entry shortly after her marriage. Dyrerisan was intrigued to read that she'd married a near stranger, a man she specifically did *not* love. It seemed she'd had her own way of fighting the curse, hoping a loveless marriage would give her more time. For the first year, it seemed to work. Then she had Ember.

Dyrerisan read closely as, in a tired, broken scrawl, Agnes

described the difficulties of her pregnancy and the patient care of her husband. After Ember's birth, the tone of Agnes's writing began to change. She wrote often of her daughter, and slowly included more about her husband. It seemed that, as loveless as their marriage had begun, Agnes and her husband were well suited to one another. And what began as a partnership of convenience grew into a true joining of two souls.

Agnes first felt the curse's effects when Ember was eight and managed to hide the significance of her symptoms for over a year. It seemed she'd never told her husband the history of her family. It was when her weakness grew too serious to hide, and she finally explained the curse to her husband, that the heartache truly began. The rest of her account was stilted, bare records of Ember's growth and the curse's progression. Her husband was absent often, and it seemed he'd taken her hope with him.

Agnes's last entry was after Ember's father had died. It was only two sentences:

> *The light of my life has gone out, and I know soon I must follow. Forgive me, Ember, for not being strong enough to stay with you longer.*

And just below, in a child's shaking hand, Ember had written,

> *I forgive you, Mommy. I'll be strong enough for both of us.*

Dyrerisan stared at the page, more tearstained than many others, for a long time. So, this was what Ember had lived through. This was what formed her. Dyrerisan knew the pain of losing his parents, but he'd endured the grief as an *adult*. And it had still twisted him nearly beyond repair. He couldn't imagine bearing such a weight as a child, watching both her parents fall victim to a curse. *She knew she'd be next.*

Dyrerisan swallowed around the lump in his throat. He turned the page to escape the sight of those words, only to find one final entry. Ember must've been older when she wrote this: her hand was steadier, though her handwriting was as wild and fierce as her voice.

> *I will be the last. If my death is the sacrifice it takes to end this curse, so be it. I'll die...but I'll do it alone and unloved. And there will be no more grieving husbands. No more daughters left behind, waiting for the curse to claim them too. No more broken hearts.*

Dyrerisan closed the journal, standing stiffly. He could hear Ember's voice, whispering those words. *No more broken hearts.* And it carved a piece of his stone heart from his chest, that determination to save others but not herself. He turned, going to where she slept and kneeling beside her. After a brief hesitation, he took one of her limp hands in his own.

"I'll stay with you," he whispered, watching her sleeping face. She wouldn't do this alone, no matter what end came for them.

Ember watched Dyre, absently pushing food around her plate. He'd brought a book to the table, propped up so he could read as he ate. It was old enough Ember wouldn't have dared *touch* it, let alone risk spilling gravy on it. But he'd been consumed in its pages since she'd walked in, pausing only enough to ask how she was feeling.

"You aren't eating," Dyre said, glancing up at her as he turned a page.

"I'm not hungry."

"You need to eat." He'd returned his attention to the book, and Ember watched a moment before responding.

"And if I don't?"

Dyre looked up again with a smirk. "Do you want me to *help* you?"

"No," Ember said, looking down to stab a green bean. "But a little conversation would be nice."

Dyre closed the book, sending dust into the air, and turned toward her. Ember couldn't help the small smile as she took a bite of her dinner.

"And what would you like to talk about?" he asked.

"Anything other than my...situation."

"Care to hear predictions for the harvest?"

Ember looked up only so he'd see her roll her eyes. He leaned back in his chair, still smirking.

"You choose the conversation, then."

Ember looked to her plate, taking another bite to escape answering. She only had one topic that interested her at the moment, but she wasn't sure Dyre would humor her that far. He wouldn't let her dodge the question, though. He watched her, silent and still.

"What were you like before the curse?"

When she looked up, his eyes were shuttered.

"You already know," he muttered.

"Not really."

"What more is there to understand?"

He'd turned his eyes back to his book, brushing his hands over the cover, but Ember didn't miss the torment that had taken over his expression. She was slow to answer.

"What were you like as a child? What did you enjoy? What did you dream about? What were your parents like?" Ember finished with a shrug, staring at her plate. "I want to *know* you. That includes understanding your past."

"Even if my past is what I've fought to overcome?"

"Even then."

He stared at her a moment, and Ember resisted the urge to squirm in her seat. It wasn't wrong, to want to know *all* of him... was it?

"I dreamed of being one of the men memorialized in the great hall."

Ember blinked, tilting her head as she thought of that. *He wanted to be a hero?* She planted her chin in her hand and leaned forward.

"What about them was it that drew you?" she asked.

She knew what it would be for her: the adventure, the stories, the *victory* they claimed over evil. She'd always thought, if she could step within one of the legends she held so close she wouldn't care who she was...as long as she could be a part of the triumph, the hope those heroes brought with them. But given the way Dyre now stared at the table with a frown, his own reasons had been different.

"I wanted..." Dyre took a breath before continuing. "I wanted to live a life that would be spoken of in the generations to come. I wanted a name that would be said with reverence, with excitement."

"You wanted to be a part of the legends," Ember said, nodding.

"And now I am."

Ember's heart ached when she caught sight of Dyrerisan's face, twisted in regret and disgust. She sifted through her other questions, searching for one that would bring him back out of those darker thoughts.

"What were your favorite pastimes when you were growing up? Mine was reading, and...visiting town with my father."

Ember looked down at the table to escape the sympathy in his eyes.

"I had many, all related to training to be the Marquis. I suppose my favorite was strategy. When I was older, my father brought me along to most of his meetings, so I could observe and learn by example."

"And your mother?" Ember asked. "How did you spend time with her?"

An unconscious smile softened Dyre's face. "Mostly taking me out to visit people who lived in our domain. She taught me to remember names, faces, life stories...Her desire was that I would see them as individuals, rather than faceless masses."

"What's the story with the endless riches in the halls?" Ember asked, before Dyre could slip back into that melancholy look.

The question revitalized his smile, his eyes glinting with humor as he looked to her.

"Still bitter about your dusting?"

"And if I am?"

His smile widened, and he leaned back. "Most of them were gifts, tokens from those Nyxwood helped. I had them pulled out of storage when I became Marquis and I've been too lazy to return them in the years since."

So, it was a young Dyrerisan who'd littered the halls with riches. To impress? To awe? Helen had said there was a time when the endless guestrooms were filled. Ember couldn't help but wonder what that must've been like, to live and know Dyre *then*.

"What led to the curse?" she whispered, without thinking.

The smile slipped away, and back came that haunted look. But this time, Ember didn't search for a way to distract him. But she did turn her eyes to her hands.

"You said you were arrogant...but why? Your parents don't sound..."

She trailed off, not knowing how to finish. And she dared a glance up at Dyrerisan, who stared at her with a pained look to his eyes.

Dyre sighed, but he stood. "*This* conversation would be better held elsewhere."

Ember took Dyre's hand when he offered it, following him out of the dining room. He took her to the library, all the way to the back wall where portraits filled the stone. Ember had looked them over some, but most of her attention had been claimed by the books. Dyrerisan took her past the oldest portraits to the far corner, where

Ember found a face she recognized: Dyre, in the same formal pose, but with a smirk and eyes lit with mischief. His hair was dark, his skin a tanned olive. Ember glanced from the painting to Dyre, comparing them. But Dyre's eyes were on another painting just above, of a couple offering warm smiles to the onlooker.

"My parents," he said, nodding at the couple. "They were...everything the rulers of Nyxwood aspired to be."

Ember tilted her head, studying those two faces. Two lives who'd walked the halls she'd cleaned, who'd looked over the land she'd grown up in...who'd shaped the man beside her. They looked...kind. Brave. Loving.

"They raised me to be humble, to serve the people we protected. They would've been ashamed to see what I became without them."

"What happened to them?" she whispered.

"They died when I was twenty," he said, voice heavy with old sorrow. "A sickness was killing the populace. They gave so much helping the victims, they had no strength left to fight off the fever themselves."

"That must have been hard," Ember whispered. Losing parents was difficult enough...but becoming a leader everyone looked to at the same time? Had Dyre even had the chance to grieve?

"Their loss...broke me. I'd thought I was ready to take on more responsibility, but once they were gone..."

Dyrerisan shook his head, staring at his parents' portrait with anguish...regret. Ember watched silently, slipping her hand into his to offer a small measure of comfort. She didn't trust her voice. After a slow, ragged breath, Dyre continued.

"I wanted to be worthy of their legacy, but I didn't want to make the sacrifices they did. In my desire to be seen as a true Marquis of Nyxwood, I became conceited and ineffectual."

Ember nodded slowly, taking that in. She knew it was a difficult admission, a truth that still pained him. *Does he believe he's still that man?* She turned to look at him, finding his eyes still focused on the portrait of his parents.

"What changed?" she asked.

Dyre looked down at her, brows furrowed. "Pardon?"

"You said you only protected people for the sake of a legacy," Ember said, speaking slowly. "But now you protect them, even though no one knows you're alive. Something must be different."

He'd raised one eyebrow, his lips turned in a wry smile. "What did Collin and Izzy tell you?"

"Only what I asked."

"They're too generous to me."

Ember shrugged, not sure that she agreed. But she didn't say anything, waiting for his answer. She wouldn't let him escape this one. He looked down at her with a wry smile, an exasperated light to his eyes. But he did answer her question, looking back to the portraits as he did.

"I failed. Left with the consequences, I had more than enough time to reassess my decisions."

Ember stared up at Dyre, heart beating a little faster as his hand tightened around her own. She had another question, but she wasn't sure if she could ask. She'd already dredged up enough pain for one evening.

"Ask," Dyre said, glancing down at her. "I won't be angry at you for being curious."

Well, if he *wanted* her to say it...

"The quartz heart on your desk...did *she* give you that?"

Dyre scowled, and Ember regretted asking.

"Yes. Three years after she set the curse in place, she came for a... visit."

"What did she do?"

"Offered us another chance at escape."

"I take it the price was too high."

Dyre's scowl deepened, and his eyes were suddenly dark. "In a sense."

Ember shivered, not willing to press for more. How could she turn the conversation away from this? All she could think of was the rough feel of Dyre's hand, how it lacked the softness and give of normal flesh. She never wanted to meet the kind of human being who would curse someone as that sorceress cursed Dyre.

"Come," Dyre said, his voice gentle again as he squeezed her hand. "You need rest."

"So do you," Ember said, though she stepped back from the portrait wall.

"I'll sleep."

Ember waited for him to glance down at her and raised an eyebrow. She wasn't sure she believed him...she could easily picture him holed up in the library all night, searching through book after book in his doomed attempt to save her. But he didn't confirm or deny her suspicion, just smiled and stepped a little closer to her side. She rolled her eyes, trying to ignore how she felt a little warmer standing so close to him. And trying to ignore the way her heart faltered painfully at the contact.

*I won't let you steal this from me,* she told the curse. *Not anymore. I'll have my few months of life.*

Dyrerisan paced in the tower, glancing up to the moonlight drenched forest to gauge the time. He wasn't surprised by the cloaked figure who appeared in the doorway.

"Collin," Dyrerisan greeted, pausing before a window. "Where's your other half?"

"Passing your orders on to the others."

"Good."

Dyrerisan waited, but Collin leaned his shoulder against the wall and seemed content to watch. Dyrerisan raised his eyebrow before turning to face the window, staring at the silver night.

"You have questions?" Dyrerisan asked.

"Plenty. Will asking them land me out the window?"

Dyrerisan grunted. As if he would do such a thing.

"What's bothering you?"

"You need to ask?"

"When I saw you last you had it together pretty well...something must have changed. Is Ember alright?"

"As alright as she could be," Dyrerisan sighed, gripping the windowsill. "The journal Ember has. I've been reading through it."

"And you found something," Collin guessed.

Dyrerisan turned to face him, crossing his arms over his chest. "A complication. The family who cursed the first pair of star-crossed lovers were the *Jairvases*. The man was Mitzianna's nephew."

Collin nodded slowly, still reclined against the wall. Dyrerisan let the silence drift on until it was apparent that Collin wasn't going to say anything.

"Do you see any issue with this?" he asked.

"Depends," Collin said. "Since Izzy and I didn't find that connection, I'm assuming the lovers broke with his family after the curse?"

"Yes."

The Jairvas family had tried to bring their wayward family member back into the fold, of course. But, especially after his wife's death, he'd violently rejected their every effort.

"Then I don't see a problem," Collin said. "What connection Ember has with the Jairvases is slight, and I doubt she even knows about it."

Dyrerisan grunted in response, rearranging his arms. He glanced across the window, to the mountain looming in the darkness. Collin took a step forward, his voice piercing the darkness in a hiss.

"Don't tell me you're doubting Ember because of this."

Dyrerisan shifted, preparing to respond, but Collin went on before he had the chance.

"The only involvement she has in your curse is a desire to set you free, and if *that's* not enough to convince you she isn't like Mitzianna I don't know what would be."

Dyrerisan glanced over at Collin, eyebrows raised. “Finished?”

“That depends on what comes out of your mouth next.”

A smile flickered across Dyrerisan’s face, dying quickly. “I’m not doubting Ember. The thought occurred, of course, but...Ember is nothing like Mitzianna.”

Still, he was glad to have Collin’s confirmation. Ember wasn’t a Jairvas. She was no friend to dark magic, only a victim of it. Collin let out his breath in a huff, and Dyrerisan smirked.

“Then what’s the problem?”

“It’s twofold,” Dyrerisan said. “First is the fact that I’ve given every effort over the past two centuries to wipe out the Jairvas family. Ember’s family.”

“You’re worried she’ll resent that?”

Dyrerisan didn’t answer. He didn’t relish putting it into words. The worry felt...weak. But Collin didn’t need Dyrerisan’s answer. He snorted, shaking his head.

“I wouldn’t worry about it. If you explained it to her, she’d probably say ‘good riddance.’ What’s the second worry?”

“That it was a *Jairvas* who cast Ember’s curse.”

All traces of good humor disappeared from Collin’s face. Dyrerisan’s heart sunk, and he gestured loosely to his face.

“We both know how twisted and cunning the Jairvas’s curses could be. If this man’s father resented his son’s marriage as much as Mitzianna despised me...”

“You’re worried there’s no simple way out.”

“Precisely.”

This time Collin was slower to answer. Dyrerisan returned his attention to the windows, searching the land surrounding them for any movement. When Collin sighed, Dyrerisan stiffened.

“I can’t say much to that. You know Izzy and I will give everything we have to try and help, but the only *advice* I can really give is...don’t overcomplicate matters. Sometimes breaking a curse is less about creating a certain circumstance and more about finding what the curse *can’t* take.”

"Thank you," Dyrerisan murmured, though he wasn't sure Collin's advice did more than muddy his thoughts. What couldn't Ember's curse touch? It seemed the sort of curse that took everything.

"Need anything else?" Collin asked, drawing Dyrerisan out of his thoughts.

"No. Get some rest before tomorrow."

Collin grinned, his teeth bright in the darkness. "I won't argue with that."

Collin left the tower, and Dyrerisan heard him meet Izzy down the stairs. He stayed in place, staring out the windows as he turned Ember's situation around in his mind, examining it from all angles. *What can't the curse take?*

Ember lingered in her room, collapsed in a chair with a small square of cloth in her hands. She'd taken the embroidery from her journal before giving it to Dyre, not wanting to lose the small token. Now, she ran her fingers over those careful stitches and wondered what she'd done to deserve the love and care that had gone into it. How she wished she could see Sophia and Louisa again, just to let them know that she loved them.

A soft knock made Ember look up, as Freya poked her head in. "Are you alright?"

"Yes." Ember set the embroidery aside, moving to rise. "What time is it?"

Freya moved deeper into the room, closing the door behind her. "Less than an hour after dawn. There's no need to hurry."

Ember watched Freya take a seat across from her, nervous in spite of herself. She knew Dyre had told Helen of Ember's curse, and that Helen would've passed it along to the others. But so far none of them had mentioned it.

"I'm sorry I didn't tell any of you," Ember whispered, unable to stand it. "I've...never told anyone, until Dyre."

"It sounds like he had to pry it from you, even then," Freya said with a sad smile. "It's alright, Ember. None of us are angry with you."

Ember looked away to her hands clasped in her lap.

"Dyre said something," Freya said, "that confused me. He told Helen that being in love makes your curse worse?"

"Yes."

That one word was nearly more than Ember could manage. She didn't like discussing this...she still wished it could fade to the background, that *she* could fade to the background. But she couldn't refuse to answer Freya now, sitting right across from her. Perhaps that's why she found Ember when she was alone.

"Does that apply to us kitchen folk, too? Does our loving you make it worse?"

Ember glanced at Freya. She should've guessed that Freya, and the rest, would come to the same conclusion Dyre had. They blamed themselves. But what could she say? She knew that the curse stung a little more when she spent time with them, when they laughed and spoke in easy companionship. But was it their love causing the pain, or her own?

"Not exactly," Ember admitted in a whisper.

"But...it felt like you've been holding back. Is that not because of the curse?"

These were the days for painful conversations, apparently. Ember couldn't bear to watch Freya as she answered, so she took up that small piece of cloth again and ran her fingers over the edges.

"I did hold back, but because I...I don't want to be the reason someone's hurting."

And oh, how she had failed. How many would she leave grieving when the curse took her? How many of them would wonder if they could've done more, if they could've saved her? Hands took her own in a warm grasp, and Ember looked up to find Freya kneeling before her, her eyes full of tears.

"Loving you is our choice," Freya said, fierce even through her tears. "Our grief is *not* your burden to bear, Ember."

There was so much Ember wanted to say...but she couldn't find her voice. She settled on offering Freya a watery smile. Freya returned it, standing to pull Ember into a hug that lasted until Ember's tears had dried. And she couldn't help the pang of sorrow over all that she'd missed. She still believed her reasons were right... but she knew now how narrow her existence had been. *Why is it that I'm gaining everything just as I'm about to lose it?*

"Let's get some breakfast," Freya said, patting Ember's back as she pulled away. "Sound good?"

Ember nodded and smiled, allowing Freya to tug her out of the room. As they made their way to the kitchen, Freya drew Ember into an easy conversation, light nothings like Ember imagined normal friends would share. She also kept their pace ridiculously slow, but Ember didn't mention it. She concentrated on Freya, on spending time with her friend. *There's so much life I want to live...but how much time do I have?*

After breakfast, Dyre took her away to the parlor where she'd talked with Collin and Izzy. Someone else was waiting for them, a large and scruffy man Ember thought she'd seen walking with Dyre. Beside him was a smaller, nervous looking boy who couldn't be any older than Ember, probably younger. Both bowed to Dyre as they entered the room, and the younger boy flashed her a smile. That smile disappeared in a wink when Dyre cleared his throat, and Ember thought she caught Dyrerisan glaring at the boy. Ember resisted a smile as Dyre turned toward her.

"This is Badger and Ferret. Badger has experience with magic's effect on the body, and he's going to look you over."

Ember frowned, glancing toward Badger, who now offered her a gentle smile.

"It's not going to help anything," she muttered, looking back to Dyre.

His smile was strained. "Perhaps not. But will you allow it?"

She should refuse. It would only give him false hope. But the look in his eyes...she didn't want him to grow too desperate. She could humor him in this.

"Where do you want me?" she asked with a sigh.

Dyre guided her toward the couch, taking a seat beside her as Badger knelt on the carpet.

"May I?" he asked, reaching for her hand. Ember gave it to him, looking away as he turned it over and felt for her pulse in her wrist. The boy, Ferret, was watching Badger's actions closely. An apprentice? Ember didn't ask, distracted when Dyre took her free hand in his own. She focused on him, examining the lines around his eyes and wondering if it was her imagination that there were more of them. How much worry was she causing him?

"What are the main symptoms?" Badger asked, startling her out of thoughts.

"Headaches," Ember said. "Dizziness, fatigue, shaking..."

"When did you first begin to experience them?"

"Last winter, mostly."

"And they grow steadily worse?"

Ember glanced at Dyre. "For the most part."

Dyre raised an eyebrow at her but didn't demand more. Badger released her wrist, now taking her chin in his calloused hand and tilting her head back and forth. He stared into her eyes for an uncomfortably long moment, and only the pressure of Dyre's hand kept her from squirming away.

When he finally released her, Ember leaned against Dyre, barely resisting the temptation to turn her face into his shoulder. She didn't bother to pull away when Badger took her wrist again, frowning as he felt her pulse. She knew why...her heart had gone unsteady when she leaned against Dyre, as she considered that he felt like home. Ember stared at Badger, silently daring him to say anything.

"That's enough for now," he said gruffly, drawing back and standing. "Anything else, my lord?"

"No," Dyre said. "Report back when you have everything."

Badger bowed and left, Ferret on his heels. Ember waited until they'd left the room to look up, leaning her head against the back of the couch to meet his eyes.

"Satisfied?" she asked. "Or are you going to have someone watch me climb the stairs, later?"

Dyrerisan didn't tease back like she'd expected. Instead, he frowned, his eyebrows drawing together.

"I won't leave any stone unturned."

Ember stared at him, her heart thudding painfully in her chest, and looked away only to hug his arm.

"I know."

They stayed like that for a few minutes, until Ember's thoughts had turned too dark to continue pondering.

"What's next?" she asked, lifting her head.

"To the library?"

Ember smiled. "To the library."

She didn't care where they went, as long as she could stay by his side.

Ember sat in the kitchen chair, her fingers twined together in her lap to keep them in place. Behind her, Miri and Freya played with her hair, discussing what style would look best. She was wearing the midnight dress again, and when she'd descended Helen had suggested doing something with her hair to fit the special gown. How they'd guessed her reason for wearing that particular dress, she didn't know, but she accepted their help with gladness. Only it was taking longer than Ember had anticipated.

"Don't be so nervous," Freya said, pinning a lock of hair somewhere on the back of Ember's head. "You're not *that* late. Besides, waiting once in a while is good for him."

"It'll give you a more dramatic entrance," Miri added around the hairpins between her lips.

"I hadn't planned on anything being dramatic," Ember protested, running her fingers over the skirt.

Miri snorted, taking the pins from her mouth. "I didn't sew this dress to be worn on just any evening. Play the part, have a little fun."

"You mean *you* sewed all these gowns?" Ember asked, twisting to look at Miri. Freya caught her head and turned it back to the right position.

"Most of them," Miri said. "What can I say? Two hundred years is a *long* time. And there were all these *hideous* dresses the courtiers left behind when they fled...might as well turn them into something beautiful."

"They *are* beautiful," Ember said earnestly. If she'd known before, she would've thanked Miri earlier.

*Dyre knew, didn't he? He knew she's spent hours on all those gowns, only for them to sit in a closet...is that part of why he told me to wear them?* Ember hoped it had given Miri some joy, seeing Ember wear her creations.

"There," Freya said, sticking in one more pin. "You're finished."

Ember reached up to cautiously feel Freya and Miri's work, a mass of curls and braids on the back of her head. Some curls hung loose around her shoulders, softening the effect. She stood and turned to Freya and Miri.

"Thank you."

Both women grinned.

"Our pleasure," Freya said. "Now get in there! Your handsome prince awaits."

Ember rolled her eyes at that, but couldn't resist the soft smile that crossed her lips. And as she turned toward the door, tray in hand, she pretended not to see the worried way they all watched her. Her steps were steady, even if her heart beat a little fast.

"There you are," Dyre said as Ember shouldered the door open. "I was about to come looking for you."

"I took longer to get ready than usual," Ember explained, setting the tray on the table and turning to Dyrerisan. He was staring at her, a wistful half smile on his lips that she imagined was unconscious.

"Well?" Ember asked, taking a step away from the table to spin around. "What do you think?"

Dyre stepped forward, stopping her spinning with a hand on her elbow. When she looked up, Dyre was watching her with a fervent light to his eyes that made Ember warm all over.

"Beautiful."

Ember looked down in a vain attempt to hide her blush. "Freya and Miri did my hair...it took a while."

"That doesn't surprise me."

Dyre led her back to the table, sliding her chair in for her. And for a few minutes, neither of them spoke. Dyrerisan had brought a book again, but it sat untouched beside his place. It wasn't until Ember looked up for one of her frequent glances to Dyre and caught him watching that she convinced herself to speak.

"I want you to promise me something," she said, quiet in that large space.

Dyre set his fork aside, turning his full attention toward her. And Ember took a slow breath before meeting his eyes, before going on.

"If you can't stop my curse, I want you to promise me that you won't stop living."

Dyre's brows furrowed, and he opened his mouth to respond with what Ember was sure would be an assurance that he wouldn't fail. She went on before he could.

"I've seen people give up when their loved one dies, and I don't want that for you. I'm not the entire universe...and I don't want to be the end of anyone's life. Just...promise me you won't give up."

Dyre watched her closely, tapping his finger on the table. "Your mother gave up."

Ember swallowed painfully and nodded. She waited for Dyre to respond, watching him as he watched her.

"I'll promise, if you'll promise me something in return."

"What is it?" Ember asked, a little wary.

"It's twofold."

"That's cheating," Ember said with a smile.

Dyre grinned back. "You're welcome to exact a second promise from me to balance it out, if you wish."

"We'll see."

Dyre kept his smile, but his eyes turned grim, on the edge of sorrow with an earnestness that Ember found hard to bear.

"I want you to promise me that *you* won't give up. *Try* to live through this, even if you don't believe it will work."

Ember took a deep breath, remembering her parents. Her father had begged her mother for the same thing. And she had tried...until he'd died. *But Dyre won't leave me...he won't go get himself killed.*

"I promise," Ember said. "What's the second?"

His smile turned mischievous, though his gaze lost none of its intensity.

"That if you do live through this, you'll be my wife."

Ember's heart stuttered. That was...*not* what she'd expected. For a moment, the very concept filled her with terror. Agree to marry Dyre? They'd only known each other a few months... But then she looked back to his eyes, staring deeply in the hope that she could catch a glimpse of *his* soul. And she found herself nodding.

"I promise," she whispered.

Now if only she could live long enough to see it through.

# CHAPTER SIXTEEN

Snapping the book shut, Dyrerisan tossed it aside and grabbed the next from the pile. The papers that usually covered his desk were shuffled to the side, making room for research into anything that could help Ember. He'd learned a lot about curses in the first years of his imprisonment, seeking an escape for himself. Perhaps that research could finally be of use.

Minutes passed. Dyrerisan ran a hand through his hair, tugging on the ends as he scowled. With a growl, he tossed that book onto the rejected pile as well. The stack toppled, knocking against his morbid paperweight. Dyrerisan stared at the quartz heart for a long moment, his own heart pounding in his chest.

*"Come now, Dyrerisan. Hasn't this gone on long enough?"*

He winced at the memory of Mitzianna's voice, sultry and condescending.

*"Give in, darling. Marry me, and I'll set your pitiful fortress free."*

Dyrerisan had responded by throwing a knife at her head. She'd pouted. Claimed she'd return on the tenth anniversary of his curse, to make her offer again. And she'd left that ridiculous token as a reminder...a reminder of what the price of the curse was, if he refused her again. *A heart of stone will shatter, your love will stand on the edge of death...only then can you escape your prison of stone.*

He glared at the quartz stone, his hand digging against the wood of his desk, stone scraping deep into the surface. And a new voice rose in his memory: Ember, her violet eyes filled with tears.

*"And if you can't? Will you let* me *save* you?"

Dyrerisan snatched the quartz heart from his desk, hurling it toward the stone wall. It collided with a sharp crack and fell to the floor in fragments. And Dyrerisan stared at those broken pieces, wishing Ember's curse would break so easily.

He'd reached the edge. Two hundred years he'd endured, pressed on, turned his focus to atoning for his mistakes. But he couldn't go on like this. If he failed Ember, too...

*Almighty, show me a way. Give me a way to save her.*

Dyrerisan looked up from his book, hearing footsteps in the hall. He glanced down at Ember, sleeping with her head pillowed on his shoulder, and stayed seated. He didn't know why anyone would be coming to them here, but he wouldn't disturb her unless it was necessary.

The door swung open, and John burst into the library, running toward the couch where Dyre and Ember had settled.

"My lord," John said, out of breath. "Duke Kelan is at the gate."

Horror coursed through his veins like lightning. He glanced down to Ember, sitting up and blinking sleep from her eyes. He had to get her to safety.

"How did he get here?" Dyrerisan asked, turning back to John as he helped Ember to her feet.

"We think he has a guide."

There was only one person who knew of Nyxwood's existence

who was cowardly enough to reveal it to the Duke of Sarnere. Dyrerisan gritted his teeth against curses at Radcliff, glancing again to Ember before forcing his focus onto John.

"Get everyone down to the dungeons and go to the border tunnel. There should be a few Aerie there."

"I'm coming with you," Ember said.

Dyrerisan turned toward her, intending to say that she'd go with John if he had to drag her. But Ember's fierce look, ruined somewhat by her messy hair, sent a knife through his chest.

"I need you safe," he said instead. "And far from Duke Kelan."

"And I need *you* safe."

"Ember," he growled. "There isn't time for this. Go with John. I'll come and find you when it's safe."

Ember raised her chin, eyes flashing. Dyrerisan knew he hadn't convinced her, but he didn't expect the next words from her lips.

"If you want me to be your wife, you better get used to the idea of me standing beside you, because I'm *not* going to let you walk into danger alone."

John coughed, but Dyrerisan ignored him. *If this turns to a battle, what are the odds I could convince her to run?* But if he forced her down to the dungeons with the others, would she find her way back? Ember didn't back down, though he could see tears gathering in her eyes.

"Alright," Dyrerisan said, around the weight in his chest. "Come on."

He grabbed her hand, barely catching her fractured smile as they turned toward the door. John was already through the door, running for the kitchen. Their own pace was slower, for Ember's sake. As they passed a window, Dyrerisan glimpsed a mounted company entering the castle's gate. He gritted his teeth and reached for his sword hilt, glad he kept it with him always. *He's here for war.* He considered insisting again that Ember retreat with the others, but a glance at her convinced him that it would do no good. *Please, let her live through this.*

They made it to the foyer. The doors weren't barred, but no one had come through them yet. Dyrerisan stopped to the side and pulled a tapestry away to reveal a small door. He turned to Ember.

"You can watch from inside. Swear to me that you won't leave this room, no matter what you see."

Ember set her jaw, glaring at him and shaking her head.

"Marquis of Nyxwood," Duke Kelan shouted outside. "We have matters to discuss."

He had no time. He leaned forward, pressing a kiss to Ember's forehead before he backed away, pulling his hand from hers.

"Right now, we're both safer if I meet him alone," Dyre said, praying Ember listened.

He took another step back, waiting for her to respond. When she didn't follow him, he forced himself to turn toward the door, wrenching it open and stepping into view of his enemy.

Ember watched Dyrerisan leave the castle with her heart in her throat. Every part of her screamed to follow him, to not let him out of sight. But instead, she turned toward the small door, tugging it open and finding a tiny room with small holes drilled into the stone. *We're safer if he faces Duke Kelan alone*, Ember repeated to herself, though her heart couldn't believe it. How could they be safer apart? She finally found a hole that allowed her a sight of Dyre and Duke Kelan, and she held her breath as she watched.

Dyre stood at the top of the steps, looking completely at ease even with his hand resting on his sword hilt. It struck her all over again how *big* Dyre was. Duke Kelan, in all his dark armor, looked like a teenage boy playing knights and maidens. But then, Duke Kelan didn't need to be strong enough to defeat Dyre...he had a small army at his back. Ember bit her lip, praying for Dyre's safety as she watched.

"Speak," Dyrerisan said, in a low rumbling tone that should've made the men cower. "I want to know why you're trespassing on my lands."

"I've come to retrieve my property," Duke Kelan replied easily.

Ember flexed her hand, pressing her fingertips against the stone. He couldn't mean *her*, could he?

"Nothing here belongs to you."

"I must disagree. Your servant girl was promised to me long before Radcliff's unfortunate meeting with you."

Duke Kelan gestured over his shoulder, and two soldiers dragged forward a bruised figure in chains. Ember's stomach soured. *Radcliff.* He wouldn't raise his head, groaning as the soldiers dropped him to the ground beside the Duke of Sarnere.

"Well, Radcliff?" Duke Kelan asked. "What was our agreement?"

"That you'd have someone from my house in your service," Radcliff said.

His voice shook, and for a moment Ember felt pity for the broken man before her. What had Duke Kelan done to him? *Are my cousins alright?*

"Not just anyone," Duke Kelan said. "Ember Kendrick. You named *her* as my prize, did you not?"

"Yes."

*Of course, he did.* But Ember had no shock or anger left...he'd never defended her. *But Uncle, couldn't you have kept silent just once?*

"Nyxwood doesn't recognize such contracts," Dyrerisan said. "I paid the debt price for Ember. Take it and be satisfied."

*Yes,* Ember agreed silently. *Take it and be satisfied. Leave us alone... please.* But Duke Kelan only grinned cruelly.

"I find gold to be much less useful than a beating heart."

"But you won't take Ember's."

"And you'll stop me?" Duke Kelan scoffed, lips twisting in a smirk that Ember longed to slap from his face. "The mighty Marquis

Dyrerisan, defending a servant girl. It's a fitting way for you to die, I suppose."

The ring of metal interrupted the end of Kelan's speech, as Dyre drew his sword.

"I don't intend to die."

Dyre glanced at the wall, and Ember swore he looked straight into her eyes. Her breath caught. He didn't *intend* to die...but could he really survive this? Could he fight off the twenty, thirty men gathered behind Duke Kelan? *Where are the Aerie? Someone needs to help him...he can't fight them all at once!*

But Dyrerisan didn't appear intimidated. He watched six knights climb the stairs toward him with cold assurance, holding his sword with an ease that made Ember hesitate. She'd never seen Dyre fight, but she knew once he must have. *I won't get in the way...not yet.* She wouldn't distract him from the fight, not unless she had a way to save him.

The first knight attacked, and Ember winced. At first, she closed her eyes, but the clang of metal and a cry of pain made her pry them open again. She had to know what happened...she had to know if Dyre was alright.

The cry hadn't been Dyre's. Of the six knights who'd attacked, one was already bleeding out on the stairs. The other five were attacking Dyre...without success. Ember could hardly make sense of the wild movement, except to watch the men fall. Dyrerisan's movements were quick, assured, and deadly. Other soldiers climbed the stairs after him, as he dispatched enemies to die on the stone like they were no more than pests. A chill entered Ember's heart, watching Dyre kill so easily, so dispassionately.

*He's defending,* she reminded herself. *He's protecting.*

Duke Kelan was the true horror. Ember ripped her eyes away from the fight to look at the duke and found him watching with *boredom.* His men were running forward to their deaths for *him,* on *his* orders...and he didn't seem to care. Did he see them as disposable tools? Did he place that little value on life?

Watching Duke Kelan, she saw the skinny man who stepped up to the duke's side. He looked nothing like the muscled soldiers Dyre was fighting. This man was *skeletal*, with tattoos and scars covering most of his exposed skin. His only weapon was a dagger of black metal, which he used to slice open his own forearm. As the blood wept from that wound, the man chanted, stepping toward the fight. *A sorcerer.*

Dyre didn't see him coming. Ember didn't think there was anything he could do even if he *did*. Ember sucked in half a breath, her heart stuttering. The image of Dyre falling, of that skinny man grinning over him...it was too much. Before Ember knew what she was doing, she was out of the small room and tugging open the main door. He promised he wouldn't leave her...he *promised*. She wouldn't lose him like this.

Outside was pure chaos. Ember edged away from the door, pressing her back against the stone wall. Dyre was still fighting, still winning. Around the small battle being waged on the steps, she could see the sorcerer approaching. How did she stop him? Even if she could get around Dyre and the soldiers, she wasn't strong enough to fight anyone, let alone a sorcerer. *But I have to do something.*

Dyre's cry of pain finished it. He was still moving, still fighting... but that sound filled her with a cold resolve. She stood taller, taking a deep breath. She knew what she had to do.

"Stop this!" she shouted. Her voice could barely be heard over the fight. She tried again.

"Dyre!" She shrieked. "Duke Kelan! Listen to me!"

Dyre glanced back at her, and the look of fear in his eyes nearly sent her back into the castle. But the soldiers kept coming, and Dyre turned back to fend them off. Ember tightened her hands to fists behind her and stood strong. She edged further over to where she could see Duke Kelan beyond the fighting. The sorcerer was already climbing the stairs. Ember's breath caught.

"Duke Kelan," she shouted, taking a small step forward. "If you want a beating heart, you'll stop this and *listen* to me."

Duke Kelan watched Ember, still looking far too dispassionate. But as Ember glared down at him, he raised his hand. A whistle pierced the air, and the soldiers fell back, stumbling away from Dyre's sword.

For a moment, Ember thought Dyre would follow them. But instead, he pulled away, chest heaving as he backed to Ember's side. He half turned toward her, resting a hand on her shoulder as he met her eyes.

"Go inside," he said, eyes pleading. "I'll finish this."

"Against a sorcerer?" Ember whispered, glancing to where the skinny man stood near the base of the stairs, now surrounded by soldiers.

"I'll protect you, I swear."

He tried guiding her inside, and Ember grabbed onto his sleeve, planting her feet in place.

"I won't watch you die," Ember said, voice cracking.

"I'm not a patient man, Miss Kendrick," Duke Kelan called.

Ember didn't acknowledge him, keeping her eyes on Dyre. Their silent battle of wills lasted what felt like an eternity.

"Please," he whispered.

Ember's smile was shaky as she reached up to touch his face. *I'm sorry.* She turned toward Duke Kelan, still holding tight to Dyre.

"If you want me alive, you'll leave Dyrerisan unharmed."

"And why is that?" Duke Kelan asked indulgently, his smile mocking. Oh, how Ember longed to knock it off his face. Instead, she stood straighter, letting all her fury and loathing rise to the surface and hoping he'd recognize it.

"Kill him and my death won't be far behind."

"Ember," Dyre whispered reproachfully. Ember squeezed his arm but didn't move when he tried tugging her toward the door. He could've picked her up and been done with it. When he heard what she said next, he *might*.

"I have ways of keeping you alive."

"Ways more powerful than a Jairvas curse?" Ember challenged.

She couldn't help it: she looked to Dyre. She'd made the connection a while ago, that their curses came from the same family. She'd feared telling Dyre...but he wasn't shocked. *He already knew.* Ember's lips twisted into a broken smile against her will, as she offered another silent apology, knowing it wasn't enough.

"You think your curse can claim you that quickly?"

That pulled Ember's attention back to Duke Kelan, her brows furrowed. *How did he know about my curse?* But that troubling question wasn't hers to answer, at least not now. He might know she was cursed...he had no way of knowing what it *was*, at least not as well as Ember.

"Don't pretend you know *my* curse," Ember spat. "I watched my mother die to this magic. I know what will happen to me if Dyre dies."

Duke Kelan looked a little less assured, at least. He glanced between Dyre and Ember, and a twisted smile stole across his face. The roiling dread and terror in Ember's stomach grew, knowing that nothing good could come of such an expression.

"And if Dyrerisan lives?"

Her breath caught, fingers tightening around Dyre's arm. But she stood tall.

"Then I'll come with you willingly."

"No," Dyre growled, stepping in front of Ember to cut off her view from Duke Kelan.

He planted one hand on the wall over Ember's shoulder, leaning down so their eyes were only a hand width apart.

"I won't let you," he said. "You won't die for me."

"And I won't let *you* die for *me*," Ember replied, fighting to make her voice fierce through the tears. She was losing, but she didn't bother to dry the tears. That would mean looking away from Dyre.

"I accept your bargain," Duke Kelan called, *laughing*. Ember and Dyre ignored him.

"He'll kill you."

"Not right away," Ember said. "He'll want to have his fun...and I don't intend to give in to him."

"Is that supposed to *comfort* me?" Dyre growled. His grip on her arm tightened, but Ember didn't pull away. He had to understand... he had to let her go.

"Yes. I'll last, Dyre...I'll hold on long enough for you to *come get me.*"

She held his gaze, accepting the horrified understanding, the wild grief. But she didn't give him a chance to respond. She leaned forward, pressing her lips to his despite the agony fracturing her soul.

She'd felt it in the past few days, the fissures steadily spreading through her heart. Ember had been slowly crumbling as she finally let love in. But now...now she *swore* her heart shattered within her. Because she was breaking *his* heart...and all she could do was pray it was enough. Pray that her sacrifice, their shared heartache, was enough to satisfy the twisted magic binding Dyre to this prison of stone.

She felt it, then: that coy, grasping darkness falling away, stone fracturing to pieces. Triumph raced through her. But it did little to sooth the agony of what must come next. Ember pulled away, twisting free of Dyre before he could react and stumbling down the stairs.

"Ember," Dyre gasped.

She kept going, through the soldiers that parted before her and past the sorcerer whose presence made her shiver. A glance over her shoulder showed Dyre still beside the doors, leaning against the stone as if he couldn't stand on his own. She looked away quickly, unable to bear the way he was watching her. *I have to.*

But turning away meant facing Duke Kelan. He looked taller up close, with Ember standing within reach. He stared down at her like she was an oddity, and Ember did her best to glare through the tears still coming.

"Time to go, Miss Kendrick," he rumbled.

Before she was ready, he'd grabbed her around the waist and thrown her onto a horse. She grabbed the horse's mane, shuddering as he mounted behind her. His armor was hard and cold against her back. But she preferred the discomfort to feeling *him*.

Ember twisted, ignoring Duke Kelan as she searched for Dyre... one last glimpse. He was on his knees, watching her like she'd stolen his entire world. She could swear the gray was fading from his skin.

This time she didn't look away, not until Duke Kelan and his soldiers had ridden past the gates, out of view. Not all of the soldiers had left, nor had they bothered to drag Radcliff away with them, but she didn't say anything...she knew Duke Kelan wouldn't play fair. She could only pray that Dyrerisan recovered himself soon enough to fight off a few more men. The sorcerer, at least, rode with them.

"I wonder," Duke Kelan whispered beside her ear, "if you'll regret your sacrifice, before the end."

"I'm no stranger to pain."

Duke Kelan only laughed. And Ember raised her hand to her chest, closing her eyes as her heart pounded out its broken beat, whispering that she'd left everything that mattered behind her.

# CHAPTER SEVENTEEN

*I've failed.* Dyrerisan dug his fingers against the wall, agony pulsing through his chest as he watched Ember disappear through the gate. His entire body shuddered, rebelling against the vulnerability, the new *weakness* pervading his flesh as the curse fragmented. But that pain was nothing beside the torture of failure, of *loss.* He'd sworn to protect Ember, he'd sworn that she'd *live*...but now she'd condemned herself to save his worthless life.

The sound of a sword drawn from its scabbard forced Dyrerisan's attention back to the present, to the soldiers climbing the steps toward him. Duke Kelan had taken the path of least resistance for his prize...that didn't mean he'd believed Ember's claim. But Dyrerisan had no intention of dying today.

Dyrerisan groaned as he reached down for his sword, wrapping an aching hand around the hilt. Raising the blade made his arm tremble, but raise it he did. Just in time to deflect his first attacker's sword away from his neck. And Dyrerisan forced himself to his feet, steadying himself against the wall as he fended off another attack. Ten soldiers surrounded him. On a normal day, Dyrerisan would've laughed at those odds. But in this state...

He gritted his teeth, stepping forward to offer an attack of his own. He would survive. He would defeat Kelan's servants, and then he'd make Kelan regret he'd ever set eyes on Ember. He wouldn't have her life. Dyrerisan would make sure of it.

One soldier stepped too close. Dyrerisan retreated, barely stepping aside in time to avoid another soldier's poorly aimed thrust. Eight men left, eight swords to avoid. His heart pounded within him, the ache in his bones suggesting that it wouldn't take much to silence it.

A wolf's howl pierced the air. Dyrerisan's attackers flinched, pausing in the fight to search for the source. And Dyrerisan grinned.

Taking advantage of their distraction, he disarmed one man and killed another. By the time the others turned back to Dyrerisan, Collin and Izzy were in the courtyard. The sight of a massive wolf, with Izzy on his back, was too much for the soldiers. For good reason...Collin had made a name for himself terrorizing Sarnere's soldiers in Rausbane. He and Izzy made short work of them now, allowing Dyrerisan a chance to breathe, surveying the scene.

Beside him, the door opened. Helen, Freya, and Miri emerged, cast iron pans in hand and a fierce look to their eyes. Their searching, worried expressions were too much for Dyrerisan to face. He twisted away and stepped toward Izzy and Collin.

"Keep him alive," he ordered, as Izzy subdued the last of the soldiers.

It was unnecessary: she'd already pinned him to the cobblestones.

"Mercy," the man choked.

A growl from Collin made the man flinch, closing his eyes against the threat. And Izzy looked to Dyrerisan.

"How did Kelan know when to attack?" Dyrerisan asked.

He'd come at their most vulnerable, when none of the Aerie was close enough to come quickly to their aid. That wouldn't be a coincidence. Nor was it luck that Kelan had learned the secret to penetrating Nyxwood's borders. *Whoever gave Kelan what he needed to take Ember will pay.*

"If I tell you, will I live?" the man asked.

"Oh, you'll live," Izzy said with a dark laugh. The man flinched again.

"One of your watchers is loyal to Sarnere."

Izzy twisted the knife close to his throat, leaning toward him with a snarl. "You better have proof behind an accusation like that. One of the Aerie, loyal to a sorcerer's ally?"

Dyrerisan watched in silence, letting Izzy work. His glance to Collin wasn't encouraging. Even in wolf form, Dyrerisan could see Collin's regret. It matched his own. *If we'd taken action sooner...*

"I saw him with Duke Kelan," the man stuttered, trying to lean away from the blade at his throat. "I heard them talking, explaining what the duke needed to watch for when we came here. He said that most of your warriors were out looking into some curse, and that now was the time Nyxwood would be vulnerable."

Now Izzy looked up, her eyes meeting Dyrerisan's.

"Take him down to the cells," Dyrerisan ordered. "We'll deal with him when we return."

"We?" Collin asked, already shrugging on his cloak. His eyes were sharp as he looked Dyrerisan over.

"The curse is broken," Helen announced. "We all felt it."

"Ember's doing," Dyrerisan explained, though speaking was nearly beyond him.

"Duke Kelan has her?" Collin asked.

Dyrerisan nodded, throat tight. *Willful, misguided...* He should've forced her back inside, fought to the last man. He should've taken on that skinny sorcerer and his blood magic, no matter the risks. *She wouldn't have stayed on the sidelines.* Ember had been determined to save him, in more ways than one. Her eyes still shone in his mind, filled with unshed tears. *I'll hold on long enough for you to come get me.*

And he *would* come for her. He'd ride through whatever darkness Sarnere could conjure. He'd fight armies. But he *would* save her.

"John and Ben are already saddling the horses," Freya said.

"Do we ride now?" Collin asked.

Dyrerisan hesitated, looking again to the open gate. His heart demanded that they go after Ember now, intercept them on the road and steal her back before Kelan could even *think* of harming her. The more time she spent in his presence, the more danger she was in. But every bit of his training told him to wait, to gather his strength and attack when they were assured of victory. Riding to Ember's rescue would do no good if he died before he reached her.

"Not yet," he bit out around the panic tightening his throat. "Collin, gather the Aerie. Everyone able to make it by dusk will meet here. Send no word to those watching Sarnere."

"Yes sir."

Collin's form rippled, and in a heartbeat the wolf was running toward the boundary gate. He passed a shaking and ragged Radcliff, who fell into the bushes getting away from the wolf bounding past. Dyrerisan ignored him. Let the man go wherever he could drag his sorry carcass. Dyrerisan had more important matters to take care of. He forced himself to turn to face Helen, Freya, and Miri.

"What would you have us do?" Helen asked.

"Prepare for visitors," Dyrerisan asked. "And ready the castle for lock down. I'm afraid I'll be leaving Nyxwood vulnerable tonight."

"No one will take Nyxwood, my lord," Freya said, gripping her iron pan like a sword. "We'll make sure of it."

Dyrerisan looked over the three women, noting their unshed tears and determined looks. He wouldn't test them. Nyxwood, at least, would be safe in his absence.

"I will bring her back," he said.

"We have no doubt of it, my lord," Helen said. She turned to Freya and Miri, urging the younger women inside. "Come on. We have work to do."

Dyrerisan watched them go and turned back toward the gate. *Ember.* She shouldn't have given herself up. But sacrifice wouldn't be her final act. *Ember will live,* he vowed. *I will end this tonight.*

THE RIDE to Sarnere lasted an eternity. Ember ached with more than exhaustion as the hours stretched on, perched on a warhorse with Duke Kelan's black armor at her back. They took no rest, they offered her no comforts. Not that she would've accepted any if they had.

Ember said nothing to Duke Kelan, ignoring his few attempts at conversation. Instead, she watched the forest surrounding them for any sign of Collin or Izzy. She had to believe that Dyrerisan had called them, that he'd survived to set them on her trail. But she didn't see or hear anyone around them besides Duke Kelan's men.

*It's a good sign,* she told herself. *Duke Kelan and his soldiers would notice them following before I would.* Collin and Izzy knew what they were doing. Ember just had to hold on...hold on long enough for them to come for her. *Please, let Dyre be alive. Please let me live long enough to see his face again.*

The sun had set by the time they reached the gates of Sarnere. Ember examined the fortress in the fading light, wondering if it was her imagination that it looked more sinister than Nyxwood ever had. Those walls didn't feel like protection...they felt like a prison. Ember shivered as they passed beneath the portcullis.

Duke Kelan dismounted, dragging Ember down with him. She stumbled, planting her fists against his breastplate in an attempt to stay on her feet. He pushed her into the arms of two guards.

"Take her to a cell," he ordered.

Ember sagged in the guards' rough grip, making the mistake of meeting Kelan's gaze. His smile was cruel.

"Don't make yourself too comfortable, Miss Kendrick. I'll come for you as soon as I see to a few pressing matters."

Ember didn't waste breath responding, looking down to her feet. The guards swept her away, half carrying her to the edge of the courtyard and down a staircase to a hall that smelled of waste and death. She wrinkled her nose, not looking too closely at the barred cells they passed. The one they dragged Ember into was empty, at least, with a thin cot against one wall. She stumbled to that cot when they released her, collapsing on it as the door closed with an ominous grinding of key in lock. Ember didn't even care. She huddled on the musty straw, locking her arms around her knees to try and conserve as much body heat as she could. And she prayed.

*If you have any love for us, any pity for our fate...please let me see Dyre again.*

DYRERISAN SLOWED HIS HORSE, looking out into the shadowed forest beyond the gate. Above, the sky was still stained with the last, bloody colors of sunset. And just before him laid the invisible boundary he hadn't crossed in two centuries. The Aerie were already gathered beyond, waiting for him to join them.

Thinking of Ember, remembering her unshaking trust in him, Dyrerisan took a breath and urged his horse onward. He passed the gates unhindered, and a weight fell away from his shoulders. Dyrerisan straightened, riding to the front of the group where Collin and Izzy waited to lead them. They all watched him. For the first time in all the years he'd led the Aerie, he'd lead them to battle. *Don't let us falter*, he prayed. *Give us strength to defeat this evil, once and for all. For Ember...for all his victims.*

Collin and Izzy watched Dyrerisan as he took his place, waiting for his signal. Dyrerisan nodded, and they set out, using their enhanced night vision to guide them safely through the forest. They had a path to Sarnere that took less time than the road, one that Sarnere wouldn't know to guard against.

*Stay alive, Ember. We're coming.*

Clanking metal woke Ember from her restless sleep, and her eyes flickered open. Dark, hazy shapes stood in the door to her cell. She shivered, aching with the damp cold that seemed to reach down around her bones. But, biting her lip against a groan, she sat up as elegantly as she could manage. Blinking her eyes allowed Duke Kelan's face to come into focus, watching her with vague amusement.

"Comfortable?" he asked.

Ember swallowed, aiming for a carefree tone she hoped grated against his nerves.

"Certainly. Damp air and musty straw are just the thing for one's health. You should try it."

"Perhaps another time."

Kelan stepped aside, allowing guards to enter and drag Ember from the cot. She didn't resist, struggling to get her feet on the ground so she wouldn't be dragged. The guards followed Duke Kelan down the hall, beyond the cells and the stairs to a solid door standing open. The guards released her, as Duke Kelan gestured for Ember to enter first. The flickering lamps were just bright enough to show dried blood staining the floor in a trail leading out of that room. But with a glance at Kelan, Ember swallowed and entered.

Ember stood tall, feeling eyes on her back. Her trembling hands she wrapped in her skirt. It wasn't just fear making her shake all over. Kissing Dyre, leaving him on the steps at Nyxwood, had done *something* to her curse. She'd felt it tearing through her veins ever since, eating away at whatever strength and life it could find. She was down to days, not months.

*But I'll spend those days with Dyre,* she told herself. *I'll see him again, no matter what Duke Kelan puts me through. I will endure.*

"Take a seat," Duke Kelan said, sitting in a chair near the wall.

The only other seat in the room was a low stool, which Ember perched on reluctantly. She felt more vulnerable there, in the center of the room. She didn't doubt that was the intention. She turned her attention to glaring at Duke Kelan, hoping that would hide some of her fear. It took her a moment to notice the second figure standing behind him, hooded and shadowed beyond recognition. Ember turned away from thought of what he was doing here...she could see the whip in his hands, and that was enough to send a different chill through her.

"Before I hand you off to my allies, I have a few questions for you."

Duke Kelan paused, waiting for her answer. Ember rearranged her skirts, resisting the urge to tuck her arms around her waist.

"Oh?" she asked in frozen politeness.

"You see, the legendary *Marquis* and his paltry army have been thorns in my side ever since I rose to my position. I'd like to do away with their annoyance, but despite *everything* I've done I can't seem to find Dyrerisan's weakness."

He glared at the man beside him as he spoke, and Ember looked to the darkened form again. *Would* she recognize him, if he left the shadows? Had Dyrerisan been betrayed?

"But you," Kelan said, with a note of laughter that drew Ember's attention. "You have obviously found a way into his confidence. And now you'll show me the way to Dyrerisan's vulnerabilities. Assuming he still lives, of course."

*He still lives,* Ember whispered to her pounding heart. *He's coming.* She'd hold on to that hope until her last breath. Dyre wouldn't leave her here to die alone. But to Duke Kelan, she offered her most poisonous glare. He smirked.

"Stubbornness will only lead to more pain."

"Impatience will only kill me faster," she replied.

Kelan's smile grew, chilling Ember to the core. She held on to her glare.

"Touché," he said. "But I think you can survive *some* incentive.

My associate says you have a strong will...perhaps that will work in my favor."

Ember turned again to his companion as he stepped out from the shadow and threw back his hood. *Badger.* She recognized his face, even if his smile now was far more cruel than gentle. Ember swallowed back her chagrin.

"Familiar with magic's effect," she scoffed. "I take it you have personal experience?"

"Of a sort." He uncoiled his whip. "I'm sorry this is necessary. I enjoyed watching you shake Dyrerisan's endless confidence."

"Enough pleasantries," Kelan snapped. "What do you know of Nyxwood castle?"

Ember turned her eyes back to Kelan. His sharp gaze was easier to meet than Badger's. She hadn't ever been under the illusion that Kelan might be an ally.

"I know it gathers enough dust to fill this room," she snapped.

Kelan smirked. "What do you know of its *defenses?*"

Ember's thoughts immediately went to the dungeon and its many doors, to the passage Dyrerisan said led to a veiled entrance. Did Badger know of that? A glance in his direction revealed nothing. *Regardless, he won't hear of it from my lips.* She shrugged, smoothing her skirts.

"How would I know? It's not like Radcliff gave me lessons in defensive architecture."

"Careful, Ember," Duke Kelan purred. "It's not in your best interest to be difficult."

Ember smirked. "Being difficult is my specialty."

Kelan ignored that, leaning forward. "I'm sure you've explored. You've lived there for months...surely you know more than the occasional visitor."

That made Ember glance to Badger again, though she looked away quickly. Had he tried exploring? *How much did Dyre trust him with?* Not much, if Kelan was resorting to interrogating *her.*

"Answer, Ember."

Ember lifted her eyes to Duke Kelan, raising an eyebrow. He wanted an answer? Ember would give him one.

"The only weakness I know of in Nyxwood castle is the useless trinkets cluttering the halls. They make it so difficult to *clean* anything."

Now he looked annoyed. Before Ember could draw much satisfaction from that, Kelan flicked a hand and Badger lunged forward. Ember barely had time to flinch before a line of pain blossomed across her shoulders. She hunched over, biting her lip against the sting. And she glared at Duke Kelan. Badger stayed close, and she cringed when he shifted. But the whip didn't come down again...yet.

Duke Kelan looked *far* too satisfied for Ember's taste. But she held her silence. She couldn't provoke them too much...she had to save her strength for when it mattered.

"Then what do you know of the legendary Marquis?" Duke Kelan asked, sneering at Dyre's title. "What are his weaknesses? I'd wager my castle you're *more* than familiar with those."

Perhaps she was familiar with them. Perhaps she *was* one of his weaknesses. That didn't mean she had any intention of betraying him, no matter how much Badger's whip cut into her flesh.

"I know Dyrerisan is the most cunning and determined man I've ever met," Ember said, pleased when her voice held steady. "And I know that whatever weaknesses he has, they aren't enough to give you a fool's hope of defeating him."

Duke Kelan's smirk faltered. Seeing his mask drop gave Ember a fierce pleasure, even when Kelan flicked his hand to Badger again. Down came the whip, this time tearing through cloth and skin. She couldn't keep in her cry this time, tears stinging her eyes as blood welled up through the wound. She took a shuddering breath, digging her fingers into her legs. Her pulse fluttered under the duress, and she fought to take another breath. She would last. She had to.

"If you think you can survive this, you're mistaken," Duke Kelan said. "I'll snuff out your life without a second thought...once I get what I want."

Ember raised her head, glaring at Kelan through her tears. Every movement sent fire through her back, but she managed to speak through her clenched teeth.

"And if you think that will make me give in, *you're* mistaken. Weakness doesn't make me faithless."

*And you'll never take my hope*, she added silently. *Dyre won't leave me here. I'll keep my heart beating long enough.*

# CHAPTER EIGHTEEN

Dyrerisan watched the guard pacing along the top of the wall, oblivious to the two figures scaling the wall below him. Tigress and Leo incapacitated him before he could say a word. They ducked out of sight, and Dyrerisan shifted his feet as they waited. Beside him, Collin and Izzy whispered to their newest recruit, a boy who'd chosen the name Ferret.

"This close to dawn, the guards are tired and relaxed," Collin said. "They're not expecting anything to happen."

"Their negligence is our gain," Ferret whispered.

"Don't be overconfident," Izzy chided. "Arrogance leads to mistakes."

Dyrerisan narrowed his eyes. Yes, arrogance led to mistakes... hopefully Kelan's arrogance would be to their benefit.

A rope ladder dropped down the wall, with Leo rising above the wall just long enough to give the "all clear". Ferret shifted nervously, drawing Dyrerisan's gaze as the first pair of Aerie warriors slipped across the open field. He found Collin and Izzy holding hands, whispering their pre-battle prayer.

"If we die today, we go to the Almighty," Collin said.

Izzy added, "If we survive this day, we thank the Almighty."

Dyrerisan turned his eyes back to the wall, but he listened closely, echoing with his own prayer. *Lend me Your strength, guide my steps. May this battle be to Your glory.* And he watched closely as the couple entered the open space between the forest and the wall, running low to the ground. He reached out, grabbing Ferret's arm when he started forward.

"You'll go with me," Dyrerisan whispered when Ferret glanced nervously at him.

"Yes, sir."

This boy was the nervous sort. Dyrerisan still wasn't at ease bringing him inside Sarnere. He'd only been training with the Aerie for six months, and at seventeen was hardly the sort Dyrerisan wanted to risk in this den of sorcerers. But Collin had insisted he would be an asset...and Dyrerisan needed everyone he could get.

"Now," Dyrerisan whispered, stepping out the trees' shelter.

They made it to the base of the wall without incident, and even with his focus elsewhere Dyrerisan reveled in the lightness, the ease of his movement. It had been so long since he'd done anything without pain...

Dyrerisan had Ferret climb the ladder before him, watching in approval as he scaled the wall with ease. Dyrerisan's own movements were slower, but he didn't falter.

On the top of the wall, Dyrerisan dropped down the nearest staircase to where Collin and Izzy were waiting. The rest of the Aerie had already dispersed, blocking off the barracks and mess hall and preparing distractions to keep Sarnere's soldiers busy. Darkness still hid the fortress, where in an hour or so servants would be rising for the morning's work.

"Where's the boy?" Dyrerisan asked when he reached Collin's side.

"Sent him to have a look around."

Dyrerisan sent a skeptical look Collin's way but didn't voice his disapproval. What was done was done...he'd just have to hope Ferret didn't get himself into any trouble.

"Kelan keeps most of his important prisoners within the keep," Izzy murmured. "We're ready when you are."

Dyrerisan nodded. "Lead the way."

Collin led the way into the courtyard, Izzy taking the rear to watch their backs. Dyrerisan was grateful for their vigilance. His own mind had only one focus: Ember. *What has Kelan done with her? What has she endured while we waited for the opportune time?* Waiting was necessary...they had one chance to rescue Ember and end this for good, and they couldn't waste it in desperation. But even with that logic, his heart had beat in one refrain since his last glimpse of Ember: he had to get her back.

Collin led them in a side door. A glance in the dark showed his unease as they edged inside. Dyrerisan agreed. An entrance like this should've been guarded or locked...their way in shouldn't be so simple. But they had to keep moving forward. Dyrerisan wrapped his hand around the hilt of his sword as they moved further into the hall.

They came across sentries further in, at a junction of two halls. Collin and Izzy incapacitated them quickly, leaving them bound in a shadowed corner. Their presence should've set Dyrerisan more at ease, but it didn't. The air still tasted sour. This ease wouldn't continue.

Still, with the sentries taken care of they moved on, down the hall to a thick wooden door barred from the outside. Collin was the first to enter, Dyrerisan just behind. But the scene that greeted them wasn't what Dyre had expected...only one person occupied the room, and it wasn't Ember.

"Viper," Collin sighed.

Dyrerisan echoed his disappointment. Hints of a traitor had led back to two of the Aerie, and it would've been simpler if the culprit had been Viper. But of course, matters wouldn't be that simple. Dyrerisan set his jaw as he inspected the figure hanging limply from chains attached to the ceiling. He couldn't tell from this distance if Viper still breathed or not. And he didn't see any sign that Ember had been here. Which was good...enough torture implements filled the walls to send a chill through his blood.

Commotion from the hall made Dyrerisan turn, drawing his sword. Soldiers were pouring in from the other doors, blocking all escape. Dyrerisan watched them take their places grimly. He'd expected something like this...but he'd hoped he could find Ember and get out before Kelan sprang his trap. Dyrerisan stepped up to Collin and Izzy's side, taking his place just outside the door to Sarnere's interrogation chamber. The Duke of Sarnere was walking down the hall toward them, with a satisfied triumph that made Dyrerisan grit his teeth.

At his side, Izzy hissed her displeasure. "If it isn't the traitor."

Dyrerisan glanced to the figures at Kelan's side. One was the sorcerer he'd brought to Nyxwood. The other, looking nearly as pleased as Kelan, was Badger. Dyrerisan scowled at his warrior, once more cursing his own blindness. How much had he given Duke Kelan? Dyrerisan let this man near Ember...what had he betrayed to Kelan about her condition? But he didn't acknowledge Badger more than that, returning his attention to Duke Kelan as he stopped half a dozen steps from where Dyrerisan stood.

"Greetings," Kelan said. "I must say, it's a surprise having the Marquis of Nyxwood himself in my home. Ember must have more of a hold of you than I'd thought."

Dyrerisan gritted his teeth, gripping his sword tighter at that casual mention of Ember. He longed to demand to know where she was...but not yet. He had no reason to reveal that information now... but he would. Dyrerisan would make sure of it.

"You can trust that my presence isn't for your sake," Dyrerisan replied. "I've no desire to experience Sarnere's notorious *hospitality*."

Dyrerisan glanced at Collin and Izzy as he spoke, seeking their thoughts. Badger knew more of their curse than most...they'd be dangerously vulnerable in this fight. But neither of them showed any fear or hesitation: at Dyrerisan's glance, they nodded, waiting for his orders.

"You came here looking for Ember, I suppose," Kelan said.

"Of course."

"And I take it you *didn't* expect to find other familiar faces."

Dyrerisan raised his eyebrow. So, Kelan felt the need to gloat, did he? He must've been strongly convinced he had the situation under his control. *What gives him that assurance? That sorcerer in his shadow?* Or was there more Dyrerisan hadn't seen?

"As pleasant as this reunion is, I didn't come to talk," Dyrerisan drawled.

He didn't look away from Kelan, though Izzy had disappeared from his side. He assumed it was to free Viper...perhaps he lived after all.

"Of course, you want to see your precious Ember. She's a delight...not useful for answering questions, but so entertaining."

Kelan was trying to distract him, rile his temper and make him an easier target. *It's working.* Kelan's implication, the thought of what he might've done to Ember, summoned a hot fury that flowed through his limbs in a torrent. Rage that demanded action... vengeance. It took all of Dyrerisan's self-control to keep his reaction hidden. *He will die...but not yet.*

"What's the sorcerer's place here?" Dyrerisan asked through clenched teeth. "Do you mean for *him* to fight your battle?"

Kelan smirked. "Why not? It's so much cleaner this way. And a fitting end for the great Marquis, after all you've done to eliminate magic."

"Taking your life will be an honor," the sorcerer rumbled, fixing black eyes on Dyrerisan. "You've terrorized this land for too long."

Dyrerisan forced laughter up his throat, though it sounded more like a snarl. And he twisted his expression into disgust, even as he adjusted his grip on his sword.

"I've faced worse than you," Dyrerisan said. "I know the limitations of your power: you rely on betrayal."

Which was why Dyrerisan trapped Radcliff, why he brought Ember to Nyxwood in the first place. As Ember's *guardian*, Radcliff's betrayal would've left her vulnerable. It was also why he hadn't been free to keep Ember from Kelan's clutches. Fighting the sorcerer at Nyxwood, where he never would've stepped without a betrayal of the path, had left *Dyrerisan* vulnerable. But not here...here the advantage was his own.

"You have been betrayed," Badger said, in a satisfied rumble that drew Dyrerisan's disgust.

Dyrerisan scoffed. "Your disloyalty hardly counts as betrayal."

Badger puffed up in anger. "Betrayed by your little lover, *Dyre*."

The sound of the nickname *Ember* had given him, from the *traitor's* lips, made Dyrerisan see red. But he didn't believe for a moment that Ember had betrayed him.

"Whatever you've done to her," he said quietly. "I'll repay against you tenfold."

Badger raised his own weapon. "By all means, try."

A snarl interrupted Badger, as Izzy and Collin took a step forward as one.

"You won't touch him," Collin growled.

Before Dyrerisan could act, Kelan had grabbed Badger by the collar, holding him back. His eyes were locked on Dyrerisan, and Dyrerisan met his silent challenge head on.

"There's no need for all that," Kelan said. "If you'd like to settle this in a more *brutal* way, I'll do the honors."

"Without your lackeys interfering?"

"Of course. Take heart Dyrerisan...you'll join Ember in death soon enough."

Those words sent Dyrerisan staggering. A fracture, soul deep, turned the world to ice and stone around him. *No. She can't be dead.* Wordless grief drowned out all thought of caution. Before his heart had reconnected with the world around him, his body was moving forward, sword raised against Kelan. Against the one who'd taken his Ember. He didn't see Kelan's satisfied smile, didn't see the soldiers around him raising their own weapons for a fight. He saw Ember's eyes, saw the trust they held. She'd trusted him. *She'd trusted him to save her.*

Kelan deflected Dyrerisan's wild attack, bringing his sword around to thrust toward Dyrerisan's throat. He barely stepped aside in time, swinging his sword low at Kelan's legs. His movements were muscle memory, automatic. His ragged mind could barely see, could barely process what was happening. *If Ember is gone...*

A snarl and a war cry interrupted that thought, as Izzy and Collin attacked the soldiers trying to interfere with Dyrerisan and Kelan. That woke him up a bit, in time to deflect Kelan's next thrust and turn that defense into an attack of his own. Icy fury cut through some of the grief. He'd promised Ember he wouldn't give up...he'd keep that promise here, against Kelan. Dyrerisan wouldn't die today. *Not until the fight is finished.*

Dyrerisan bit back a snarl when Kelan's next attack opened a cut along his shoulder. Dyrerisan's arms burned as he raised his sword again, ignoring the fire to go after Kelan. The duke fended off that weak attack with ease, and Dyrerisan was forced to turn and meet a new attack. He knocked aside Badger's dagger and stepped away, putting a wall at his back. He raised his sword, bracing the blade in front of himself to stop the dagger Badger was cutting down toward his face. Dyrerisan grimaced at the strength of that strike, but held.

Ferret appeared behind, stabbing Badger between his ribs before he had a chance to pull his dagger free of Dyrerisan's. Badger roared, turning toward Ferret. Dyrerisan didn't stop to wonder where the boy had come from, giving his attention to Kelan and the sword coming down for his head. Dyrerisan stepped to the side, using his blade to redirect Kelan's sword toward the wall. Kelan twisted his sword back up, pausing to grin at Dyrerisan.

"Do you want to hear her last words?" he asked. "They were to you."

Dyrerisan faltered, his heart stuttering under the weight of anguish. Kelan took advantage of that pause. But a new form leaped between Kelan and Dyrerisan, clashing metal ringing through the air as Viper locked his blade with Kelan's. He glanced to Dyrerisan just long enough to nod. Then he shoved at Kelan, freeing the blade in his hands to thrust toward Kelan's stomach.

Dyrerisan straightened, gritting his teeth against the trembling weakness as he raised his sword again.

"Dyrerisan." Ferret grabbed his arm.

"How did you get in here?" Dyrerisan asked, shaking him off.

Ferret grinned, eyes bright. "That's not important. I found Ember. She's alive, in a cell downstairs."

He stilled, those words sending a shock down to his bones. *Alive.* Dyrerisan forced his petrified lungs to take a breath. But he didn't let relief take him yet. The crack in his soul wouldn't be healed so easily.

"You're sure?" he asked harshly, glaring at the boy. Ferret didn't flinch.

"I'm sure. It's Ember, and she's breathing. Duke Kelan's a rotten liar."

Dyrerisan smirked numbly at the loathing in Ferret's voice. *She's alive.* Then he would finish this.

"Help Wolf and Fox with that sorcerer," Dyrerisan ordered, jerking his head to where Collin and Izzy were cornering the magic user, staying clear of the black knife he wielded.

"Yes, sir."

Dyrerisan turned away from the boy, new strength entering him. Alive. *Please, Almighty, let it be true.*

Kelan was pulling his sword from Viper's lifeless body by the time Dyrerisan turned his attention back to the duke. He stepped over Viper's corpse like it was no more than waste, raising a bloodied sword against Dyrerisan's attack. But no grief crippled Dyrerisan this time. His mind was sharp, resolved. He wouldn't falter.

Dyrerisan pulled himself back, allowing Kelan to make his own attack. When the expected thrust came toward his gut, Dyrerisan stepped slightly to the side, letting the sword pass a hair's breadth from his flesh. Then he pinned the sword to his side, seizing the cross guard to hold Kelan close. His own sword was already between them, raised to the level of Kelan's neck. Dyrerisan slit his throat.

The duke's eyes widened as he choked, and Dyrerisan shoved him backwards. He stumbled over Viper's body, falling to his back, sword dropping from his hand. And Dyrerisan turned from the duke bleeding out on stone to his warriors. The sorcerer was on the floor with his throat ripped out, and what few soldiers remained were fleeing. Dyrerisan met Ferret's eyes.

"Take me to Ember."

Somewhere far above her, Ember heard shouting and harsh clanging polluting the air. She pried her eyes open, seeing only flickering torchlight around her. Was there a fight? Or did Duke Kelan have other prisoners to torture?

Ember shifted to sit up, freezing when that slight movement awoke a wildfire of pain across her back. She squeezed her eyes shut, biting her lip and wondering if maybe she should just go back to sleep. But then there were footsteps pounding the floor, drawing closer. Duke Kelan? One of his lackeys? She couldn't help the nauseating fear that arose at the concept of more "interviews." She'd barely survived the first.

The lock ground open, and Ember rolled onto her side to face whoever was entering her cell. Then her breath caught, and she raised her head to get a better look at the man striding toward her.

*Dyre.* She'd know his face anywhere. But even in the flickering light, he looked so *different.* His skin had softened to the same shade as his portrait, his hair darkened to near black. As he knelt beside her cot, she noted that the lines around his eyes remained. She wondered with a silent laugh if that was her fault. He reached out to touch her face, hesitantly as if he couldn't quite believe she was real.

She made an effort to smile. "It worked."

He huffed an exasperated sigh. "Yes, your reckless plan worked. Don't ever do that to me again."

"Don't go fighting any more sorcerers," she replied, more breathlessly than she meant to.

Dyrerisan was inspecting her back, and the barest brush of his hand against her broken skin felt like a thousand needles stabbing her at once. She bit her lip again, focusing on that small pain over the sharp agony. Dyre had gone still.

"*Ember*," he whispered, his voice raw. Ember swallowed enough of her pain to answer.

"That bad?"

Her wry tone wasn't convincing. When Dyre met her eyes, his face was twisted in agony.

"I failed you," he choked out. "I came too late."

"None of that," Ember said, trying to sound stern and failing. "You came right on time."

Ember could see he wanted to argue. But he just shook his head, unhooking his cloak.

"I'm afraid this will hurt, but I don't have time to bandage it."

"Do what you need to," Ember said, bracing for more fire. "I want out of this place."

Even being prepared, tears stung her eyes. She bit down harder when he laid the fabric across her broken skin, tasting blood. He scooped her into his arms before she had time to prepare, and Ember wasted no time burying her head against his chest to hide her pain. She took a slow, shuddering breath and willed her heart to stay steady. *I'm alright. Everything's alright now...he came.*

Time seemed to blur, each step a new agony. Ember wrapped her fingers in the fabric of Dyre's shirt, concentrating on her breathing. She knew when they stepped outside, as the sound of pandemonium sharpened. A piercing whistle cut through the air, and Ember looked up to see people rushing toward them from all directions. Before she could panic, those people turned outward, circling around Dyre and Ember as a guard through the wasteland Sarnere's courtyard had turned into. She tried not to look too closely at the destruction around her, especially the bodies lying far too still on the stone. She turned her face back to Dyre's chest.

Her eyes flicked open when his warmth disappeared, as he lifted her to the back of a horse. Ember wrapped her hands in the horse's mane and fought to stay upright. Dyre climbed up behind her, wrapping the other around her waist. And Ember ignored the pain to lean back against him. She closed her eyes to revel in the *safety* of being near him. Even with the sounds of a battle around her, even when every step the horse took sent a new flash of pain, Ember held on to that feeling. It would be alright now...Dyre had her. He wouldn't let her go.

She wasn't aware when she faded away, only when she heard Dyre saying her name. They were still moving, at a rocking beat that threatened to lull her to sleep. But Dyre was still saying her name, and Ember fought to rise from that mire, to reply. She couldn't find her voice. Why couldn't she speak?

"Ember, listen to me," Dyre said. "Stay awake. Just hold on a little longer. Once we reach Nyxwood, I'll find a way...I'll save you."

*Oh Dyre...* Ember fought again for her voice, to say his name. But the curse was hard at work now, stealing everything she had left to her. *Months to days, days to hours...* But Dyre was still speaking. She wouldn't miss a single word, not now.

"You survived breaking my curse, you'll survive this too. We haven't come this far for you to give up now. *Fight,* Ember."

She was fighting. But she didn't have much left to fight *with. How can you ever hope to win a war fought within yourself?*

"Ember."

She tried again to respond, to reassure him, but she failed. The horse slowed, and in a moment Ember was in Dyre's arms again. She forced her eyes open as he laid her on the ground, propped against a tree. His face was inches from hers, his hands wrapped around her arms to hold her steady. His voice trembled as he whispered her name again, cradling her face in his hand.

Ember grasped at whatever strength she had left, finding enough to tilt her lips into a smile. But when she tried to raise her hand to *his* face, that was beyond her: it stayed beside her, barely twitching against the ground. She could hear her heartbeat, slow and uneven. It fought against the curse, a desperate final stand against the darkness rising to swallow her.

Ember wanted to rage, to weep. Would this be how her story ended? Here, so soon after finding the best part of her limited life? She stared up at Dyre, tears spilling down her cheeks at the raw grief she could see in his face. Memories flashed through her mind, brief moments with every person she'd ever known.

*I'm sorry,* she cried out to all those voices, all those faces. *I'm sorry I never loved you as I should have!* And she was sorry perhaps most of all that she hadn't gotten the chance to love Dyre as she could have...

And with that she realized: she'd only said the words once. Dyre was still staring down at her, begging her to stay with him. *If only I could.* But she wouldn't leave without telling him... she scraped together every bit of strength she could find, fighting the darkness for a moment more. *You won't take* this *from me.*

She took back her voice just long enough to whisper, "I love you."

Dyre's eyes tightened with new agony, pulling her into his arms.

"I love you," he whispered beside her ear. "I love you."

Ember closed her eyes, pierced through.

*Please, can't I have another chance? More time? I'd spend it wisely this time...I'd love without thought to the cost.*

But her time was up. Her heart fluttered with a final, weak protest...and fell silent.

Dyrerisan listened to Ember's heart fade. He glanced up to Collin and Izzy kneeling nearby, even as his arms tightened around her. Their eyes held only pain, no hope. *No.* He turned his face away, closing his eyes. It couldn't be too late; he couldn't lose her now, after all they'd been through.

"Please, Almighty," he gasped. "Please, let her live. If only one of our hearts can keep beating, let it be hers."

His voice broke. He continued in silence, still holding her. *Don't take her yet...don't let this curse have its satisfaction. Take me instead, give her what's left of my life, anything!*

He kissed Ember's hair, listening vainly for any sign that she lived. More broken pleas passed through his mind, meeting only silence.

Then the world dulled around him. The sound of the forest, of Collin and Izzy, faded away. The feel of Ember in his arms, the burn of unshed tears...it all numbed beneath the weight of a new presence reaching within and searching out every crevice of Dyrerisan's existence. He quaked beneath the magnitude, tempted to pull away, to hide who he was. But he knew better. He knew he wasn't worthy of anything. But still he asked for mercy, for himself and especially for Ember. He held to his plea, offering his own life dripping through his fingers.

The Almighty accepted what was offered, but even as Dyrerisan felt his own life fade that weighty presence poured it back in. For the smallest sliver of a moment, Dyrerisan glimpsed something *other*, an existence far beyond. Then he fell back through the layers of reality, to his own body, as the Almighty gave back all that was offered, mended and made new. A spark lit just before him, rekindling something lost.

Dyrerisan struggled to take it in, to reconnect to the fractured world around him. Until he felt the weight of Ember in his arms, and he remembered himself.

Ember took a breath.

# CHAPTER NINETEEN

*It's strangely beautiful, the paradoxes of this world. A heart that's safe from grief can't serve its purpose. Receiving your life means giving it away. And sometimes it takes a broken heart to see what it means to be whole. The curse couldn't break until I was willing to give my life and heart away no matter the consequences, until Dyre offered the same. I wonder now what would've happened if I'd been willing to love that selflessly from the beginning. But regardless, I was right in one thing: the curse has ended.*

*And to all the daughters and sons that read this worn-out journal, learn my lesson. Love freely, love fiercely. A heart hardened to stone isn't much of a heart at all.*

Ember smiled down at the fresh ink, signing her name with a flourish before setting the pen aside. She leaned back in her chair with a sigh, glancing toward the tall windows. Outside, the sky was bright and clear. She glimpsed a carriage on the road, which was far more visible now that Nyxwood wasn't hidden, and knew she'd need to leave soon. But not yet.

For now, she breathed deep, enjoying how easy it was to stand and take her journal to the nearest bookshelf. There, she slid it into place beside other personal records from past rulers of Nyxwood. Staring at it resting there, she prayed that whoever read it after her would understand what she hadn't: that loving isn't a weakness. And she prayed that somewhere, somehow, all those women who wrote before her knew that the curse was finally broken.

She was still lost in thought when an arm snaked around her waist. A smile slipped across her face as she leaned back against Dyre, placing her hand over his own.

"Hello, Dear Heart," she whispered.

He didn't react to the endearment, but leaned down so his lips were close to her ear. "Radcliff and his brood have arrived. You won't escape helping me greet them by hiding in the library."

Ember laughed, twisting to look up at him. "I wasn't hiding. I was...finishing something."

Dyre's eyes flicked to the bookshelf, where the journal now rested, and she knew he'd read her words soon enough. But for now, he looked back to her, his eyes dancing even as he tried to look stern.

"Perhaps you're hiding from Miri, then. I heard she has new creations she's waiting to dress you up in."

Ember's face warmed at that. Before he could notice and prod at her, she offered him a mischievous smile.

"Or perhaps *you're* hiding. I heard Collin and Izzy have some suggestions for what the Aerie should do next...and that you're avoiding talking about it."

He raised an eyebrow, tightening his grip on her waist. "That's because their suggestions all involve my presence, and I have no intention of letting you out of my sight."

That made Ember ache, as memories of that dreadful day rose in her mind. The feeling of her life fading away, the pain of *returning* to a body still broken, still weak... Ember forced them away, turning to face Dyre so she could take his face in her hands.

"It's been three months," she whispered. "I'm alive, and I'm healthy. The curse isn't coming back."

Dyre exhaled, and Ember felt some of the tension leave his shoulders. He leaned down to press his forehead to hers, his arms still encircling her waist.

"I know," he said. "But can't I have my wife to myself for a year, at least?"

Ember liked the sound of that. But even as she threatened to melt against him, she knew now wasn't the time. She forced herself to chuckle instead.

"I doubt the surrounding nobles will let us have that long."

Dyrerisan sighed. "You never know. Acknowledging Nyxwood's return means giving back all of *my* land they've been happily making use of. My guess is they're waiting for the king to return to make *him* sort it all out."

"So, we have a little peace and quiet left."

"In theory." Dyre pulled back just enough for Ember to meet his eyes. "That reminds me...why are we welcoming Radcliff into our home, again?"

Ember smiled. "So I can spend time with my cousins. I have a lot of years to make up for."

"Your cousins I'll accept, but I hope your uncle and aunt decide to return home *quickly*."

"Don't worry...keep that tone, and they'll leave within the week."

"And your cousins?" Dyre asked, in a pleading voice that belayed the severe set to his mouth.

"We talked about this," Ember said, trying not to laugh. "You said they can stay for a few weeks, maybe even a few months."

"But now I'm wondering if you're expecting me to *entertain* them. I don't have experience with children."

Ember fought to set her expression into something serious, though her lips kept twitching with a smile.

"Then you should get some practice while you can."

Dyre drew back, raising an eyebrow. "Are you teasing me, my wife?"

"Perhaps," Ember said.

Dyre narrowed his eyes, but now he was smiling. Ember gave in and grinned.

"We should start putting away trinkets now," she said. "Maybe we'll get them all in storage before our own child starts walk—"

She cut off with a laugh when Dyrerisan picked her up and spun her around. He was laughing himself, and Ember's heart overflowed with pure joy when he set her down, pressing his forehead to hers again.

"I love you," he said fervently.

"And I love you," she replied. "Always."

The rest of her response was lost as he kissed her, and Ember quietly rejoiced in all that her second chance at life had brought so far...and all it would bring in the years to come.

# BONUS CHAPTER: CELEBRATIONS

***Author's Note:***

*After publishing Stone Heart's second edition, I received several comments on the abrupt ending of the book. It got me thinking what more I could've included to soften that last page and give readers more time to process the conclusion of the story. Below is what I've come up with.*

*This chapter takes place between Chapters 18 and 19, giving you insight into some of the aftermath of Ember's curse breaking. I hope it softens the landing and makes the ending of Dyre and Ember's story a little more satisfying.*

Ember let the book fall shut, warm and satisfied as the final words echoed through her mind. She looked up, intending to insist Dyre read the book in her hands regardless what he thought of novels, but she found him asleep.

*Of course he is,* she thought, as a soft smile crept across her face. *He's gotten so little rest lately.*

The days since Ember's curse had been broken had been busy and chaotic, at least for Dyre. He'd tried to shield her from most of it, but there was only so much he could hide when he'd moved half his study to the library to keep Ember within sight.

Members of the Aerie came and went often to report to Dyre. Though he was free to leave Nyxwood's grounds, the Aerie continued to act as Dyre's eyes and sword to clean up the mess Duke Kelan left behind. Dyrerisan had refused to leave Ember's side to see to it personally.

She certainly wasn't complaining about *that*: if she had her way, she'd never have to leave him again. But a haunted look had dwelt in his eyes, one that she hadn't found a way to banish yet. Though Ember's heart was stronger than she ever remembered it being, the rest of her weakness was proving slower to disappear. Ember knew it worried him. It seemed that, though both curses were broken, they had left a scar.

She had promised the Almighty that if she lived, she would love without thought to the cost. But how could she rid herself of the fear of grief? Having come so close to losing Dyre, after she had quite literally died in his arms before being brought back...how did they release that terror of being torn apart again? Her parents had never learned to release that fear. She didn't want to follow their example.

From the stories he told her, Dyre's parents had shared the sort of love Ember wanted to have...but they weren't here to teach Ember and Dyre how they did it. Where did that leave them? She didn't want to spend her whole life haunted by a curse that no longer existed.

*One day at a time*, she told herself, taking a deep breath. That's what Izzy had advised when Ember confessed her worries to her. What Ember and Dyre had gone through wasn't something that could be erased in a few short weeks...she needed to give them time to heal. Perhaps when the remnants of her curse-induced weakness were gone, and when Dyre stopped staring at the back of his hand like he expected to see gray stone instead of skin, then that fear would be easier to leave behind.

After a moment more of staring at Dyre, Ember leaned over to grab the writing desk on the nearby table. She scratched out a short note to Dyre explaining where she'd gone. He might still worry when he awoke to find her missing, but this was the best she could do. She imagined Miri and Freya were already waiting for her downstairs.

The note written and folded on top of her book, Ember stood, gripping the back of the settee as she waited for her head to settle. The dizziness faded more quickly than it had a few days ago, bolstering Ember's confidence as she walked quietly toward the door. The curse *was* broken...she simply needed time to recover before she'd run up any staircases.

As Ember stepped into the hall, she breathed deep and reveled in the lack of dust and decay. The curtains were drawn back, flooding the halls with light as Ember made her way to the Silver Parlor where Freya and Miri waited. There was a lightness to Nyxwood that Ember had never seen before: a taste of freedom.

Although Nyxwood's sudden reappearance had understandably left people disconcerted and wary, curiosity was proving the stronger influence. Dyre had already hired over a dozen servants to free Nyxwood from centuries of disuse.

He'd also hired people to relieve Helen and the rest, insisting that after all this time Nyxwood was their home, not their place of employment. But, to Ember's amusement, every one of them had disobeyed Dyre's orders and were hard at work training the new servants and setting the castle to rights.

However, they had also claimed suites on the second floor, and now spent their evenings with Dyre and Ember in a warm companionship that Ember treasured. Those were the only moments that Dyre seemed to truly relax: with Ember tucked against his side, and their friends chatting and laughing around them.

Freya and Miri had also proven invaluable help to Ember, taking on most of the labor of preparing for her and Dyre's wedding in a few days.

Dyre had suggested they wait longer to marry, to give them more time to know each other. But Ember had refused. She knew she wanted Dyre. Their lives together would have challenges whether they married now or in a year...and now that Ember had decided, she didn't want to wait. Once she'd assured Dyre that she was ready to be his wife, he'd made it clear that he didn't want to wait either.

But *planning* a wedding in only three weeks was no easy task, especially when Ember's friends insisted on making it an event worthy of the king himself.

When Ember reached the stretch of hall with the silver parlor, she found the door propped open. Freya and Miri's voices filtered out as Ember approached.

"The hydrangeas should be blooming by then," Freya was saying. "And John made sure there will be plenty of roses...now we just need to talk Ember into actually carrying a bouquet."

"And hide her magnificent dress?" Miri teased.

Freya scoffed. "Not hide, *complement.*"

"And there's the bride herself," Miri said, as Ember stepped inside. "Did Dyrerisan try to hold you hostage?"

Her eyes glinted with humor from where she sat, surrounded by mounds of white and pale blue fabric.

"He's asleep," Ember said, closing the door behind her.

Freya looked up from her lists, her eyebrows furrowed. "Dyrerisan, asleep? In the middle of the day?"

"I know...he needs it."

"Enough about that," Miri said. "Let's get you into this dress before he comes looking."

It took all three of them to get Ember cinched into Miri's creation. The dress was massive, with dozens of layers falling over each other like petals on a rose. The sweetheart neckline felt daring to Ember, though Miri assured her it was tame, and the sleeves were loose and airy around her arms. It was also, surprisingly, one of the most comfortable dresses Ember had worn.

"You have enough to worry about on your wedding day without your dress giving you fits," was how Miri had explained it, when Ember had first tried it on a few days before.

Trying it on again, for what Miri claimed was the last time before she donned it for the ceremony, Ember struggled to comprehend it all. A large mirror dominated the back wall of the parlor, and Ember found herself staring at her reflection as Miri walked around her, making small adjustments and muttering under her breath. The ice blue layers within the skirt and slightly darker needlework curling around the bodice made her eyes appear more cobalt than lavender. The splashes of color also brought a little life back to Ember's skin, which was almost translucent when surrounded by so much white. It made her look like a fairy princess fit for an ice palace.

Like everything else Miri and Freya were planning, it felt like too much. But after seeing the bright joy in their eyes as they discussed flower arrangements and menus, Ember had long given up trying to rein them in. If Miri wanted to dress her in diamonds and Freya decided to bake a dozen cakes, Ember would let them. They deserved a bit of fun more than anyone.

"I'm still worried that it's too heavy," Freya says, eyeing the dress critically. "Ember, are you sure it isn't too much?"

Ember was saved from reassuring Freya, yet again, that she could handle the heavy skirts by Miri scoffing.

"It'll be *fine.* She only has to walk down the aisle, and then Dyrerisan can carry her everywhere."

Freya glanced at Ember, her lips twitching with a hidden smile. "I don't know...do you think Dyrerisan can really carry her with so much *fluff* in the way?"

Miri straightened, planting her hands on her hips. Ember looked away to hide her own smile.

"Who's the seamstress, here?" Miri asked.

"You, but you're biased."

"It's beautiful, Miri," Ember said, though she saw well enough that there was no true heat to their argument.

"Of course, it's beautiful," Miri said, turning back to Ember. "More importantly, *you're* beautiful."

Ember's face warmed as she muttered her thanks.

"That's what you need," Freya said. "A bit of color in your cheeks."

Miri muttered conspiratorially, "I don't think we'll have to worry about that once Dyrerisan sees her."

That only made her blush more, much to Miri and Freya's amusement.

"I'm finished," Miri said. "Let's get you back into your normal clothes before you faint on us."

Ember rolled her eyes as she followed Miri behind the dressing screen set up in a corner.

"Izzy sent word back," Freya said, as she helped undo the row of tiny buttons running down Ember's back. "She and Collin should return in time to come."

"Good," Ember said.

She wanted as many of the Aerie to be there as possible. After all they'd done for Dyre, and for *her*, she wanted them to have a chance to relax and celebrate for an evening.

"What's your opinion on ribbon?" Freya asked.

Ember glanced over her shoulder, only for Miri to turn her head back forward.

"It depends on what you're using it for," Ember said.

"Tying around flowers and candlesticks, mostly."

"It sounds beautiful."

"Truly?" Freya asked, helping Ember step back into her day dress. "Or are you trying to appease me?"

"Truly," Ember laughed.

"Then I'll go with John into town this afternoon and choose some." Freya sighed contentedly. "I love that I can say that again."

"Me too," Miri said. "Though I'll enjoy it more once people stop staring at us like we're ghosts."

Ember slipped her shoes back on and stepped around the screen. "Give it a few months. Something new will come along and they'll forget to be wary of you."

"In the meantime, I'll make sure to act peculiar to give them something to gossip about."

Ember laughed as she backed toward the door. "I should go check on Dyre."

Miri and Freya exchanged a knowing look as Freya replied, "By all means, return to your fiancé before he starts pining."

Ember laughed again. Her smile only grew when she found Dyre waiting for her in the hall, wearing a narrow-eyed look that indicated he'd heard Freya's comment. But that look melted away as his eyes rested on Ember, and he stepped forward to take her into his arms. Ember melted against his chest gladly.

"You should've awoken me," he whispered near her ear, sending shivers across Ember's skin.

"You need rest," she replied.

"So do you."

Ember tilted her head up so Dyre could see her raised eyebrow. "I've been doing little more than resting."

"Regardless."

Dyre scooped her into his arms without warning, and a surprised laugh slipped through her lips as she grabbed onto his shoulders.

"I'm not going to regain strength as quickly if you carry me everywhere," she warned him.

He raised his eyebrows. "Would you like me to put you down?"

"I didn't say that."

"That's what I thought."

Dyre turned back toward the library, and Ember shifted in his arms so she could lay her head against his shoulder.

"I received word regarding your family," he said, climbing the stairs slowly. "Your cousins are safe."

"Good," Ember breathed.

That had been the thorn in the midst of her bliss. Fear for Sophia and Louisa had plagued her since she'd seen her uncle in Duke Kellan's custody.

"Your aunt is fine, as well. Radcliff seems to be the only one harmed by the ordeal, and he's recovering without issue."

"I'm glad," Ember said, with some reluctance. Or perhaps it was guilt.

She could invite them to the wedding; Dyre had offered to bring them to Nyxwood for the occasion. But as much as she knew Sophia and Louisa would regret missing it...she wasn't ready to face her aunt and uncle again. That reconciliation would come eventually, but not yet. Not on her wedding day. She wanted this celebration to belong to those who truly cared about Ember and Dyre. She wanted it to be a commemoration of their freedom from curses and Sarnere alike.

"What are you thinking?" Dyre asked, as they entered the library.

Ember forced thoughts of her family from her mind, smiling up at Dyre.

"That our wedding can't come soon enough."

Dyre sat on their settee, positioning Ember on his lap. The position felt deliciously intimate, though she sincerely hoped no one caught them like this. Dyre dropped his head, his lips ghosting across Ember's cheek toward her ear.

"Agreed," he whispered.

Ember closed her eyes, surrendering thoughts of all except Dyre's gentle kisses. Right then, a few days felt like an eternity.

Wandering among towering bookshelves, Ember hummed to herself and ran her fingers over leather spines. Most of them were hundreds of years old, though occasionally she spotted a newer volume the Aerie had brought Dyre. Most of those newer books came from the precarious piles in Dyre's study; she'd used his insistence on keeping Ember in his sight as an excuse to bring order to some of his towers of books. He'd grumbled at first, but he couldn't deny that he found things much faster now.

Toward the front of the room, Ember heard the shuffle of papers as Dyre read through reports and took notes. She smiled as she continued her meandering search. It wasn't long before she found herself at the back wall, where the portraits of Dyre's ancestors hung. Her eyes lingered longest on the portrait of Dyre himself...and his parents. She wished desperately that she could've met them.

Perhaps there was another way she could get to know them.

Ember turned her back on the portraits, to the books shelved beside them. She thought she remembered Dyre saying some Marquis kept journals or wrote memoirs later in life. Perhaps his parents wrote *something*. Ember ran her fingers over the spines of the books just below eye level, pulling a few to check if it was arranged in chronological order.

But Ember paused when she opened the cover of the second book. Someone had written a title on the first page: A Life Lived in Love. Ember didn't recognize the name written below, other than that she was related to Dyre. The date on the first entry was a little over a century before Dyre's birth. Any records Dyrerisan's parents left behind were probably a little further along the shelf, but... Ember's eyes fell on the first line and she knew she had to read it.

Shutting the book gently, Ember hugged it to her chest and wove her way back to where Dyre worked. She had a nest of blankets and pillows on one of the settees perfect for reading.

"What did you find this time?" Dyre asked, glancing up from his reports.

Ember held up the clothbound book. "A journal written by one of your ancestors. Have you read this one?"

"Not that I remember. If you discover any dark family secrets, don't hold it against me."

Ember matched his smile, settling into her seat with the book propped on a pillow. "I'll try not to."

As Dyre returned to his work, Ember opened the cover again, her eyes falling to the top of that first entry.

*Today we've finally reached our sunrise: today I marry my Marquis.*

Ember glanced at Dyre once more, just to reassure herself that he was there. And hoping that he wasn't watching her read. She had no idea what expression she wore. She shouldn't have worried: he was engrossed in a letter, comparing it against one of his maps. Ember returned her eyes to the page before her.

The journal was hardly the warm, happy account she expected it to be at the beginning.

Beatrix began the diary on the suggestion of her mother-in-law, and it began with all the happiness Ember had expected. Beatrix had faced obstacles before marrying her husband, Lucien, and she didn't take their union for granted. They were wholeheartedly in love with one another. For two years, Beatrix's entries mainly consisted of recording small moments of marital bliss, or her work at her husband's side.

But after the birth of their first son, things began taking a darker turn. Beatrix described trouble on the edges of Rausbane forest... disappearances and word of dark magic. Then trolls on the northern edges killing travelers. Her husband was gone more and more, and slowly storm clouds descended over their happy sunrise.

Ember was six years into Beatrix's story and everything was going wrong. But unlike Ember's story, she didn't believe there was a happy ending coming. Part of her wanted to shut the book and pretend she had never found it.

"Don't feel like you need to read every dusty page merely because I'm related to the author," Dyre said, glancing up.

Ember smiled with effort. "I do if I want to unearth those family secrets."

Dyre huffed, a smile edging his lips as he returned to his own reading. Ember took a deep and continued.

She was right. There was no second dawn.

Tears burned her eyes, blurring her vision, as Ember read Beatrix's grief at losing Lucien. The sorcerers troubling Rausbane had come to Nyxwood, and Lucien had sacrificed his life to vanquish them. He saved his family and the people under his protection...but he didn't live to see it. Beatrix's heartbreak felt far too familiar, and again Ember nearly closed the book. What more could there be to tell?

Except the following pages were filled with the same, looping handwriting. The tone of Beatrix's entries were different, more somber and tinged with grief, but Ember couldn't take her eyes away as she watched joy slowly creep back into Beatrix's life. She poured love into her children, she ruled Nyxwood with all the compassion and wisdom she'd learned from her husband, and she *kept living.*

Ember was transfixed, unaware of anything else as she raced through the long years of Beatrix's life. It wasn't until the final entry that she came back to herself, aware of her racing heart as she took in Beatrix's parting words.

*As my eyes dim, and I know my time to depart draws near, it seems natural that I reflect on my life. I have come to a realization as I read these many pages: I am blessed. For my life has been full of love, and what better life can one hope for?*

*I can leave in peace, knowing I've lived the life Lucien left for me as well as I could. Our love has never faltered, not even in these long years apart, and the time is coming for me to finally rejoin my love in the eternity beyond. I do long to see his smile again.*

The handwriting on the next page was different, and Ember shut the book. She didn't want to read the words of whatever son or daughter closed Beatrix's life story. She was already overwhelmed. She stared at the towering shelves, her mind ringing with Beatrix's words as her heart struggled to comprehend all that she'd read.

Perhaps Beatrix's life wasn't the tragedy Ember had thought it. Perhaps she had her answer now.

Dyre dropped his pen, and the clack of it hitting the desk made Ember jump. She wiped her eyes quickly and turned to face Dyre.

"I need some air," he said, setting paperweights on scattered papers. "Will you join me?"

The way he was looking at her was careful, and Ember knew that he'd been paying more attention to her than she'd guessed. The smile she offered him was weak, but genuine.

"Of course. Where are we going?"

"The gardens, I think."

He helped her stand, taking both of her hands in his and staring at her a moment. Ember let out a breath, and some weight fell from her shoulders as she stared up at Dyre: *her* Marquis. There were no great threats standing against them now, and she thanked the Almighty for that. Her smile was a little easier to hold afterward, and Dyre nodded in approval.

But even as Ember and Dyre walked into the sunlight, Ember's mind was caught on Beatrix and Lucien...on the kind of love that outlasted even death.

Ember took a slow, shaking breath as Miri straightened the many layers of her skirt. Freya stood in front of her, watching Ember with a soft smile that didn't hide the worry drawing lines around her eyes.

"Are you ready?" she asked.

Ember nodded, not trusting her voice. Freya handed her a bouquet of white roses, carefully wrapped in blue ribbon. She and Miri both offered Ember sympathetic looks as Ember continued to fight to keep her breathing steady.

"Just keep your eyes on Dyrerisan," Freya said, squeezing Ember's elbow. "You'll do fine."

Ember sincerely hoped so. Her heart was beating far too fast at the moment, and she was praying fervently that she wouldn't faint halfway to the altar. She wasn't sure she could recover from that kind of embarrassment, even if it was only friends watching.

Miri and Freya left her to join their husbands in the garden. Alone, she found it harder not to hyperventilate.

Was she sure about this? Was this really the right time to be married? *What if Dyre changes his mind now that I'm not someone in need of saving?*

"No," she whispered savagely, tightening her grip on her bouquet until she was sure the flowers would fall to pieces.

She wouldn't doubt Dyre. After all they'd been through, after all he'd done for her...she trusted him with everything. She'd allowed fear to rule her life for so long...would she really let it mold her mind now? No...she loved Dyre. He loved her. And she was going to step forward and vow to spend the rest of her life at his side, even if she trembled every step of the way.

Holding that promise in her mind, she took a step forward and knocked on the door that stood between her and the garden. It opened silently, and two new servants stood on either side as Ember stepped through.

Beyond, well over a dozen familiar faces turned to watch her. They stood gathered in a stone courtyard, surrounded by countless flowers bedecked in bright ribbons fluttering in the breeze. They all smiled as she stepped toward them. But as glad as she was to see their faces surrounding her, *they* weren't who she was searching for.

She cast her eyes over the clear aisle strewn with rose petals, to the arch of flowers where Dyrerisan and the minister stood. Then, taking another deep breath, she raised her eyes to his face.

Immediately Dyre's bright, love-filled gaze captured her. He stood tall, and as she watched his mouth spread in a wide grin. For the first time in far too long there was no shadow of fear in his eyes, nothing but joy. Ember found herself smiling. Her steps were a little steadier as she walked toward him.

After that, the ceremony passed in a haze. She must've said the right words, though, for the next thing she was aware of was Dyre kissing her and everyone cheering. As he pulled back to smile down at her, Ember felt she could breathe again.

The rest of the day passed with congratulations, embraces, and shared tears that all made Ember feel like she was spinning through the sky. But Dyre never let go of her hand, and that kept her tied to the ground. It was dusk, and Freya had enlisted everyone's help in lighting hundreds of candles, before Ember and Dyre managed to slip into the corner and sit together.

Ember leaned against Dyre, sighing in bliss as she watched their friends dance and eat and laugh. She was glad they were enjoying themselves, no matter how exhausting this celebration was turning out to be. Freya might not have been joking about Dyre carrying her away...her massive skirt felt far heavier now than it had when she first put it on.

"Are you ready to disappear?" Dyre whispered, running his fingers down her arm in a way that sent pleasant shivers across her skin.

"Yes."

It had been a while since anyone had come over to speak to them. She didn't think anyone would mind if they quietly left. As Dyre helped her stand, Ember looked over the party once more. In the mingled light of the moon and candles, she could just make out their smiles. She followed Dyre gratefully into the shadows. Ember preferred to slip away quietly and leave everyone to their celebration.

Away from the party, Ember and Dyre walked slowly through the garden, circling around to an entrance hidden from Freya's thousands of candles.

But when they were nearing the door, Dyre tugged her sideways into a hidden alcove. Before Ember could ask what they were doing, he'd captured her lips with his in a kiss *far* more intimate than their kiss after the ceremony. Ember's knees went weak, and he was half carrying her by the time he pulled back to press his forehead to hers.

"Have I mentioned today how much I love you?" he whispered breathlessly.

"Not in words," Ember replied. "Another kiss might make up for it."

Dyre didn't need to be asked twice. And when they broke apart again, Dyre scooped her into his arms to carry her toward the door.

"Dratted dress," he muttered, struggling to get the door open around the fabric of Ember's skirt.

Ember giggled.

He wrestled it open, and as he stepped into the dimly lit hall, Ember laid her head on his shoulder and breathed deep. *Sunrise, indeed.*

Perhaps loving fully didn't mean being fearless...perhaps it meant being determined to love and *keep* loving. Perhaps it meant using that love to batter down any walls fear tried to build.

Ember would always fear losing Dyre, just as he would always fear losing her. But that didn't mean they had to let that fear rule their lives. As long as they *were* together, Ember was going to offer him every part of her heart again and again. And she wouldn't take a single moment for granted.

# WANT FREE STORIES?

**Sign up for my newsletter on my website!**
You'll receive a collection of short stories, including...

- "Dreams and Vows," a bonus story from Memories of Salt and Stone,
- A journey into the mind of a storyteller with too many stories to tell,
- The story of the Blood-born Champion and the Stuttering Songbird who follows him,
- And an Ashton Legacies short story following the events of *Aderes in Karkhana*

My newsletter will give you updates on my author adventures, recommendations from my bookshelf, and glimpses of the wonder saturating the world around us.

# ALSO BY MAEGAN M. SIMPSON

*CHANGED HEARTS COLLECTION*

Wolf Heart

*LEGENDS OF EMYR*

Memories of Salt and Stone

Memories of Sea and Sky

Memories of Blood and Bone

Memories of Truth and Terror

*THE AGONIZOMAI SERIES:*

Frosted Fire

Born in Darkness

Broken Healer

Menacing Whispers

Winds of Wrath

Shrouded Hope

Heir Eternal

*ASHTON LEGACIES:*

Aderes in Karkhana

Viggo in Orlin

*SECRETS OF THE NATIONAL PARKS SERIES:*

Shadow of Memory

Dragon's Flight

Midnight's Wings

# About the Author

Maegan M. Simpson accepts many titles, including Daydreamer, Mountain Girl, and Indie Author of 16 books. She believes that God created our world full of beauty and wonder, even in the broken pieces, and endeavors to capture that wonder in her writing.

Maegan's life so far has been full of adventures, whether it's finishing college, taming dragons (alright, they're cats), or devouring every book she can get her hands on. When she's not exploring fantasy lands or searching for faeries in the shadows, Maegan lives in rural New Mexico with her family. There, she enjoys gardening, painting, and exploring the mountains she calls home.

For more books and updates visit https://maeganmsimpson.com/

www.ingramcontent.com/pod-product-compliance
Lightning Source LLC
Chambersburg PA
CBHW020500310726
48979CB00016B/2734/J

* 9 7 8 1 9 6 6 4 2 0 0 1 9 *